BLACK CLOUDS

A BRACKISH WATERS NOVEL

JODIE CAIN SMITH

AETHON THRILLS

aethonbooks.com

ALSO BY JODIE CAIN SMITH

BRACKISH WATERS

Splintered Reeds

Black Clouds

———

Want to discuss our books with other readers and even the authors?

JOIN THE AETHON DISCORD!

———

You can also join our non-spam mailing list by visiting Thriller Books: https://aethonbooks.com/thriller-newsletter/ and never miss out on future releases. You'll also receive five full books completely free as our thanks to you.

For Mama and Daddy

1

I am the queen of poor decisions.

Summer is in its crankiest month. Avoiding starvation is the only reason I'm in the garden in this heat. That and needing quiet this morning. Between the state of our food supply (grim at best), and a rocking hangover (buckets of blackberry wine), I chose the heat and sun over hours spent inside the house with the family today. Mama thinks turning on the AC is a waste of precious resources, so there's no cooling off inside the house, only noise. Noise about food. Noise about rain-soaked crops and hot, still water. Noise about whether the power's back on for good, or if this is just another unfunny joke from God. Noise about noise. A hangover plus a house like a kiln has the potential for all sorts of arguments and hurt feelings, and I'm ill-equipped for either today.

I could go for a swim in the Bay, but the warm water does nothing to cool off the body. It's also jellyfish season. No such thing as a refreshing swim in July. Not here. A warm bath peppered with stinging tentacles is not my preferred escape. Not that I'm getting in the water at all, as that idea still conjures a trauma response and mental images of being torn to bits by hammerhead sharks. No, I wasn't attacked by sharks while paddling away from the Middle Bay Lighthouse a year ago, but I imagined their pointed fins and sharp teeth with every stroke atop my makeshift raft.

When I do sleep, I have nightmares. In those nightmares, the sharks have faces. Dave Richardson's face. Clem Richardson's. Troy Cowart's ugly mug and stringy hair. All the faces that wanted me dead.

Thanks to the blackberry wine—such a bad decision—my head is pounding, so much so that if I lean too far left or right when bending to pluck cherry tomatoes off the vines, I risk falling into dirt. I thought I sweated out all the demon wine last night as I thrashed around on my cot in the garage-slash-oven, but I didn't. Plenty of the demon swill swims in my veins this morning.

I only have myself to blame for where I am right now—and the fact that Cole is here, too. I forced him to work with me today in the garden because, even though I want to be on my own, I'm scared to be alone. Safety in numbers is now a core value.

Together, I thought we'd work in the sun, and I'd burn the toxins out. There are weeds to pull, drainage to dig, tomatoes to harvest, and a bunch of hungry people to feed. Also, being in the garden would get me out of fertilizer duty today. The thought of cleaning the chicken shit out of the coup roils my suspect stomach, ushering in a potential return appearance of last night's modest meal and all that wine.

But if I were back at the house, shoveling shit and immersed in the chaos of survival with a dozen other people, I wouldn't be looking at four soldiers with the words *Military Police* displayed across their chest. Three stand near the military contraption that brought them here. One waits just outside the garden gate. Three carry rifles, which would make number four the man in charge. He has a nine-millimeter strapped to his thigh to prove his commander status. He's at the gate, waiting to be granted entrance.

Do they know what a threatening display this is? They probably get their rocks off by scaring the bejeezus out of the locals. I wonder what they would do if I fought back? How would they react if I lunged at them with my trowel and spade? Bullet through my brain? *Chicken shit, indeed.*

Swallowing my mounting nausea, I place my hand in the crook of Cole's arm, giving him a gentle squeeze, and pray he hears my silent warning. *Say nothing.*

"May I help you?" I ask the men. I think it's a better, more innocent greeting than, *you can't take this boy* or *get the hell away from that gate.*

"I'm Captain Shahin of the 128th Military Police Unit, Alabama National Guard," the man with the pistol says. He places his hand on the metal fence as if he intends to open it without my permission.

"That's quite a mouthful." My smile is forced.

"Yes, Ma'am. Jules Martin, right?"

"Jules Martin *Jones*," I correct. "You're National Guard? What happened to the regular Army unit?"

"And the boy?" Shahin asks, skipping right past my question.

"Cole." I don't offer a last name, but I do squeeze Cole's arm tighter. Cole responds by pressing his lips together as tight as an oyster shell.

"Impressive garden," Shahin says, gesturing at the rows of bell peppers, cucumbers, and pole beans. He removes his sunglasses so I can see his golden-brown eyes and dark, envy-inducing lashes. His skin is smooth, except for a few laugh lines, and tan. Very tan.

I need to look away, because if I keep looking at him, things might get weird. Of course, isn't this already weird? How long has it been since I spoke? *Oh, for fuck's sake, get your head right, woman*. Perhaps the heat is affecting my judgment. Or I'm still drunk. I must be drunk. "Gotta keep the family fed," I spit out. Good. No slurring. Or maybe that's bad because if I'm not drunk, then I've completely lost my mind.

"And a large family at that."

"You didn't answer my question. The one about the regular unit that was here. Before. I asked you a question that you didn't answer." *Perfect.* Stammering makes this situation much better.

"I was surprised to learn how much land your father owns. I always thought it was just the one plot on the water."

"My father and mother. They own it all together. You seem quite informed to be the new guy, Captain." I feel Cole cower just the slightest bit, so I take my hand from his arm and place it on his shoulder. *Everything is fine, kid. I'll get rid of him.*

"I'm not new to Bellefontaine."

"Oh. Okay. Well. We have a lot to do, and it is not getting any cooler. So, unless there's something you need, or you'd like to answer my question about why you are here—"

"Of course," he says and smiles again, relaxed and welcoming. In another place and time, and if he wore anything other than an Army uniform, I would like his smile. But this isn't that place or time, and he displays one word that chills me to the core ever since bringing Cole into my life and home—*police*.

"Bellefontaine is now my area of concern." Shahin appears even taller with the words *area of concern.*

"Yours?"

"Yes. The official handover was a couple of days ago."

"Congrats." There is no smile, no emotion, in the word.

With my trowel hand, I adjust the brim of my sun hat to better look Shahin in the eyes. I borrowed the hat from Mama after she told me that I'd look like one of her Dooney & Burke purses soon if I don't protect my skin. She didn't say "Protect your face, Jules. It's your money maker if you want to land another man." I bet she wanted to, though. I should check her lips for bite marks. But she knows better because Jacob hasn't been gone that long, and I'm still in the mood for Victorian mourning clothes—if I had any and wouldn't pass out dead from overheating. Black clothing doesn't really suit this heat. Of course, melting into the dirt and mud would fertilize the plants well, probably even better than guano.

Shit. I let my brain do that wandering thing again and have no idea what new guy has been saying. Because he has been talking. At least those pretty, pretty lips are moving. *Stop that.*

"I'm sorry. What were you saying?"

Shahin gives me a curious look. "Just that we settled in quickly and I'm surprised you were unaware that a new unit is now securing the area."

"We're a bit isolated here."

"The road to the combat outpost is right there." Shahin gestures to the road that leads to the COP. "I'd think you'd have noticed all the equipment coming and going."

"Well, if you've seen one Humvee, you've seen them all." And I'm a grown woman whose every move is monitored by her parents because a year ago a bunch of psychos tried to kill me.

"I was told the change was all over the radio."

"We don't listen much."

Dammit, Daddy. This is why we can't isolate ourselves. Isolation leads to long conversations with arrogant men with broad shoulders and muscular hands that could wrap around my waist and rip off my…*Oh, for fuck's sake. Stop it.*

"I hear you're missing quite the listen from that Libby Lefty on the mic." On cue, the other soldiers chuckle at the boss's joke. "She's supposedly a whole vibe."

"Yes. A *vibe.*" Thank you, new guy. That one word breaks the spell, bringing all sexy thoughts to a halt. I turn to Cole, handing him the trowel. "Why don't you look for weeds near the peppers? Get the whole root out or they'll just grow back." I wait for Cole to walk far enough away, then turn back to Shahin. "So, like I said, we've got a lot of work to do."

The questions that I want to ask this man fire in my brain. *Did you stare at that boy long enough to know who he is? Were you given a list of the most dangerous children in Bellefontaine and where you can find them before they bring this whole hellscape to its scratched knees? Are you just toying with me before you snatch Cole away for stealing crab traps, nets, and dried fish off the lines months ago while he was two missed meals away from starving to death?*

This trainwreck of thought is doing nothing for my headache. In fact, the pain has moved into my neck and shoulders. I wonder if CPT Shahin gives a good massage? His hands look quite capable. *Holy hell, how dehydrated am I?* I glance upward and clock the sun, trying to calculate how long we've been out here.

"Miss Jones, are you okay? Maybe you shouldn't be out in this heat."

"I'm fine."

"After what you went through last summer, I don't think your family wants to lose you to heatstroke."

"What I went through?"

"Being abandoned at Middle Bay Lighthouse. From the story I was told, that was quite the escape on your part. I don't know if I could have managed it."

"We do what we must. Now, I *must* get back to work."

Shahin pauses, then looks at me. "And I must do my work."

"Which is?"

"You seem rather put out that my men and I stopped to intro-duce ourselves."

"Not put out. Just busy." I close my eyes for a moment, trying to steady my legs.

"Miss, your coloring has changed."

"Maybe I'm a chameleon lizard, adapting to my surroundings." Wooziness rushes over me.

"Do you have water out here?"

"Of course, I do," I tell Shahin. I don't tell him that I polished off the bottle right before he showed up.

Shahin dips his head and, I swear to God, softens his eyes to look at me. Maybe this is his attempt at charm, which would probably work on a woman who isn't broken to her core and doesn't feel like she's about to fertilize the tomatoes with vomit.

"Are you always so…observant?" I ask, trying to break his laser stare.

"Observant?" Shahin rubs his chin, which is showing a bit of a stubbly shadow.

"Yes, and proper. Your manner of speaking. Very polished. That Ivy League posture of yours. Slick even. It's not what we're used to around here."

"Slick?

"Yes. Slick." *Too slick*. And he still hasn't answered my main question of why the hell the National Guard is here. At least not fully. The regular Army raided the Knights' compound. All those lunatics are locked up. Steel cages on Brookley. The key's been thrown away or swallowed or buried. "Why is the Alabama National Guard here?"

"It's about time the state took over here, don't you think?"

"Friedman ordered you here? She's still the governor, right?" I lean against the fence, hoping the support will do the trick. "I thought we were safe now. Electric is restored. Somewhat stable even." My jaw tightens and my mouth fills with saliva. I'm going to be sick. In front of this man. On this man if he doesn't back the hell up. "I'd think it was time for all of you to go away. Let us be."

"Miss, you don't look well."

"The Knights are gone, right?"

"We were mobilized to keep the peace around here."

"Keep the peas?" Okay, that was a bit slurred. "Peace," I say with too much effort for such a simple one.

"Yes. It is peaceful around here lately, isn't it?" Shahin snaps his fingers at one of the soldiers. "Water. Now."

"Yeah. It's been good." Mama, please forgive me because I really need to spit. And lie down. Right here. Spit, then lay down.

Shahin cracks open a bottle of water and hands it to me. I drink it down like I've never had water before in my life.

"Slow down," he cautions.

Shahin needs to go before I do or say something stupid. I made so many wrong moves with Brandon Johnson, the regular Army commander. I went off half-cocked and blamed him for failings that weren't his. I blamed him for Billy's death, even though I knew he had nothing to do with the Knights lynching Billy. I blamed Johnson for my abduction even though he had nothing to do with that either. I even blamed Johnson for the Knights' power over the people here, but none of that was his fault. Not really. And I'm trying to be more intentional. Less half-cocked and more full-cocked.

Is that a thing? Full-cocked?

And I'm trying to accept my responsibility in Billy's death. If Billy hadn't been off the base by himself to talk to me, the Knights wouldn't have snatched him. They wouldn't have beat him to death and hanged him from the boathouse rafters for me to find.

Also, I'm trying to accept the order of events that led to this situation in the first place. If domestic terrorism hadn't shut down supply lines leaving the people of Bellefontaine to starve, they wouldn't have had to accept the Knights' offerings of food and potable water. They wouldn't have been forced to exchange loyalty for their lives.

But then it comes back to me. My share of the blame. If I

hadn't pissed off the Knights, they never would have come after me. Johnson wouldn't have had to waste time on my safety. Billy wouldn't have had to worry about me. Johnson, Billy, and everybody else would still be healthy and alive. So, no, Johnson is the last person I should have blamed. He's paying to know me with injuries from head to toe. At least that's what it looked like the last time I saw him.

This new guy standing in front of me, fulfilling the duties of what is more than likely his first command, might not even know about Clem Richardson manipulating all those people. He may not know who Clem's son Dave is and that he's who drove me to the middle of the bay and dumped me on a rickety lighthouse deck to die. Shahin may not even know that Dave is a wanted man or that he's still in hiding.

I want to ask Shahin if Dave Richardson is still alive, but I don't. My stomach cramps at the thought, making my muscles weak. I really need to sit down, but I can't. Not with this new captain still here. Weak women draw attention, especially from men with savior complexes. I don't need regular checkups from an Army officer with higher ups to brief with all the good he's doing. *Strong, Jules. If you can't be strong, for the love of God, look strong.*

I take a cue from Cole and keep my words to myself, then drain the bottle. If Shahin thinks all is well, maybe he'll tell the higher ups, and they'll decide all is well. Then, these soldiers can go home without being replaced by a new group. And who knows if this new captain can be trusted. In the end, I trusted Johnson because I knew whose side he was on. But I don't know this new guy. I know he's in the National Guard, so I know he's at least from Alabama. What if he's far more local? What if he knows the Knights? What if some of Shahin's troops are Knight sympathizers or even Knights themselves?

The cool water in my stomach swirls around, shooting a

swimmy imbalance to my head. Get it together, woman! But the thoughts just keep coming. A long-forgotten saying drifts into my mind. *One man's terrorist is another man's freedom fighter.*

And with that, the strength I pretend to have flies away on the convection-oven wind. I vomit, giving into my hangover. Not quite Exorcist level spewing, but every bit of the water mixed with a little bile splash on the ground and on Shahin's boots. My vision tunnels as I feel my body limp.

On the ground, I blink, but the flashes of light are fuzzy. Men's voices sound miles away as I am lifted into the air. Someone or some ones carry me. Through the gate and to the military vehicle. A door creaks then opens, and I'm lifted into the vehicle. The leather-like seat is hard beneath my body. Memory slips in. Jacob smiling with a pint of Guinness in his hand. He takes a long sip then says, looking straight into my eyes, "Only soft thing in a tank are the four people inside it." But I'm not in a tank, and Jacob's not here. A hand slips out from beneath my head. When I open my eyes, Cole sits next to me.

"Cole, get all the way in. Close the door. Seatbelt."

"I'm in, Jules. I'm fine."

I hear the engine start and feel a vibration as the vehicle moves. Through the windows, I see two soldiers walking beside the vehicle. They pick up speed to jog alongside our transport. Beyond the soldiers are the trees, shrubs, and kudzu of Bay Aire Road. Through the windshield, I see Mobile Bay creeping closer, or rather, we're creeping closer to it.

"No, Cole! They cannot take us home!"

"Where else are we supposed to go? Miz Martin is going to want to help you."

"But they don't know. Mama and Daddy don't know."

"Of course they don't know you passed out. That's why we're taking you home."

"No, Cole. They don't know who these men are."

CPT Shahin turns, staring at me from the front passenger seat, an alarmed look on his face. "And who exactly are we to you?"

Shit. I pull myself up in time to see Matt pulling the driveway gate open. As we pass, Matt makes eye contact with me.

Double shit.

———

Yes, I am the queen of poor decisions. If I'd kept my mouth shut, Shahin and his soldiers wouldn't be touring our property right now. Once Matt unlocked the gate, allowing the Army vehicle access to our driveway and to park next to our carport, Shahin asked for a tour. Requesting a tour sounds much better than, "We need to search your property." Refusing the request of a tour would be downright inhospitable and break the southern hostess' etiquette guide my mother has followed her entire life. And Shahin seemed to know that.

Thanks to Matt's natural born curiosity, I learned that my ride home was in a Mine-Resistant Ambush Protected All-Terrain Vehicle, or MATV for short. Matt asked what kind of vehicle it was as soon as I staggered from the back seat. I'm almost offended by how uninterested he was in my health. But now I want to know why such a heavily mechanized vehicle is necessary for securing a fishing village.

"How long have you lived here?" Shahin asked as Mama led him from the carport to the back door.

"Thirty years," Mama said.

"What did you do for work before everything shut down?"

"I was a bank teller. A head teller," Mama said, having led him through the house to the front porch. She then stepped back inside the house, leaving Shahin, Daddy, and me on the porch, which is where we are now. All I want to do is sleep, but there's no way I'm doing that until these soldiers, these military police officers, are off our property.

"And you, sir?" Shahin asks Daddy.

"Civil engineer."

"Hmm, hmm." Shahin appears preoccupied, looking from the house to the pier and back.

"Do you or any member of your family have a connection to local militia?"

I'm woozy still, but this is beyond the pale. "No! None of us do. The Knights tried to kill me, remember?"

"Julianne, go lie down." Daddy looks at me like I'm a kid in need of a nap.

"Daddy, I—"

"Go." Being done with me, Daddy turns to Shahin. "What else on my property would you like to see?"

"What's the view like from the pier?" Shahin asks, seeming unaffected by Daddy chastising me.

"Be my guest." Daddy motions toward the pier, then follows Shahin down the slight hill and onto the wooden walkway.

I walk inside and straight to the living room sofa. Mama is waiting with a damp towel for my head and strict orders to drink every ounce of water from the mason jar in her hand.

"What were you thinking, Julianne? First, you put yourself in harm's way by being out in that heat without enough water, and then—"

"I thought I was plenty hydrated."

"What if you had passed out with only Cole to get you home?"

"We would have figured it out."

"Or you would have suffered a full heatstroke, dead in the garden. Your Daddy would have died of a broken heart if that had happened."

I look out the front windows at Daddy. He's a shadowy figure at the end of the pier standing next to another, taller shadow. It will be a bit before he feels he can speak to me without losing his shit. That's my parents' way. One of us got hurt, they got angry because chances were likely that we got hurt because we were doing something stupid. That premise hasn't changed since we all aged out of hide-and-seek and games of tag. We're still supposed to use the "sense God gave a goat," and I didn't do that today.

Mama's not patient like Daddy, though. She won't wait for her pulse to slow before the exasperation comes out, loud and fast. "Jules, I swear you have some sort of death wish. The dangers you put yourself in."

"Mama, I'm fine. Please sit. You're getting upset—"

Mama cuts her gaze at me. "Not getting. I'm there. What were you thinking saying such a thing to Captain Shahin? 'They don't know who these men are!'"

"How do you know that?"

"Cole told Matt. Matt told me."

"Wow. Y'all don't waste any time, do you?"

"Are you trying to get this entire family locked up? For what? Nothing. We've done nothing wrong. But you. You insinuate that we don't want those men here."

"One of the soldiers was a woman."

"Do not get cute with me, young lady."

"Mama, please sit. You're way too worked up."

Mama puts a hand to her chest and lowers herself into her chair, the plaid upholstered rocker with matching glider that no one sits in except her, at least not when she is inside the house. "Jules, what on earth did you mean by that? What don't we know? We've been living around soldiers for so long. Why would this be any different?"

I sit up straighter on the sofa, gulp the last of the water, and set the mason jar on the table. "Shahin and his guys are National

Guard, not regular Army. That means that the federal government has deemed it safe enough to leave."

"But that's a good thing."

"It would be if the National Guard wasn't here. Their being here means that even though the feds aren't too concerned anymore, the state of Alabama, Governor Friedman, has decided we still need to be watched, that some sort of emergency still exists here. Either the governor has decided we still need to be under someone's thumb, or she's not sharing what is still brewing around here. As far as we know, she's on the side of the Knights and wants to make sure that they win out over any other militia or movement that may be at play here. And the National Guard are locals. Just how local, I don't know yet."

"Oh." Mama slumps in her chair, pursing her lips as she digests what I've said. "Well, that sounds a bit paranoid to me. We can't overreact to this. It's still a smaller unit and military police instead of warfighters, right? That's a good sign, isn't it?"

Just as Mama seems to relax, Matt busts through the front door like his hair's on fire and all the water in the world is inside this house. "The National Guard? We've got local boys playing Billy Badass soldier now, watching their own?"

Good going, Matt. Let's make this situation worse.

2

R ight or wrong, I'm further away from the house than I've been in a long time, which isn't saying much since the garden has served as my personal boundary since returning from the clinic a year ago. No market days or ration distribution lines for this woman. I became an official homebody. Until today.

"Matt, this doesn't feel right."

Matt raises an eyebrow but says nothing.

"This screams turkey shoot."

"Jules, this is the same as it is every week. We're perfectly safe." Matt gestures toward the dozen or so soldiers lined up in front of the ration distribution tables.

I envy Matt. Here he is in his uniform for the apocalypse— khaki shorts, fishing shirt, and Crocs—without a thought at all to the dense woods that flank the asphalt road. All those hiding places. Matt sees a dozen guards and thinks no one will try anything with that much fire power on display. I see their positioning—a wide formation facing the line, rather than dispersed down it. They prevent entry into the COP, rather than protect the residents waiting for food. Their formation prevents any of us from rushing the stacks of rice and flour, not from someone rushing out of the woods, armed and dangerous.

"I shouldn't have come." I rub my throat, trying to massage out the panic.

Lauren, Matt's wife, strokes my back. "We'll be fine, honey. Matt and I are here every week and nothing ever happens. Well, except that." Lauren gestures right. "Oh lord, here they come," Lauren says, nudging Matt's side and throwing a smirk at me over her shoulder.

I follow her gaze to a truck parking in the grassy shoulder. About ten people pile out of the cab and back. *Fantastic*, the weird protestor people are here because God likes to give with both hands. According to Matt and Lauren, these freaks show up every week to the ration line. Until this moment, I thought Matt exaggerated how odd they are. Like any good southerner, Matt embellishes while spinning a yarn. Now, I think he downplayed the creep factor. Ten red-faced people with signs reading "Blood stains your hands" stare at the us, the citizens in line. I'm guessing they used beets mixed with clay because the red stuff on their faces is clumpy, dry and cracked like clay, with a watery substance dripping down their necks. "That red shit turned to mud in two seconds flat and slid right off their faces," Matt had said after a popup thunderstorm soaked everyone in the ration line two weeks ago, including the freaks. Matt laughed about that all afternoon. But looking at them now—their crazed stares gleaming from red faces—I don't find them funny at all.

"Who are they protesting—us or the Army?" I ask, but neither Matt nor Lauren answer me. It would make sense that the red-faced freaks are protesting the Army because the Army killed a handful of Knights during the raid on Mon Louis Island. So, maybe they're Knight sympathizers. But as each one breaks through the line to sit in the middle of the road, they face us, the people in line. They need to revise their signs to make it clear who has blood on their hands. Facing us with their signs suggests that we, the people in line, are at fault. But the only blood I've spilled belonged to Troy Cowart, and I don't feel a bit of guilt for that. And much to my dismay, I'm not the one that killed him.

Three protesters pass through the line directly in front of me, all wearing similar T-Shirts—old, dingy, but with freshly painted, bright lettering that reads BDEL. These three also carry themselves with an importance absent from the others. These freaks walk with their shoulders back and chins up. Silent like the others, but this silence carries intention laced with self-righteousness.

A red-faced woman shoulder-checks me as she passes. "Excuse you," I say. She stops and turns her head to glare at me. "Go on. Please," I say. Every bit of my badassery left my body the moment I locked eyes with her. I take a step back and bump into the person behind me. "Sorry. Sorry," I tell the stranger, but he only grunts a response. "I need this line to get moving," I say to Matt and Lauren. "The air is bad today."

"That's a constant." Matt speaks to me over his shoulder, dismissing my concern. "It's all that sulfur bubbling in the swamp. Should ease with high tide."

"Not the smell. Something in the air *feels* different."

As if on cue, and a big part of me thinks it is just that, the opening chords of "God Bless the USA blast over the crowd. If the patriotic blaring was supposed to affect the red-faced freaks, the shot misses its mark. They seem to have resolve, one impenetrable by Lee Greenwood's warbling.

"That's new," Matt says. "Has the COP always had surround sound?"

"Not that I know of," I practically shout back. The volume is way too loud. Uncomfortably loud. Unnecessarily loud. Loud enough to make a woman with a crying baby step out of the line and break down the road as if fleeing the noise. When I glance behind, my gaze following the mother as she jogs away, Clem Richardson stares at me.

I snap back around. "Fuck. Fuck," I whisper, frozen to my spot.

Clem Richardson? I glance back again, long enough to confirm that, yes, Clem Richardson is in this line. Just standing there like he belongs in a ration line and not the cafeteria line of a prison. One more glance, real quick, just to triple check. He catches my eye and smiles. That motherfucker is here and smiling at me.

My breath quickens. "I need to go. I have to go," I whisper.

Lauren glances behind us. I see in her face the moment she finds Clem in line. "What the hell? Matt," Lauren nudges her husband.

"Don't do or say anything," I command them. "Stay here. Right here." I take two steps forward, then stop short. "The kids. Cole and Jessie. They're in the truck." I look left down the line at Daddy's old truck, waiting for the bed to be filled with rations of food and fuel. Through the windows I see one flash of red hair and one of blond. "Why the hell did we bring them?"

"I'll get them." Lauren takes off to the truck, as I stand paralyzed.

I knew Cole should have stayed home. Jessie, too, but Cole is mine. My responsibility. I don't like him being anywhere near soldiers. I don't know if he's on some list or not, but I do know that stealing during martial law is a dumb move. One Cole made time and again before I caught him and gave him a real chance of survival. But can I really confine a twelve-year-old boy to our house all the time? That seems cruel, and he's already suffered enough cruelty for a lifetime. But I hadn't considered that Knights would be in this line. They're all supposed to be under lock and key, not walking around like they didn't try to kill all sorts of people here—most importantly to my neck, me.

I look at Matt. "I'll be back."

Before my brain intervenes, I march to the soldiers near the security checkpoint and straight to CPT Shahin. He'll do something about this. Their radios should be blowing up with some sort of jailbreak.

"Shahin," I say, winded from terror. "Clem Richardson is here. In line."

"And?" he asks.

I can't see what emotion, if any, plays on his face because his sunglasses are too dark. "He's supposed to be in lockup on Brookley."

"Miss Jones, I understand that seeing him may be distressing to you—"

"Distressing? Yeah. It's a hell of a lot more than distressing. Do something."

"Has Mr. Richardson done something to harass you today?"

"No, but—"

"Then, there's nothing to be done. Governor Friedman ordered the Knights released. All charges dropped."

I swear to God the pavement shifted. Liquified. Bubbled. "Dropped? No trial? No investigation? Just dropped?"

"That's right. In the spirit of reconciliation, she had the charges dropped."

"Reconciliation?" I blink away the bullshit of that statement. "How many of them are here?" I scan the line, trying to recognize faces, piece together eyes and browbones and noses into the faces of my backwoods-justice trial on the Knight compound. There's too many and my legs are mush, and I think I may hyperventilate, but there's no way I'm pulling two medical emergencies in front of this asshole. Two in two days.

"You should return to the line, Miss Jones. There's nothing more to do about Mr. Richardson here today."

As I stand there, stupefied again, a soldier motions a couple forward. The man stands with his arms out like a T as another soldier pats him down. The woman shows her ID, then presses one fingertip onto a little contraption connected to what looks like a cell phone.

"What are they doing?" I motion to the soldier with the fingerprint machine.

"Scanning biometrics."

Again, the total lack of concern or any emotion at all in Shahin's voice is disturbing. Mix his nonchalance with the blaring music, the heat, the red-faced freaks, and Clem Richardson hanging out a hundred feet away, and this is an aneurysm-inducing clusterfuck.

"Do you have all our fingerprints? How?"

"Well, not yet, Miss Jones. We just got this tech. It's been around awhile, but the old commander didn't think about it, I guess. So, new tech, new security. All we have to do is scan a fingerprint into the system, match the name and address, and we know exactly who should be here and who shouldn't. You wouldn't believe the number of non-residents that were allowed rations under the last unit. Despicable, really."

"Wow." That's all I've got. One syllable.

"Is there a reason you don't want yours or your family's data recorded? As far as I know, you are all here legally with your parents. Is this not true?" Shahin slips off his glasses and stares down at me. The moment or two that passes while he stares me down tells me all I need to know: Clem Richardson isn't the only asshole here.

"I'm going to rejoin my brother."

"Do that."

Matt's eyes are like fire when I step back in line. Lauren stands between the kids, an arm linked through one each of theirs.

"Well?" Matt asks.

"Friedman let them all out. She let them off the hook."

"Garbage." Matt keeps his voice low, so I must strain to hear him over the music.

"There must be more to it than that. They committed some heinous crimes. Terrorism, murder, attempted murder." I tap my own chest on the last one. "And Shahin's taking biometrics. Collecting fingerprints from everyone now."

"Everyone?" Lauren asks, then glances at Cole.

"Everyone, I think. I don't know. I just saw a couple get theirs scanned, but don't know if they're taking the kids' prints also. They scan them into this little machine. It matches your print to a name or builds a new item in the system. Shahin called it his 'new tech' and seems damned proud to have it."

"Maybe you should take Cole home," Matt says. "Lauren and Jessie and I can stay for the rations."

"I don't know," I say, swallowing hard. Vomit fights to make an appearance. Puking in the honeysuckle along the side of this road will definitely cause a scene, and I cannot be a scene right now. Not as long as Shahin and Clem Richardson are so near. And why is it that every time I get myself into some stressful situation, I want to puke?

"I wonder how long Clem's been out," Lauren says.

"Does it matter?" I snap, and Lauren flinches. My tone causes me to cringe. "Sorry. Sorry. Just look straight ahead, please."

It doesn't matter how long Clem has been free. What matters is if there are still people here who believe in him. He's only a threat if people still admire him. Admiration clouds judgement, and I need everyone thinking clearly. I need everyone in Belle-fontaine to see Clem for who he is—the true leader of the people responsible for so much destruction. I can go back home. Live in the garage forever. Keep Cole there with me and keep his finger-prints out of some Big Brother system. But if Clem ends up with the same hold on this town as before, we won't be safe anywhere, even locked up in the garage at home.

"Cole," I say over Matt's shoulder. "Cole?"

"Cole, Jules is speaking to you," Matt says.

"Matt, it's fine. He doesn't have to speak to me right now. I need to think." But every minute we stay in this line while I *think*, we inch closer to that fingerprint scan.

Matt shakes his head and lets out a sigh, which I take as his opinion of my parenting—poor at best. Well, he can save his judgement for another time, because right now I have to figure out how to get Cole and me far away from that machine and Clem. But my scrambled brain offers zero solutions, only a jumbled recap of this morning.

Before me, Cole had the run of all of Bellefontaine. Wild child of the trees and water. As long as he brought that bitch Martha stolen goods to trade, he could do whatever he wanted and had the bare necessities to survive. Alone in the woods. No one to love or who loved him. But he's got me now along with my whole family who are willing to treat him like one of us. So, he should listen to me. He should've listened to me and stayed home. More so, I should've acted like a real guardian, a parent, and stuck to my initial plan—for Cole to stay home, protected from the gaze and technology of the 128th Military Police Unit. Protected from Clem.

But Cole's face when I told him.

Earlier today, in the garage, I thought he would understand. I was wrong.

"So, all of you get to go where you want, but I'm trapped here? I can't even go to the ration line with you?" Cole stood next to his cot, squeezing his folded blanket to his chest.

"Cole, I have a bad feeling about this Shahin guy. Captain Johnson let you slide because he had bigger problems."

"And this new guy doesn't? Nobody's looking for me anymore."

I watched as confusion turned into anger on Cole's face. "We don't know that. We don't know anything about this guy."

"This is bullshit."

"Language, Cole."

"You're such a hypocrite."

"Maybe so, but that's not the point. I need you to understand that it is not safe for you to leave here. Not right now. Not until I know more about this new unit."

"Bull. Shit."

"Cole Aarons! You will not speak to me or any other adult that way. Yes, you are angry that I won't let you leave the property, but that's how it is right now. Don't you get it? I'm protecting you from what you used to do. Chances are there's a warrant for your arrest. Don't you get that? I can't walk up to a soldier and say, 'This is Cole Aarons. You may recognize that name because he was one heck of a looter. But he lives with me now, so it's all cool.' Cole, your actions have consequences."

Cole flushed, even his nose went red, then he swiped at a tear on his cheek. "So do yours!" He threw the blanket on the bed and kicked his cot until it flipped over, spilling the blanket onto the floor. "You're not my mom!" Then he ran out of the garage.

He fled, and I followed. He ran, and I chased him. He ran faster. All the way to the end of the pier. When I finally caught up with him, he kicked off his shoes and jumped into the water.

I wanted to jump in after him. To wrap him in my arms and tell him that, no, I am not his mother, and I would never replace his mother. That I wouldn't even try to replace her. I imagine she was the kind of mother that would do anything for her boy. I bet she was attentive and loving and did all those mom things like cook him dinner and read to him at bedtime when he was little. Maybe she sang soft lullabies to him and hugged him so tightly that he begged for air, then laughed when she finally agreed to let him go.

I should have told him all of that while standing waist deep in the water and holding him until all his tears were spent. But I didn't. Like a ninny, I stood at the edge of the crab deck and begged him to get back on dry land. *Because I'm afraid of the water.*

"Cole, I need to go, but I don't want to leave you like this," I yelled to him from the safety of the deck.

Cole turned away from me and sank below the surface. The water was so murky from an early morning storm that I could barely make out his shape.

"What is he doing?" Jessie, my niece, asked beside me. She'd appeared as if by magic.

I glanced around the boathouse and crab deck. "Have you been out here this whole time?"

"Nah. Ran out here when I saw you chasing him down the walkway. Wha'd'ya do to him?"

"Nothing. He's mad at me and knows I won't go in the water, so—"

"So, you did do something."

"Not really."

Jessie blew a red curl out of her eye and gave me the perfect pre-teen *you're so dumb* look. "So, he's just going to sit there under the water and you're going to let him?"

"Till he runs out of breath. I guess that's what I've got to do. He's going to need to breathe, eventually."

Jessie kicked off her flip-flops and pulled her T-Shirt over her head, revealing a striped one-piece bathing suit. "Don't worry. I'll get him." She smiled and did a perfect cannonball into the water, which caused Cole to pop up, undrowned but surprised by the intrusion. Floating on her back, her hair creating a flaming, curly halo around her head, Jessie looked up at me. "My dad says we'll be leaving soon, so you better get ready."

"You're going with us?"

"Yeah. Dad said Cole and I can hang out in the truck and help y'all load up after you go through the line."

"He did, did he?"

"Yes, Ma'am. Nobody's gonna notice two kids lounging in the truck bed." Jessie laced her arms behind her head, floating in the water as if her natural state.

"Matt doesn't make decisions for Cole. I do."

"Then take that up with Dad. But first, pants would be good."

I looked down and realized I wore only my underwear and favorite sleep shirt—Jacob's oversized Auburn University T-Shirt. No pants or bra. The shirt is soft as silk and threadbare in places and hangs to my knees because Jacob was so tall. But it's hardly appropriate attire outside of the garage. That's when I noticed the bottoms of my bare feet burning on the sun-drenched decking. "I guess I took off after him without realizing," I called back, skittering to a shaded spot on the balls of my feet.

"I know. We all watched you two from the windows." I followed Jessie's arm as she pointed to the house where several members of the Martin clan stood at the picture windows, watching me.

"Matt," I say, staring at my brother and hoping my face shows exactly how pissed off I am in this moment. "Next time, I need you to leave parenting Cole up to me. Okay? He shouldn't be here, and I knew that."

"So, take him home, Sis. Nobody's stopping you."

I'd like to punch Matt in the face, but that will have to wait. Right now, I need to figure out how to get Cole out of here without Shahin noticing and without Clem Richardson seeing how unarmed and vulnerable I am right now. Shahin is about forty feet ahead of me. Clem Richardson looms somewhere behind me. The red-faced freaks are sitting along the line to my left, making that exit a giant spotlight—who wouldn't stare at a bunch of people with beet juice on their faces, statue-stiff posture, and their lips practically sewn shut. So going left is a no. Forward is a no. Backward is a question.

"What the hell did you just do?" A man's voice thunders over the music and noise of the line.

Looking forward, I see a woman on her knees. When she stands, stepping away from the soldier towering over here, tears stream down her face.

"You can't touch her like that!" The man pushes the soldier then steps in front of his wife, protecting her from whatever the soldier just did and might do again.

At that, even a few of the freaks turn toward the commotion, breaking their protest. Two more soldiers engage, wrapping the man up and throwing him to the ground, knocking over the woman in the shuffle. The other soldiers close ranks around them, blocking whatever's happening on the ground from view.

"Shut it down!" Shahin's voice booms over everything. The music cuts out. "Shut it all down. You're done here. Go home!"

The crowd surges forward, panicked by the denial of food. For so many here, rations are their only source of food for the week. Some people in line cry out for food until the sound no one wants to hear: the spray of gunfire.

3

The muscles in my forearms burn. Sitting on the floor, out of sight of anyone who may pass by the window, I crank the radio for a good five minutes to ensure battery life for the entirety of Lefty Libby's afternoon broadcast. Daddy doesn't want us listening to the radio except for storm updates. He thinks the political talk stresses us all out, without benefit. Being uninformed stresses me out more, and the ration line fiasco earlier today proves just how uninformed I am. So, I'm going to crank this thing until my arm falls off.

Earlier, after returning from the ration line, I checked Cole for bullet holes. Three times. Three times, I clutched him in my arms, until he yelled at me to stop. Jessie intervened, having broken free of Matt's and Lauren's embrace. The adults agreed to let them go out front for a swim. So, I stood at the window and watched that redhead girl lead my boy down the pier and into the water. Maybe the water will ease Cole's mind, because I know from the rabid look in his eyes that he is not okay. Why would he be?

I wish I had Jessie's constitution. I wish we all did. As far as I can tell, she's already tucked away "soldier fired his rifle into the air" into a tiny box in the recesses of her mind, forever compartmentalized where the incident belongs. To her, *no harm, no foul* rings true. But I can't stop running all the what-ifs through my mind.

What if Cole had been shot? What if medical intervention didn't arrive in time? What if I couldn't save him? What if I am the reason I bury him? What if I'd stayed out of his life?

Because if it weren't for me, he wouldn't have been at the ration line at all. Ever. He wouldn't have had to leave the safety of the truck to be "safe" from Clem Richardson. If it weren't for me, Clem Richardson wouldn't know who he is. Maybe Cole should've stayed in his little clearing in the woods, sleeping under the shade of that live oak. And what's weighing heaviest on my heart, pressing on my breastbone until I can't breathe is this: Did I bring Cole to live with us for his sake or my own? Did I save Cole, or is his being here saving me?

After staring out the window for far too long, watching Cole grin as he and Jessie performed cannonballs off the crab deck, Mama started in on the lack of rations for this week. The panic in your voice over how to feed all of us without a week's worth of rice, flour, yeast, and oil was too much for me to digest. So, I told the family that my first excursion outside of the safety of home wore me out. That wasn't a lie. My bones were tired, as if all the life and vitality had been squeezed out of them. But as soon as I closed the garage door behind me and let the silence of this space envelop me, lightning surged through my veins.

Something is happening here, or something is about to happen. Or something isn't right. I don't know exactly what, but I know something is off. We can all tell ourselves that we're safe. That today was nothing more than one soldier overreacting. That the Knights are no longer a threat. And maybe Governor Friedman believes that all those people were acting out of desperation. If so, maybe she's right. Fear makes people act badly but it isn't who they are at their core. Maybe that soldier today was scared. Maybe most of the people on the Knights' compound a year ago were afraid of life on their own. But that doesn't erase what the Knights did, and I can't twist my brain into believing that Friedman let the Knights walk out of jail out of some misdirected compassion. *Spirit of Reconciliation. Bullshit.*

What if the Knights are bigger than I thought a year ago? What if Clem Richardson isn't the tip of the spear but a tentacle connected to a much larger body?

The only remedy I can think of for curing this anxiety is listening to Libby's show. Become informed. And I need to listen alone. No comments from the peanut gallery. No questions from the family members who may not get that all is not quiet on the western shore of Mobile Bay. No one to make excuses for the actions of that soldier today. Just me, a locked door, the radio, and Libby's voice.

I wiggle the antennae, stretch it to its maximum length, and finally, a static pop and Libby's voice breaks through, strong and as rich as ever. And loud. *Shit.* I turn the volume dial down.

Good afternoon, my darlings. I'm coming on the air today with a weight on my chest. Heavy, heavy, heavy. What has transpired over the last few hours makes me question who the real enemy is. First, and brace yourselves for this one in case you haven't heard, Governor Friedman has dropped all charges related to the Knights and their criminal enterprise in Bellefontaine.

Yes, I know this is hard to learn and confusing for any law-abiding citizen, and I agree with you. I'm confused. I also feel Bellefontaine is a lot less safe today now that these lunatics are back among us. Does the Governor think they will all behave like good little boys and girls again? That their days of blowing up bridges, abducting women, and terrorizing the good people of our community are just over and done with? Are we to believe that a few months in jail have rehabilitated all of them? Especially after what transpired today at the ration line?

Wait. Was Libby Lefty in that line today?

That display of brutality against one of our own cannot be tolerated. From what I witnessed—

She was there! Right there, and I had no idea. I'm not sure why I thought she's been holed up in some basement this whole time, especially since basements are pretty much nonexistent around here, but I did.

...that soldier manhandled that woman, which caused the man with her to push back, as any decent person who witnesses such an act would. For his trouble, the man—I have not confirmed his name—was thrown to the ground and cuffed. For her trouble of simply being there, the woman was shoved out of the way when more soldiers joined in this display of brutality. What happened next can only be described as an unexperienced man playing at leader. Captain Shahin, without a second thought to all of us standing in line so we won't starve to death, shut down the ration line. So, if you came and went before this incident count yourself as lucky.

But what about the unlucky ones? What are we supposed to do?

Captain Shahin should count himself as very lucky that the hothead soldier spraying bullets above that crowd didn't hit anyone. That, my darlings, is what you call an Act of God. Capital A, capital G. It is amazing that no one was injured or killed. But if blood was shed today, it would be on Shahin's hands. He needs to get ahold of his soldiers, and now, before we all end up dead.

Seriously. I can't imagine Jacob allowing that reaction out of his soldiers. Granted, I was never in combat areas with him, but the whole scene seemed so undisciplined.

Are we supposed to go back to the ration line? Try again to get the aid promised to us by our government? If I had any other way to feed myself, I would stay far away because I don't trust this new unit one bit. Not after today. And does Shahin not understand that this kind of chaos and fear was exactly what led to the Knights fooling so many around here with their "We'll take care of you" bullshit rhetoric. This is beyond the pale, Captain Shahin. Beyond the pale.

Yes, it is. So, what are we supposed to do about it? I need guidance, not a Libby rant.

But buckle up and hunker down, because this Shahin guy isn't done ruining this day for all of us. Not two seconds before I came on the air, a flyer drifted onto my patio.

Leaving the radio on the ground, I rise up on my knees and peek out the window. Nothing but green grass and—*oh shit*—Kate and Garrett on the side porch swing. I hit the floor and turn down the radio volume to barely audible.

...I am sick and tired of cleaning up all this trash every time the Army decides to disseminate information. So, just in case the choppers haven't reached you yet, let me read to you this hot garbage: Effective immediately: Unauthorized travel to and from Bellefontaine is prohibited until further notice. All residents should remain within the boundaries of Bellefontaine. Any unauthorized attempt to travel north of Baker Sorrell Road, west of County Road 59, or south of Highway 188, will be deemed hostile movement. Violators will be detained.

What the hell? We're trapped here? I know I don't have plans to leave or go anywhere else, but having the option made me feel better.

Take a moment. Digest. But, as I've said before, my darlings, compliance is key. Yes, that is a hard pill to swallow—complying with everything the National Guard demands of us is hard. But we must comply. Even when they tell us we are no longer free to come and go as we please. I know no other way forward than compliance. And I must keep the faith that if we abide by their rules for just a bit longer, just a little while longer, my darlings, eventually Governor Friedman will pull the soldiers out of here and send them home. Eventually, life must return to normal. I just pray we can all hold on until then.

"Your grand plan is compliance?" I say out loud. And as if Libby heard me, she answers.

Compliance means not fighting back. Do not challenge their laws. Compliance means following this travel ban. If you had somewhere to go, you don't now. Plain and simple. Do not risk your life trying to leave Bellefontaine. After what Shahin's soldiers did today at the ration line over a man trying to protect his partner, I don't know what they will do if you try to blatantly break one of their laws. Your life isn't worth it.

And I know many of you are not happy about the biometrics situation—my god there's just so much to deal with today—but you must comply. Yes, there are privacy and usage concerns. I have them too. But I'm not in charge. We're still living under martial law, and if the law states we must scan our fingerprint at ration lines and checkpoints and lord knows where else, then that is what we will do. We will remain compliant until they leave. Compliance is our best form of resistance.

Lastly, we will not, not a single one of us, act out any form of revenge on any former member of the Knights. I cannot stress this enough. Any act of retaliation will only encourage the Army to stay. Peaceful living. That is our best bet to being left to live our lives freely under our Constitution without this continued occupation. The tide will turn in our favor. It just has to.

Our hard days are far from over, but if we lose our patience now, if we submit to our worst urges, we fail. All that we have gone through these last many, many months—hunger, fear of a known terrorist, greater fear of the unknown devils among us, losing loved ones—my God the grief we've all endured—will all be for nothing, if we can't keep our anger in check now... I'm sorry... I need a moment.

Was that a choke in her voice? Libby's upset washes me in dread. In the past, Libby was always controlled, so effortless with her updates and witty observations. Today's broadcast hasn't offered a single moment of levity, not an ounce of wit. And since when did she believe we must accept all of this? *Compliance?* For fuck's sake, Libby.

The sound of Libby clearing her throat too close to the microphone makes me jump, and I nearly bump the radio on the floor in front of me.

Thank you for that, darlings. I apologize. I guess even your old gal Libby needs a good emotional breakdown once in a while. Emotional bloodletting is good for the soul, right? I wonder how many of you, like me, thought this would be over by now. How many of you thought we would be back to grocery shopping, sitting through school plays, Friday night lights, community fish fries? I did. I guess my being so horribly wrong is getting to me today. Do you know that I still have the phone right next to my chair in the studio. It's right here. I want to reach out and press a button for a caller. Say, "Hello, darling, you're on the air with Libby," but no one calls. None of those buttons light up. It's just me. Alone. Talking into this microphone. I assume I have an audience. I assume you're out there, listening to me. That's what my sources tell me. They tell me that you're listening, but I don't know that for sure. I don't know anything for sure anymore.

It must sound like I've lost my mind. Maybe I have. Maybe this is all too much for me today. I promise I'm trying to keep it together. I promise. I'm keeping my eyes and ears open so that I can relay every important detail to you, my faithful listeners. So, stay strong. Stay vigilant. Stay compliant. Until next time. This is Libby Lefty signing off.

Libby sniffs and clears her throat. The last sound from the

radio is a nervous laugh then static. What the hell did I just listen to? And who in that line today goes by the name Libby Lefty? I should have paid more attention to the people around me because she had to be standing close to us to have had the view she did.

The sound of a door handle rattling startles me. I flip off the radio and sit still with my back pressed against the wall.

"Jules, you in there?" Cole's voice sounds from outside the locked door.

"Yes, yes. Hold on." Sliding the radio under the table, I pull myself up to standing. "I'm coming."

"What's going on?" Cole asks, as I let him in through the doorway. "You just sitting in here in the dark?"

"It's not too dark in here." I look around the garage, where I've spent so much time over the last year and a half. First, it was my sanctuary, where I could hide from my family and entertain my ghosts. Then, with the addition of one boy, two cots, and a sheet hung between them for privacy, it became Cole's and my home. It is our shelter from everything outside these walls that could harm us.

"I guess I'm not used to having the lights on anymore." I flip the switch next to the door, illuminating the space with all its dust and clutter.

"Missus Martin wants our dirty clothes. She's going to wash them." Cole steps behind the curtain to his side of our sleeping area. A few moments later, he reappears in fresh clothing and walks toward the door, a pile of dirty laundry in his arms.

"Cole, I'm so sorry."

"For what?"

"I guess for not knowing you well enough to know what you need. I promise I will not replace your mother. I'm not trying to do that, and I couldn't do that anymore than someone could replace mine. We only get one. But... I want to keep you safe. I must keep you safe. Maybe your mom would want that, too."

Cole drops the armload of laundry on the table and sits on Jacob's trunk, in its permanent spot near the table. I can't see Cole's face, but I hear jagged whimpering, the kind that doesn't come freely, the kind every muscle in your body tries to suffocate. I sit next to him and drape my arm across his shoulders.

Leaning into me, he speaks. "I miss her so much."

"I know you do."

"If she were here, I wouldn't—" Cole cuts himself off and scoots away from me.

"I know," I say. "You wouldn't be here. You wouldn't have gone through everything you've been through. You wouldn't have been in that scary scene today."

"I wouldn't have done the things I did!" Cole stands, looking like he wants to run from the garage or blast himself through the ceiling. He squeezes his hands into fists and punches his own thighs.

"Cole, you did what you had to do to survive. And don't forget you were a little kid, a child, following Miss Martha's orders. She is to blame for you stealing from people. Not you."

"That's crap." The certainty in his eyes nearly breaks me. "I knew what I was doing. I stole all that stuff. And for what? Some bread and a little deer meat?"

"It kept you alive."

"It made me a thief." Cole stares at the ceiling, a mixture of regret and disbelief showing on his face.

"No, Cole. That's what you did. It's not who you are."

"Now, because of that, because of what I did, I can't leave here." Cole glances up at me then away again. "Not that I want to leave. I mean I'm grateful for everything you're doing—"

"I know what you meant, Cole. When you're older, when it's time for you to get on with your life, you don't know if you ever will get the chance. If you will have the freedom to leave when it's time for you to go."

Cole sniffs his agreement, and I don't have the heart to tell him that right now, none of us can go anywhere. Whether we had somewhere to go or not, like Libby said, we don't now. Sitting on the trunk next to Cole, the reality of a travel ban starts to sink in, and that reality is bleak. If we can't leave, then neither can Clem or any of the other Knights who may—probably—still want revenge for what I did to them. For better or worse, we're all stuck here together.

I grab Cole's hand and pull him back down on the trunk beside me. "For now, I think you need to stay here. Those finger-print scanners…I don't know how connected they are to anything that happened last year. Like, I don't know if the old Army unit has fingerprints from any of your old crimes. I don't know how much investigating they did. Hopefully, I'm being paranoid, and they have plenty of other things to worry about than a kid that used to steal things."

Cole looks at me. "Is this you being helpful?"

I nudge him with my elbow, laughing at his dry humor. "It's just, right now, I don't want the soldiers to know about you."

Cole's mood changes on a dime from calming down to abso-lute frustration. He stands, grabs an old plastic grocery bag from the shelf, and shoves his dirty laundry in it, piece by piece. "Why does Clem Richardson get to walk around like he ain't done nothing?"

"Clem Richardson?"

"I saw him today. He was in line behind us."

"Yes, but—"

"He gets to be free after everything he did." He pokes his chest with one finger. "I know what he did. I saw him. Doesn't he have to pay for what he did? I'm paying for my crimes. He should, too."

"He should, yes."

"He's dangerous. Way more dangerous than me. If the Army won't do anything about him, then I will."

"No."

"Somebody has to do something."

"Not you."

"Then who?"

"Not you, Cole. Promise me. Promise me or I swear to God, I will lock you up somewhere and not let you out until—"

"Until when, Jules? When will it be safe for us to leave here while Clem Richardson is walking around free? He's out there." Cole points at the window. The fear on his face is too real for me to hold his gaze.

I want to tell him anything but the truth. But a lie won't make the situation better, and, above all else, I need Cole to trust me. I need him to believe I will keep him safe. Lies won't do that. "I don't know, Cole. I don't know when normal life will be safe again. I don't know what the world will be like after all of this is over. But I promise I will keep you safe. Now and in whatever the future brings. I will not abandon you. But I need you to take a breath. I need you to breathe and leave Clem to the adults. You are to do nothing." Now, I sound like Libby. Maybe she's right. "Please, please, Cole. Do nothing."

"Fine." He shoves the last of his laundry into the bag.

"Promise?"

"I promise. Cross my heart and hope to die." Cole flings the door open and storms out of the garage with an exasperated sigh.

When I look through the open doorway, crisp white flyers litter the ground.

4

"Trust me, Jules," Daddy says, "the way through this is through this."

I grind my molars and nod at Daddy's so-called wisdom while sliding the second kayak from the rafters beneath the deck. He woke me at sunrise with his *I'm done waiting* look plastered across his face. I should take back his copy of the garage key. Yes, he owns this place, but I'm still entitled to privacy. Now it seems, along with a loss of privacy, I've lost all autonomy, and being awakened at dawn puts me in a piss and vinegar mood.

Before I can mount another protest, I hear a splash as Daddy lowers the first kayak into the water. I've already tried several *I'm not ready, Daddy's* and one *You can't force a person through trauma.* The latter garnered a smirk from Daddy.

"Julianne, get in the water." Instead of tying the kayak rope to the deck, Daddy drops it into the water. "You better get that before it drifts off." He lowers himself into a plastic chair and leans back, with no apparent intention of retrieving the wayward vessel himself.

Each of my past attempts to get back into the water ignites the same reaction. Lightning pings through my veins. My throat tightens and my tongue feels thick. Drowning. I feel like I'm drowning. I hold my breath, afraid to let go of the little air I have.

"Get the boat, Julianne. Jump in and get the boat."

"You get it." I cannot believe he is trying this shit with me. "Daddy, I am not—"

Cole pushes past me in a sprint, stopping the words in my mouth. He leaps off the lower deck and into the water, and I am left watching as he swims to the adrift kayak.

"Mothers have to be stronger than their children." Daddy says from the comfort of his chair. "It's not fair to that boy to make him be your rescuer. It's not right to burden him with your wellbeing."

"I'm not doing that."

Cole reaches the kayak and turns to drag it back to the pier. His chin is barely above water as the sun glistens off the high tide.

"Really? I'm betting that boy just saw you standing on the end of the pier and saw that kayak drifting away. He ran out here to save the kayak so you wouldn't have to. He knows you won't go in the water. He knows you're scared."

"Of course I'm scared. I get to be scared."

"Yes, you do. We all get to be scared. But the grownups have to be the grownups and let the children feel safe. Children feel safe when they trust the adults can take care of themselves *and* them. You're not giving that to Cole. Do you understand that? Kids need to see their parents doing hard things. That's how they learn to do hard things."

"Don't worry, Jules," Cole calls from the water. "I got it!" He climbs the ladder with the rope in his hand, then tries to pull the 12-foot boat up and onto the pier by himself.

"Cole, stop." I take the rope from him. "I've got it. You'll pull yourself back into the water."

Cole looks up at me. "I'm stronger than I look."

"I know."

"And you don't get in the water anymore, so I wanted—"

I muss his wet hair, trying like hell to stop the tears forming in my eyes. *Sweet boy.*

"Are you going out with your dad?"

"Um… maybe. I don't know. I don't think it's the right time."

Cole gives me a pitiful look.

"Cole, don't. Thank you for your help, but you may go now."

His look of pity turns into one of hurt. "I was trying to help you." Cole charges up the three steps from the crab pier to the main deck.

The guilt is immediate. "I'm sorry. I shouldn't snap at you."

He turns to me and spreads his arms, motioning to the calm water surrounding us. "You know what? If you can't make yourself get in the water, you never will. Stay out of it forever. Be hurt forever!" He turns and walks toward the house, his footfalls so hard that the pier shakes with each step.

"Great," I mutter to myself. Holding tight to the rope, the kayak bobbing in the water below me, I watch Cole for several moments, then look at the calm water. *From the mouths of babes.* "Daddy, are we going or not?"

"There was never any question," Daddy grabs two fishing rods and the green, short-handled net. "Get your butt in your boat."

In my red kayak, bobbing on the gentle chop of the water, my muscles know what to do even while I'm screaming on the inside. The paddle feels hard and stiff in my hands, foreign against my soft skin. My callouses earned from months of paddling softened while I obeyed my fear and stayed clear of the water. My skin may be as new as a baby's butt, but my muscles remember what to do. Without thought, my right arm, then left, dips and glides. My torso twists with the paddle, pushing the kayak forward, away from the safety of our pier.

"Let's head up shore, past the first set of piers. I've got a feeling about the second set."

As I paddle by the first pier—nothing more than a storm-damaged deck and walkway pylons stripped clean of boards—I am aware of how far we are from our pier, and how far Daddy intends for us to go. The second set of mostly abandoned piers is a mile from home. That's a lot of water. A lot of time for something to go wrong.

As we clear a third ramshackle pier, Daddy paddles up alongside me. Without turning to look at him, because turning my head might throw my balance off and send me plunging into the water, which would lead to the freak-out to beat all freak-outs, I ask a question of which I know the answer. "Did you ever run on a treadmill?"

"What do you think?"

"So, no." I rest my paddle on my lap and float with the current as I've done a thousand times before. Only now, I'm aware of the growing chop of the water beneath me, that feeling of teetering on disaster. *Just talk. Talking is a good distraction. Talking staves off panic.* "Jacob hated running inside. Well, he kind of hated running altogether, but especially inside on a treadmill." My voice is as choppy as the water—an unsteady rhythm with sudden peaks and valleys.

"I can't say I see the point of running myself unless there's a ball or bear involved."

I laugh at Daddy's joke and at the thought of Jacob's disdain for gym cardio rooms. "He thought nothing was more boring than running on a treadmill. If he had to run, and he did because he had to pass his PT tests, he'd rather run while looking at interesting things. Outside. He preferred running in the woods. Trail running. But he also didn't like treadmills because he thought it was too easy to quit. Not so outside."

"How come?" Daddy asks.

"If you run outside, no matter how far you run, you have to run back."

"Jacob was a smart man."

"Yes, he was."

"A good'n."

"Yes," I say, smiling at Daddy's use of such a country-fried phrase.

"As soon as you brought him home for that first family dinner, your mama and me knew it was over."

"What was over?"

"Your being ours. We knew you'd made up your mind. How would Jessie put it? 'You'd found your person.'"

"And just look at me now." Sarcasm is my favorite coping method.

"Yes, look at you now."

I turn to look Daddy in the eye and regret the move as soon as I feel the pang in my chest. Kindness and love from others tighten my chest. I don't know why. I wish I could be one of those people who accept compliments and words of affirmation without embarrassment, or worse, ending up a puddle in the corner of a room.

"Jules, you were tough to begin with. I've told you that before. But Jacob made you even stronger. I'm grateful to him for that. He loved you enough to let you grow into the most capable woman I've ever met."

I swipe a tear from my cheek and let out the breath I was holding. "So that's why you've got us paddling all this way, isn't it? Because you think the longer I paddle, the more comfortable I will become. That I'll remember."

Daddy grins, so proud of himself.

"Well, we're not back home yet. I could surprise you. You think I couldn't live on what's left of these piers? That's where you're wrong, old man. I am very resourceful and could set up shop under any old roof."

Daddy smiles at me. It is a smile that I love more and more the older I get. As a child, it was the smile that told me he was proud of me, the one that celebrated As on tests, hard-earned Bs, and goals scored in basketball games. Now, it is the smile that tells me I can do this. I can build a new life. I can give Cole a life of love and support. I can conquer this fear.

"That's what I'm hoping happens, Julianne. That you remember yourself. That you paddle back."

"And if you keep me talking about Jacob, I'll forget to be scared?"

"That, too. Talking about Jacob might remind you of who you actually are. Because you are more than you're giving yourself credit for lately."

"I know, Daddy." An annoyance that I meant to disguise is loud and clear in my tone. "I'm sorry. I didn't—"

"I'm serious, Julianne. The things you went through with Jacob. All those separations. Moving every two years. New places. Constant new people, new jobs, new ways of living. And you were both so young. But the two of you did it. You thrived in all that uncertainty."

"I loved Jacob."

"Takes more than love. Devotion through absence and constant change takes a strength few have. But you have it. I need you to remember that. Your experiences, even losing Jacob, have given you a toughness few people know."

I chew on the idea of toughness while Daddy and I paddle further away from home. Am I as tough as Daddy seems to think? The last year has made me feel anything but strong. In this storm of grief, I'm prone to a litany of trauma-related symptoms. Emotional outbursts, erratic mood swings, cynicism; that's all printed on my DNA now. Some days, I'm so fatigued that rising from my cot to lumber to the outhouse seems the only task I can complete, and that's only because the alternative is too humiliating to consider. My brain is goulash, all meat and noodles drowning in a thick roux. None of that sounds like toughness to me. Rather, this all describes a woman in need of a padded cell and psychotropic medication. If only that were an option.

At the second set of storm-ravished piers, we tie off to two pylons. Barnacles cover the weathered poles. The tiny creatures emit bubbles from their shells as they struggle to breathe in between soft waves splashing against the poles. As a kid, I was careful not to brush up against the barnacles when swimming or to step barefooted on the barnacle-covered rocks that revealed themselves at low tide. Not because I felt protective of the little creatures. I didn't really consider them living beings at all, just pieces of shell that would puncture my skin. But as I watch them now, a kinship forms between us. Like them, I am in a constant state of unrest, a depletion of oxygen as wave after wave of grief and fear wash over me.

"The fish aren't gonna jump in your kayak, Julianne. Get your line in the water." Daddy watches his cork float on the surface as he speaks.

Embarrassed again at my wandering mind, I cast my line down along the pylons, then reel the line back one slow crank at a time. This, according to Matt, is supposed to make the brown metal lure at the end of my line resemble something alive that a fish would want to eat. More often than not, this method is an exercise in failure for me, but it works for Matt. And it works for Daddy, evident by a sharp whirring sound behind me.

"Got something," Daddy says, his voice straining against the exertion of cranking his reel. Whatever is on his line struggles against the hook in its mouth. Daddy's pole is bent into a full arc, and his words come out in mostly pants and snips. "This is either very big or very strong."

I secure my fishing pole to my kayak with a bungee cord and

paddle closer to Daddy. Grabbing the net from Daddy's stern, I watch as the fish breaks the surface in an angry thrash.

"Get that net under him." Daddy pulls and yanks the line—a mighty battle between beast and man. "Now, Juliane, now!"

I let go of my paddle and hold the net handle so tight that I am sure my knuckles are white. I thrust the net beneath the surface, beneath the fish, and feel it fight against the green mesh. My paddle falls into the water, but I let it drift. *Get the catch. Get the catch. Do not allow this fish freedom.* With both arms, I heave the net out of the water and set my eyes on the biggest speckled trout I have ever seen.

"Hot damn! Look at it!" Elated by the sight, Daddy sets down his rod and takes the net from me. Blood oozes from the mouth of the fish, a shiny, spotted trout of possibly three feet long.

"Daddy, I didn't know trout could be that big."

"Me neither." With the fish laying on the bottom of his kayak, Daddy removes the hook from the trout's bloody lip and drops the fish into the live-well in the bow of his boat. "Julianne, your paddle." Daddy points a few feet away, where my paddle is attempting escape.

"Shit." I lean forward and paddle with my hands, catching the loose end of the oar's rope. The combination of posture and movement recalls a memory—desperate paddling across the shipping channel on a wooden door. I squash the mental intrusion and snag the wayward oar by the tip of one blade. When I turn back to Daddy, paddle securely in my lap, he's rocking back with laughter.

"Stop laughing." I protest but Daddy's laughter is contagious. "I was trying to help you get that thing in the boat without flipping both of us over."

A rare but familiar sensation flows through my muscles and over my skin. It is the feeling of being unburdened, of agony leaving my body. *Happy*. This is what happiness feels like. But happiness is fleeting.

———

After an hour of casting and reeling, Daddy scored three more trout for a total of four. I reeled in one nasty catfish. Daddy was kind and dubbed it good bait for the crab traps, so I guess my fishing effort wasn't in vain. And fishing wasn't the actual goal of this excursion, was it? Today is about ripping off Band-Aids. So, I peel up the corner of another.

"Daddy?" I ask and wait as he rotates in his kayak to face me. "Daddy, what do you think about the National Guard being here rather than regular Army?"

"I'd like to think this means things are settling down. That now, soldiers are here to maintain peace and safety while we rebuild. Like after a hurricane."

"You're not concerned that Governor Friedman did this to keep tabs on us?" I know Daddy is not a fan of speculation, but this needs to be discussed.

"Oh, I don't doubt that for a second. But she has to consider the safety of the entire state. If Mobile, especially the port, isn't safe, then the state isn't."

"I see that. But, if the regular Army is gone, what happens with the Knights? Clem Richardson is walking around a free man. The rest of the Knights are free as well."

"I'm sure she had her reasons for letting them go. And I don't want anyone turning Brookley Field into another Guantanamo Bay. Do you?"

"I don't think the man calling the shots for a criminal group should roam around. Do you?"

"No, I don't. But it's not our decision to make."

"Why aren't you angry about this? You should be angry, Daddy. He wanted me dead!"

Daddy locks his gaze to mine and the rage in his eyes stops my breath for a moment. "I am angry," he says through clinched teeth. "I want that man locked away for the rest of his life. But I can't make that happen. Do you know how that feels? To not be able to protect your child? Can you imagine that feeling, Julianne?"

I have no words. It's hard to even look at Daddy, seeing the hurt in his eyes. Watching the tick in his hand start up. I did this to him.

"Sweetheart, all I can do is keep you safe now, away from him. And pray. I pray every day that no one will listen to Clem after what became of the Knights' compound."

"You've seen it?" A flash of irritability prickles my cheeks. "When?"

"Only from the water. I haven't been on Mon Luis Island in over a year, maybe two."

"Oh." I breathe in and out to calm my nerves. They're so easily frayed. "So, no one is living there?"

"Not that I could see. All the houses and outbuildings are boarded up."

"I wonder where Clem is living."

"I don't want you to worry about him."

"I have to worry about him! Because apparently, he still has rights, even under martial law, which I thought suspended those things."

"We're not making the rules, Julianne."

"That's why I have to worry!"

"I know you will, you're going to worry. Twist yourself into knots, just like your mama, but try not to. You will never be alone with Clem again."

"I bet Freidman blamed all of this on Troy and Dave. One

dead, one alive in hiding as far as we know. That's almost a tidy bow on the whole mess."

"Dave Richardson is probably dead."

"He's out there, Daddy. Somewhere."

Silence falls between us for several moments. It's heavy and thick with anxiety.

"So, all I'm left with is to keep looking over my shoulder. I get to spend the rest of my life searching for the boogeyman."

"No. This will pass. In the meantime, you do as I ask and don't leave our property by yourself. We will keep you safe. I will keep you safe."

"So, Clem is free, Dave is free, but I'll have a chaperone for the rest of my life."

"That's a little dramatic, don't you think?"

"Dramatic or not. It's true." I reel in my line, losing faith that anything else will bite today. I assume that with the sun high in the sky, the fish have gone somewhere cooler to hide from the heat.

Daddy does the same with his line, looking quite satisfied with the day's catch. "I guess none of us will be going much of anywhere, what with the travel ban in effect."

"Surely that concerns you? They've trapped us all here, the criminal and the law-abiding, to duke it out until one side is demolished. Removed from the Earth while Dave hides in a cave somewhere."

Yes, happiness is fleeting. The peace that washed over me an hour ago slips away, sinking to the bottom of the bay.

I face the shore as my kayak turns with the current. As I rock with the slight waves, my mind conjures Dave Richardson's face. He's peering down at me as I cower on the bottom of his boat, he wants me erased. I squeeze my eyes shut to dispel the image.

When I open my eyes, I spot them. Two men step out of the tree line, causing my breath to catch in my throat. One man carries a bundle. I can't tell what from this distance, but it's definitely white or wrapped in white. In another time, two men emerging from the woods on a clear day wouldn't cause alarm. That time feels so long ago that I wonder if I ever felt so safe as to not worry about the appearance of two strangers. *Was that ever real life?*

"Daddy, who is that?"

"Not sure."

I watch as the man with the bundle unfurls it. "Is that a sheet?"

Sitting there, bobbing in my kayak, the men acknowledge us, giving a quick wave. I don't wave back. The last thing I want is actual contact with these two. The men turn away from us and back toward their task. "What are they doing? Are they hanging something?"

The men hammer the ends into two trees, leaving it stretched between them. Then, the men wave again and disappear back into the woods. Even from this distance, some hundred yards away, I can read what they've left behind—a banner.

"What is The Way?" I ask, not expecting an answer, and Daddy doesn't offer one. Instead, we both stare at the words—*By Dawns Early Light. The Way.*

The first letter in each word is painted in red: B-D-E-L.

"Daddy… I…the protesters had that on their shirts at the ration line."

"Untie the ropes, Julianne. We need to get home."

5

Whoever makes banners for The Way didn't win the English prize in high school. The three banners I know of—two I've seen over the last week and one that Matt saw—have said the same grammatically incorrect phrase: *BY DAWNS EARLY LIGHT*. On two of the banners–the ones I saw–the words were painted in red capital letters without the apostrophe in the word "dawn's." I asked Matt if there was an apostrophe on the banner he saw. His right eyebrow shot up to his hairline at the question. Matt's never been a stickler for grammar, so he didn't have a definitive answer. I assume the creator is consistent in their mistake, and I'd love to tell The Way that Francis Scott Key was not referring to multiple dawns when he wrote that famous line.

The error bothers me.

I can't correct the error unless I paint or insert an apostrophe on the banners myself, which will not happen. Also, does the use of all caps still mean yelling? If so, why is the banner yelling at me?

Yes, I am fixating on it.

It's a lot safer to fixate on a missing apostrophe and the yelling caps than what the banners mean. And I know the creator also omitted "the" in the line, as in "by *the* dawn's early light," but that doesn't bother me as much as the missing apostrophe. The missing apostrophe feels intentionally ignorant. Somewhere in The Way is someone who knows that's wrong and is keeping their mouth shut. Where's your grammatical courage, *The Way*?

Also, is something coming at dawn? Which dawn? It could be a literal dawn, but if that's the case, I wish The Way would provide a date. Also, details. If something is coming at dawn, what is that something? A brief description and exact date would inform me if I should stick around for the mysterious something, or head for the hills. Not that Bellefontaine has many hills. It's pretty much swamp, rivers, and flat land that becomes swampy if it rains too much, and a slope to the Bay. The one hill I know of is on Bay Aire Road near the garden and wouldn't protect us for long, as it's in the middle of a fairly busy road.

As I sit here on the crab pier, skimming the warm water below me with my bare feet, I know I am no closer to discovering who The Way is and what they mean by invoking the second line of The Star-Spangled Banner. Wait. Are the red-faced freaks The Way? That was the first time I saw mention of BDEL, but only three members wore shirts inscribed with those letters. Still, three out of a dozen feels substantial. Maybe they only had paint enough for three shirts and three banners. It's not like there's a Lowe's or Home Depot or craft store within the travel boundaries. I wonder if there's a single hardware store open on the entire Gulf Coast. Does anyone have cash to pay for home DIY supplies?

Or maybe the red-faced freaks mean something entirely different with those letters BDEL? *But did everyone lie? Bald dude eats lemons? Big dick energy leads?* Maybe the red-faced freaks are really proud of their lemon consumption and protective of the patriarchy. If that's the case, they needn't worry. I'm fairly certain most everyone likes lemons and the patriarchy's here to stay. *Dumbasses*. Trying to work out the acronym gives me a headache and reminds me too much of my first months as a new Army spouse bombarded with undefined abbreviations. It was a merciless death by acronym.

The locations of the banners give no substantial clues as to the identity or definition of The Way. The first banner was the one Daddy and I saw hanging from on an insignificant point of the shoreline. That stretch of deserted beach isn't of any importance that I know of. It's not facing a channel marker in the Bay or marking a path to an intersection of roads. It's not at a point on the shoreline useful for navigation or near a house or a meeting place. The second one I spotted was on the road leading to the Army's combat outpost on the lagoon, near the intersection with Bay Aire Road and the garden and our singular hill. That could be a warning or message to the National Guard, but it's also a frequented stretch because of ration distribution—that is, when Shahin allows distribution and doesn't throw a fit. With everyone in town lining up on that road once a week, the artist could just be going for mass exposure. It's certainly prominent, being the size of a twin bedsheet.

The third hangs at the Holy T—reported to me by Matt— where a good many Bellefontaine residents find themselves on Sunday morning, as the intersection is home to the two largest churches in Bellefontaine. So, hanging one there will get the attention of most of the Catholics and Baptists in town, which covers most of the population. Well, the population we know of. Who knows who is living here now? Maybe that's what Shahin is trying to figure out with the biometrics data collection.

The Way could be harmless. Maybe they're a group of well-intentioned Protestants telling us to keep the faith. *The country will survive! We just have to make it to dawn!* I'm assuming they're Protestant because no Catholics I know would refer to themselves as a member of *The Way*. We use phrases like the flock, the Church (uppercase C), or the Faithful (uppercase F). If that's the case—a group of well-intentioned Protestants—I won't worry about it. Spreading religious messages via billboards is commonplace in the South. I bet even with the chaos of the last year and a half, the *Go to church or the devil will get you!* sign is still standing alongside I-65 North. But something about the message *By Dawns Early Light* and group name—*The Way*—tells me this is not a bunch of mild-mannered Methodists trying to keep up morale. Does Bellefontaine even have a Methodist church?

My gut says The Way is The Knights, version two-point-oh-my-god. A rebranding. A fresh start. Being known for bombings, abductions, and murder is not a great look. I'd say The Knights need a rebranding. And turning to religious fanaticism and Bible thumping when your nuts are in a vice reek of the Richardson way. I'm sure Clem Richardson could cherry-pick a Bible verse to justify his every action.

Also, has any political conflict ever ended with the whole movement agreeing that they were wrong and promising to be more agreeable citizens? Not that I recall. I can't recall a single terrorist group that abandoned its cause after the long arm of the law bitch-slapped them. All that raid a year ago achieved was the complete radicalization of every one of The Knights. I'd bet my life on it, if I had a life worth betting on.

Yes, I am chin-deep in self-pity today, well that and obsessing over banners and Jesus-freak cults. Daddy's keeping his word about me keeping my butt at home. Sure, I can go to the garden if accompanied (Daddy's orders) and if I bring two jugs of water with me (Mama's orders), but I cannot leave the Martin Family footprint altogether. I might as well be a princess in a tower. If only I had ridiculously long hair or a friendly dragon to whisk me away. The dragon would probably chew me up with its monstrous teeth, then spit me out because I'm sure that by this point, I taste fishy.

I wonder if Cole feels like a princess in a tower, too. The hypocrisy of my actions—keeping Cole hidden as Daddy hides me—isn't lost on me. Or Cole.

So, here I sit. Fixating on things out of my control. Turning over in my mind images of all the potential boogeymen that lay beyond our property and barbed-wire fencing. Daydreaming of how I will rid the Earth of the Knights if they decide to attack our little slice of paradise. Imagining a dragon gagging after trying to eat me. Fantasizing over thumping the creator of those stupid banners right in the middle of his stupid apostrophe-less forehead. All while moving my legs back and forth so my toes drag through the warm bathwater that fills Mobile Bay in July.

But at least the Bay and the idea of being in the brackish water no longer results in a PTSD-like episode. Daddy's plot worked. He ripped off my fear Band-Aid and grinned while doing it. Maybe he didn't grin, but he was sure proud of himself.

The *thwap, thwap* of a helicopter interrupts my pity party. I look to the sky and watch as one flies just above the tree line. When it reaches the bayfront homes of Bay Aire Road, white leaflets float out the open door. I watch the paper disperse in the wind, falling in all directions. "Hey!" I stand, my balance compromised by my half-asleep legs, and wave my arms before grabbing hold of the deck railing. "Not in the water, idiots!"

As I watch the helicopter fly south, dumping more and more trash on my beautiful coastline, I rotate my ankles and slide my feet back into my flip-flops. The words "What fresh hell is this?" run through my mind like a banner towed by a prop plane.

The banner in my imagination undulates in the high-altitude air, whipping back and forth over the white coastline of the Gulf. Imaginary tourists look up from their beach chairs, blankets, and towels, hoping to read about the newest all-you-can-eat-shrimp special at the Hang Out or Live Bait or Flora Bama, but they read unexpected words instead—*What fresh hell is this?* Alarmed, they abandon their chairs, tents, coolers, and beach toys, and run inland. In my daydream, Matt appears on the beach. He saw the prop plane and banner, too. He waves his arms like a madman, desperate for my attention. The wind picks up his voice, and I hear him. "Jules! Now!"

Oh, shit! That's real. Matt's real.

Shaking out the last of the pins and needles in my legs, I rush down the pier as fast as I can in flip-flops without flipping myself out of my flops and into the water. Seriously, what fresh hell is this?

In the lush grass, I snatch a flyer from the ground. The words stare up at me: *Mandatory Town Hall Meeting.*

"All of us?" I ask Matt, reading the flyer in my hand. Matt's eyes show every bit of alarm that I feel. "We all have to attend? If we're all ordered to attend, Daddy has to let me go."

"Really, Jules? That's your reaction? I love ya, sis, but you're getting a bit selfish in your old age."

"I'm not old," I tell Matt.

"But being called selfish is cool with you?"

"I've been called worse," I say, shrugging off the insult. "You try being grounded in your thirties and tell me how much you like it."

"Anyway, Jules, yes. The order states the household must attend, and I don't like the idea of no one being here. That's asking for trouble. Open season on everything we have."

"I bet people are getting more and more desperate with rations shrinking."

"Exactly. We can't leave this place unprotected. No way in Hell."

―――――

Our conversation was quick, and I hope Matt didn't feel dismissed as I rushed through our discussion about the Town Hall order. I promise you, baby brother, I wasn't being dismissive, but right now, I need more information, even if it's laced with bias and speculation. I need Libby.

I rush around the side of the house. I could have cut through the house, the more direct route to the garage and radio, but Mama and a slew of others are inside. I can't risk being sucked into their speculations and worries. When I round the corner of the house, twenty feet from sweet privacy and a good dose of pirate radio, I stop short.

"Captain Shahin," I say, offering our visitor and Daddy a tight smile. My fist closes around the flyer in my hand. "Delivering an engraved invitation? You didn't have to do that. We'll be there."

"We'll discuss that later," Daddy tells me.

Oh, hell no. I'm going. The Great Grounding of Jules Martin Jones is done.

"I had an important matter to discuss with Mister Martin prior to the town hall meeting." Shahin swats a fly away from his face, but it comes right back. Persistent little nuisance. *Good job, buddy.*

Daddy looks at me, then back to Shahin. "I'll let you know my answer at the town hall." Daddy walks toward the house, calling to me over his shoulder. "Your mother will be ready with lunch soon. Come inside, Julianne."

"Sure, Daddy. I'll be inside in a few minutes."

"Now."

My cheeks flush as Shahin's face reacts to Daddy treating me like a child. "Daddy, I need to speak to Captain Shahin. Nothing bad will happen to me standing in our carport speaking to an Army officer. And I'm old enough to be alone with a boy."

Daddy grimaces but turns back toward the house. As soon as

the door closes behind Daddy, I look at Shahin. "What did you need to discuss with my father?"

"Well, I guess this won't be privileged information for long, and it's really not a secret, so—"

The house door flings open and out pops Matt and Mallie. Matt palms a cheap, plastic ball, the kind thrown by the dozens from Mardi Gras floats. He dips his chin to Shahin as he passes, then looks down at his daughter. "Come on, little girl. Let's play a little catch."

Mallie cannot catch a ball, and everybody knows it. She can roll a ball, bump one, even kick one with her short legs and pudgy feet, but she cannot catch.

"I don't need a babysitter, Matt," I call over to him.

"I don't know what you're talking about, Jules." Matt grins at me, then tosses the ball to Mallie, who reacts how I knew she would. She watches the ball float through the air, lets it bounce off her head, then collapses in the grass in a fit of giggles.

"Please continue," I tell Shahin.

"Why is your family guarding you? Is this about you fainting the other day?" Shahin asks, breaking out of his stuffy officer-speak for a moment.

"The fainting didn't help, but no, that's not it. They are all concerned now that Clem Richardson is walking around free. I may be in danger. Clem may want a little revenge. Did anyone think about that before he was released?" I stare at him with as much venom I can muster. And I muster considerable venom, enough to put down an elephant.

"So, as I was saying, you will probably learn about all of this as soon as you go inside, that is–"

"Nothing about Clem, huh?"

"I'm not your enemy, Miss Jones."

"You sure about that?"

"You don't know anything about me or my plan for Belle-fontaine."

"So, enlighten me."

"I came here today to ask your father to be on the Belle-fontaine Stabilization Council. I thought it best to include a member of your family in Bellefontaine's future. Don't you?"

Shock and suspicion. These two emotions compete for space in my chest. I am shocked that Shahin would think to include residents in his plan. Suspicious because that is my go-to reaction, especially for anyone in power, no matter how miniscule that power may be.

Before I can form a response, Shahin speaks. "Wow. So that's how it's done."

"How what's done?"

"Convincing you to close your mouth."

"Rude."

"Maybe," Shahin says, then offers me a boyish grin. "But you have to admit, this is the first time you haven't had a comeback at the ready."

"Well, how's this one? My first thought regarding your Belle-fontaine Stabilization Council is B. S. C. Bull shit cometh." Another acronym for me to play with.

Shahin laughs, appearing to relax into our exchange. "I hope it doesn't turn into that. But it's time to look forward. And I need your dad to do that."

"And now you want me to convince him to join your council?"

"Not want. I *need* you to convince him."

"What did my dad say exactly when you asked him to do this?"

"Not much at all, really. He's a man of few words and defi-nitely hard to read."

"A man of few words, yes. Hard to read? No. When he forms

an opinion, or in this case, makes his decision, you'll know it. He just likes to think over things before reacting."

"That!" Shahin's expression lifts, his eyes alight with his intentions. "That's why I need him. We're never going to move out of this… this… limbo without community leaders. Leaders who think instead of panic."

"Ready to go back home? Slap a Band-Aid on this and leave? Is that your plan?"

Shahin shakes his head. "You've got me all wrong. Sure, I'd love to be at home in my bed, but that's not an option for me. What I really want is for Bellefontaine to get back to what it used to be."

"How do you know anything about that?"

"My family has a fishing camp a little ways south of here. On Fowl River. I spent every summer here as a kid, fishing and crabbing off my granddad's pier."

"I didn't know that."

"Well, I did. We spent Sunday mornings at St. Philip's, just like you."

"I don't remember that."

"Of course you don't. You and Kate and Matt, y'all were older than me."

"So where is home?"

"Mobile. That's what I'm trying to tell you. This place. It's my second home. And since my first home, Mobile, is in shambles, this place, what happens to it matters to me."

A foggy memory comes to my mind. A boy with three friends on a makeshift talent show stage in a high school gym. "Are you *Georgie* Shahin?"

"Yes."

"Why did you act like you didn't know me when we first met? All that *I'm Captain Shahin*. You just… weren't we in chorus together? Why did—"

Shahin's blush—a surprising emotion coming from the CPT Shahin I thought I was getting to know—leaves the words in my mouth unsaid.

"Because you're Jules Martin," he says. "I recognized you from the start, but you clearly didn't recognize me."

"Well, in my defense, Georgie Shahin didn't look like this." I gesture to the expanse of the tall, broad-shouldered man standing before me. "Georgie was—"

"Short," Shahin says. An old hurt dims his eyes. "Small. Skinny. A joke. And I don't go by Georgie anymore."

"You weren't a joke, George. Is it George now?" I ask and Shahin nods. "And at that talent show, you were, what, a freshman?"

"So, you remember that?"

"Yeah. You have a good voice."

"We were laughed off stage. It was humiliating." Shahin's countenance shifts from Army captain to fourteen-year-old boy. The moment is brief, but there.

"I remember thinking how cruel that was. The jeering. The heckling. We went to school with a lot of jerks."

"All those seniors. Right in front. Laughing."

"Not all of us were laughing."

"Yeah, well, I'm not that kid anymore." Shahin rolls his shoulders back, like he's dismissing the ghosts of bullies past.

"Does my dad know your connection to Bellefontaine?"

"No."

"You should tell him. You should let people here know that this place is important to you. That we're not just an assignment for you."

"Maybe."

Something about this side of CPT George Shahin—his remembering a humiliation from high school and how much that humiliation still seems to bother him—softens my resentment towards him. He seems almost vulnerable. I understand being vulnerable. My vulnerability has been on display for so long now that I often feel like I'm walking through a lion's den, only I'm already skinned. Bare and bloody for all the world to see.

"I'll talk to him," I say. "I can't promise that I'll be successful, but I'll try. Consider it my penance for not telling the shitheads to shut the hell up back then."

Shahin nods. "I'd appreciate that."

"And you do have a good voice. Really good."

"Will I see you at the Town Hall?"

"It's mandatory, isn't it?"

"For the household, yes, but not every member needs to attend. Maybe the order was unclear." Shahin indicates the flyer, still crumpled in my fist. "I'd recommend one or two of you stay here to watch the place. Just to be safe."

"Oh. That makes sense."

"You look disappointed."

"Well, I haven't gone beyond Bay Aire Road for months." I open my arms wide and motion to the concrete floor of the carport. "Grounded."

"I could tell your dad that I want you there."

Now it's my turn to blush. "No need. I'll convince him." I raise my voice loud enough for Matt to hear me as he rolls the ball to Mallie in the grass. "It's time for all of them to treat me like an adult again."

"It's hard for them not to look at us as children still."

"Them?"

"Everyone our parents age." Shahin's expression slides back into military mode. "If you could persuade your father to join the committee, I would be grateful."

"I'll do it if you promise to keep rations coming. This community can't handle going without again."

"I can promise you that I will keep insisting on lawful and peaceful distributions."

With that, Shahin puts his helmet on and adjusts his chin strap. He nods his goodbye and walks to the MATV parked in our driveway. That's when I notice the soldier sitting in the driver's seat. He smiles at me, white teeth surrounded by acne-pocked skin. He can't be more than nineteen. At nineteen, I was a part-time waitress and a fulltime student. I carried a cellphone in my back pocket rather than a rifle across my chest. At nineteen, I had a crush on the busboy. That baby-faced busboy—Jacob—wasn't even thinking about guns, bullets, and orders to shoot straight at nineteen. He was too busy convincing the older servers to buy us beer and saving his tips to take me for a cheeseburger and Coke to think about his future self. Maybe I should offer Shahin a little grace as he leads not-yet men, but not-quite boys either. Maybe we're all in transition here from whatever we used to be to our future selves.

The MATV kicks up dust as it rolls down the oyster shell driveway. I watch as Shahin hops out and closes our gate, waving to me as he climbs back into the armored vehicle and rolls around the bend in the road, out of sight.

———

"Maybe I've been wrong about Shahin." Matt and I walk down the driveway, breaking the cicada song with my voice. "It wouldn't be crazy to think that the last eighteen months have made me paranoid, and that paranoia is affecting my judgment."

"You've got reason to be paranoid. Just because Shahin, in a way, grew up here doesn't mean he's good at his job."

"Just because he wears that uniform doesn't mean we should trust him outright."

Matt shoos a cloud of gnats away from his face. Even at night, the gnats and mosquitoes look to feed. "I'd like a better explanation for releasing all the Knights than…what did Shahin say?"

"Spirit of reconciliation."

"Yeah. I don't buy that." At the driveway gate, Matt checks the combination padlock. "At least Shahin knows how to close a padlock. That's something, right?"

"Definitely," I laugh. "He must have it all figured out if he can manage a Home Depot special."

"Shh," Matt says and crouches down.

On instinct, I do the same, listening to the, I presume, same odd sound. A heavy whirring. Tires crunching asphalt. An engine. Looking left then right, I can't see anything in the darkness. Bay Aire Road doesn't have security lights, so I can't see a vehicle. But I hear one. Big. Solid. And the sound is getting louder.

"What the hell is—" Matt motions left just as a MATV appears on the road.

No headlights, just a green glow bathing the undercarriage. No sound other than the engine and tires. Out of the shadows and past our driveway, the MATV roars through the night like a ghost, like an alien ship, speeding down the road. Through the bars of the gate, I watch the vehicle hug the bend in the road.

"Blackout lights," I tell Matt. "I think that's what they're called. Patrolling with only light the driver can see."

"They're going too fast for a patrol," Matt whispers back, as if the soldiers can hear us.

"Jacob told me about this, but I don't think he—"

My recollection is cut short by the sound of gunfire—loud and sudden—tires screeching, then several loud crashes—metal meeting asphalt. I'm on my feet when I hear more blasts. Machine guns. Rapid explosions in the dark. Shouting. Male voices barking commands.

"Let's go," I say. "Now."

Matt and I retreat down the driveway, sprinting away from

whatever is happening further down the street. Playing out in darkness. Too close.

Under the carport, I stop short, panting as I look back toward the sound. Where it was but isn't now. The world returns to cicada song and soft waves. Water rolling in and out over the rocks like Matt and I didn't just hear an execution. Because what else could that gunfire mean?

"Someone…someone…I think they just…" I whisper to Matt, scared that if I break the renewed silence we might be next.

"Do you think they saw us?"

"No idea, Matt. Hopefully not."

"Were they chasing someone? Did you see another car?"

"No. I didn't see shit until they flew past us."

"Should we get the others?"

"No." I pace back and forth, trying to give my adrenaline somewhere to go. "Just go to bed. Try to sleep."

Matt's face contorts. "I don't know, Jules."

"Don't say shit, Matt. Just go to bed."

6

Evidence of last night rests in the ditch near the intersection of Bay Aire and the unnamed road that leads to the COP. The truck, a cherry red Nissan, lies on its side, roof and cab pancaked, merely feet from the garden. A mangled bumper is in the tall grass across the street.

"Julianne, come with me." Daddy hops out of the driver's side of his truck.

"Check if the driver's hurt," Mama says.

"That's what we're doing," Daddy calls back. He glances at me while I climb out after him. "I don't know how anyone could walk away from that."

They didn't, I think. Stepping closer, I gaze into the ditch, crouching to peer into the twisted heap. "It's abandoned," I call to my parents.

"Get a closer look!"

"Mama, no one is inside that truck!"

"Shouldn't we let that captain know about this?"

"I'm sure he knows, Mama. The COP is right there." I motion toward the COP, its entrance just out of sight. And, for all I know, Shahin was in that MATV last night. Those shots we heard were likely fired on his command. "He's probably seen this already. And he should be at the Town Hall by now. He had to pass by here on his way."

No, I haven't told Mama and Daddy what I heard last night. Neither has Matt. Hopefully, Matt, like me, has filed last night under "Things we won't worry the parents with."

"Let's go," Daddy says with one last look at the street.

The mandated town hall meeting starts in half an hour. Today would be the first day in my life I'd welcome Daddy's typical turtle-like driving. I want time to look around. Check for other vehicles in ditches. If Jacob was correct, and he seemed to know Army tactics well, use of blackout lights rarely ends without incident.

Even more than that, I want to examine the overgrown shrubbery, dense woods, and vine-covered roofs along Dauphin Island Parkway. Months have passed since I last rode along DIP, and Mother Nature's free-range child is showing out. No boundaries or limitations on her precious offspring. My yearning to examine and behold what has changed—and what hasn't—gnaws at my insides, but we're speeding down the road so fast that the world is all green and brown blurs. A slurry of yellow wildflowers. A whoosh of dogwood trees deep in knee-high grass. To my annoyance, Daddy has thrown off his tortoise shell and become the hare.

Daddy slows behind an Army Humvee, enough for me to read the new-to-me graffiti. Street signs tagged with BDEL. A wooden sign that used to display the name of our local salon—one half of the building dedicated to human grooming, the other half to dog grooming—now asks in red letters, "Do you know The Way?"

We pass a second Way banner with a Bible verse on it. All I caught was *Thou shall,* but in my corner of the world thou is always followed with something biblical.

"How long has all this graffiti been here?"

"Just in the last few weeks," Daddy says. "I think."

Mama blots her lipstick on an old receipt dug from her purse. "I can't say exactly when it started popping up." She flips down the vanity mirror and checks her face.

"Mama, how old is that lipstick? It must be expired by now. And anyway, you are beautiful without it."

"It makes me feel human." Glancing in the mirror again, she adjusts her Miraculous Medal pendant, then flips the mirror shut and visor back into its resting position.

I touch my own face with my fingertips and try to remember the last time I wore makeup. It had to be before Jacob died. Primping hasn't been part of my survival plan. But Mama has standards she refuses to let die. I'm sure in Mama's mind, she is presenting herself today as Mrs. Matthew Martin, wife of a Bellefontaine Stability Council member.

Before I made it inside for lunch after Shahin's visit yesterday, Daddy had told Mama what Shahin wanted from him. Mama told him we must help stabilize and repair Bellefontaine. *No member of my family is going to sit by, doing nothing but complaining, when their country asks for help.* Mama can get super patriotic. On the other hand, when the summer heat and ongoing devastation sit heavy in her lap, she's been known to say that all humankind "can go the way of the devil!" I swear she enjoys keeping us guessing.

But Shahin picked a good day to make a request—one that saw Mama in a good mood. That's why Daddy, Mama, and I are enroute to the St. Phillip's Community Center. Well, that's why Mama and Daddy are in the truck. I'm here because I told Daddy I was going. He said no. I insisted. He refused again. I almost mentioned what I heard last night and that I have questions for Shahin, but I didn't. Instead, I changed course and told Mama that I needed to go to prove to myself that I'm not a victim. Mama agreed.

And yes, before anyone mentions it, I know I am a grown-ass woman who can just pick up and go wherever I want to because that's what adults do, but that's not how it's done in the Martin family. Call it tradition or culture, but we defer to our parents, even as adults. I don't always like it, but that's what it is.

As we approach Holy T—the intersection of two major roads and the two major religions of Bellefontaine—I see a banner hanging in front of the church. Our church. Not that I am anything but an argumentative Catholic, but I'm pretty sure The Way isn't Catholic, so what business do they have hanging their propaganda here? *Join the Way by dawns early light.* No apostrophe. Grammar-deficient fuckers.

My rebellious side itches to be five minutes late to the meeting, but thanks to Daddy, we are early, despite the delay with the red truck. I swear Daddy would be first in line for the apocalypse if the asteroid sent invitations with a specific start time. But there was no invitation to the town hall meeting. There was an order.

The Community Center sits at the rear of a large parking lot behind the St. Philip's parish rectory. We pull into a spot near the door. Mama's knees have been acting up, so the closer the better. Since we are some of the first residents here, there are plenty of open spaces in the weather-worn lot.

Daddy hops out of the truck, agile for a man his age. Mama grips the *oh shit* handle and lowers herself down from the truck. Her process takes so long I lose patience, peel my sweaty thighs lose from the vinyl seat, and slide along the bench to the driver's seat, my knees skimming the steering wheel as I escape the hotbox of the cabin.

Outside the truck, steam rises from the black asphalt, the result of an afternoon thunderstorm followed by unincumbered sunshine. No pesky trees or awnings to block the sun here, just a long lot leading to the large, square metal building. It's been home to wedding receptions, parish dinners, election day voting, and anything else requiring the residents of Bellefontaine to gather in large numbers. But I can't remember the last time I stepped into the building or why. Was it for Kate's wedding reception? Has it really been that long?

"Well, shall we go in?" Mama says, her purse tucked under her right arm.

"What's in that thing?" I gesture to her quilted, summer Vera Bradley bag. "It's not like you need cash or a checkbook."

"For your information, Miss Smart-aleck, I have a fan, my I.D., a handkerchief for your father, and a thermos of water."

"Receipts from two years ago, a melted lipstick, old Kleenex… " Mama's purses are sinkholes, cluttered with the evidence of her comings and goings stretching back years.

Mama nudges me in the ribs as she heads toward the propped open glass doors. "You are welcome to walk your butt home anytime."

"No, you're not," Daddy says. "We need to stick together the entire time we are here."

"I promise not to wander off."

"That's enough from you, young lady," Mama says, digging in her purse for the fan she is sure is in there. Triumphant, she pulls her hand from the bag. "Got it!" She waves the closed accordion fan for Daddy and me to see, then pats both of us on our bottoms with it.

I flatten my expression as I approach the guards. Two soldiers stand on either side of the open front doors. One soldier on each side holds a fingerprint scanner. When we approach, Daddy offers our names—Matthew and Marian Martin and Julianne Martin Jones.

"Place your right index finger on the pad," one soldier tells Daddy.

"I know the drill," Daddy says.

Mama does the same, and they are both allowed entry without

incident, after a soldier pats them both down and pilfers through the contents of Mama's purse. When it's my turn, I place my finger on the pad and wait.

"Are you a resident of Bellefontaine?" The soldier stares at me, seemingly locked on my face.

"Yes."

"Name?"

"Jules Martin Jones." I hand over my expired military dependent I.D.

"Address?"

I rattle off the address and repeat myself as the soldier enters the information into the small device.

"That checks out." The soldier returns my I.D. to me and motions me to step forward for a pat-down. I'm not sure how or why my information "checks out," but I'm glad for it. I'm not sure how I'd prove my identity or address otherwise.

As I cross the threshold of the community center, I walk into a thick wall of hot air. The linoleum floor is slick with condensation from the humidity, making me grateful I wore tennis shoes rather than flops. I hold Mama's elbow, ready to catch her if she hits a particularly wet spot. She was smart to bring that fan.

Inside, a soldier with lieutenant bars on her shirt stops us. "Missus Martin, Miss Jones, you may have a seat in the main hall. Mister Martin, please wait here. Captain Shahin would like a word with you."

After the lieutenant walks away, I whisper to Mama. "How did she know who we are?"

"It's their job to know us," Daddy says.

"Well, it's creepy."

The inside of the building has changed little since I was last here, at least to my memory. The windowless structure is still entirely beige, from the beige linoleum floor to the beige walls, broken only by pictures of ex-popes. Pope John Paul, II, Pope

Benedict, and Pope Francis all smile at us from behind framed glass. Above the pictures, a white ceiling should contrast the walls, but it's grown dingy over the years to another, you guessed it, shade of beige.

Through another double doorway, the beige foyer gives way to the beige main hall. To the right is a stainless steel, commercial-grade kitchen with pass-through windows for serving. Sadly, nothing is cooking. All I smell is a touch of mildew and body odor wafting from the few neighbors seated in white, plastic folding chairs facing a podium. They've sprinkled themselves about the rows of chairs. I choose a row and seat furthest from any of them—right side, front row, last chair. I have no interest in sharing sweaty arm space with a stranger.

To the left of my chair are racks of folding tables. Cobwebs peek out between the tables, vertically stacked like slats in wainscoting. The painted sheetrock is peeling in places, the back wall shows water damage, and a weed grows from a crack in a baseboard. If you let something sit in one place long enough here, nature will claim it for its own.

The lights are on along with several big box fans, which I guess is better than sitting in still, dark air. The fans, including Mama's handheld that she's whipping back and forth two inches from her face, churn the hot air around rather than cool the space. In the few minutes I've been inside this building, I can report that I know what living inside a convection oven feels like.

"Mama," I ask once she has saved Daddy a seat by placing her purse in the chair next to her. "Did you and Daddy report to the Army who all lives in our house?"

"What now?" she asks, too distracted with looking around the room to pay attention to me.

"With the data collection? Did you or Daddy report to the Army that I live with you."

"I'm not sure about your father, but they already knew that the first time they took my fingerprint."

"Oh. Did you tell them that Cole is living with us?"

"I don't think so. Like I told you, they already had you kids in their system. I'm not sure about the grandkids."

"Mama, you have got to be more observant." First, she pays little attention to the graffiti and now she can't remember the details of being fingerprinted for the first time in her G-rated life. Or maybe it wasn't the first time. "So, is being fingerprinted old hat in your life? Lots of crimes in your checkered past?"

"Perhaps the heat in here robbed you of your ability to speak to me appropriately."

"That's not an answer." I stare at Mama for a full ten seconds before cracking a smile.

"Jules, I am in no mood for your weird humor."

Weighing the option to pinch her hard on the arm or just look apologetic, I decide instead to stand and walk away. I head to the back door, right in front of my seat. If I can get it open, it should be enough to allow fresh air to blow through the meeting hall. *Seriously, has anyone in the 128th ever heard of a cross-breeze?* After a good shove, the door pops open, and I tumble out of the building, off the concrete exterior step, and onto the grass. The door produces a slapping sound as it swings closed behind me.

"George!" I say, surprised when I look up to see Captain Shahin standing in the grass I'm kneeling in.

"Jules, what are you doing?" Shahin asks, rather curtly, and extends his hand for me to stand.

"I'm creating a cross—" I stop short when I see a man step from behind Shahin. The man removes his sun visor and rubs one meaty paw across his balding head. "Clem."

Just his name escapes my lips. No other words, not a single syllable finds my tongue. Clem Richardson stands four feet from me. Four feet and close enough for me to tackle. *Scratch his eyes out. Pound his face and throat until he coughs up blood.*

Clem steps toward me. His face morphs into local politician mode, slick and syrupy with disingenuous concern. "Miss Jones, so good to see you. How have you been?"

The audacity of the question leaves me speechless.

"It's good to see you looking so healthy," he says.

My feet move before my brain registers the action. With arms outstretched and fingers like talons, I leap toward Clem, but Shahin's thick arm catches me mid-air.

"Put me down!" I struggle against Shahin's arm as my feet scramble to find the ground.

"Jules, stop." Shahin wraps both arms around me and carries me to the doorway, at last setting me on the concrete step. "You need to—"

"You're out here talking to him? To this psychopath? Why?"

"You need to take your seat. We'll be starting soon." Shahin reaches behind me and opens the door, pushing me inside.

"Don't touch me." I let the door slap the frame behind me and walk to my seat.

"Honey?" Mama fans my face, so close she nearly clips my nose. "I heard you talking to someone outside. Who's out there?"

I push the fan away. "I'm fine. Fine."

"No. You're clearly not fine."

I lean forward, hold my head in my hands, try to become invisible. Try to breathe.

"Jules, what happened?"

My earlier words to Mama, the ones that convinced her that I needed to be here today, loop in my mind. *I am not a victim. Not a victim. Not a victim.* Tears hit my bare legs and dot the cotton fabric of my shorts. "Clem."

Mama sits straight up in her chair and twists right and left, looking around the room. Then she glares at the door. "Where? Outside?"

"Yes." I gesture to the backdoor, which smacks back and forth against the frame. "I'll get that."

Mama places a hand on my knee, forcing me back into my chair. "Don't you move." She scurries to the door, pulls it closed, then returns and sits next to me. She twists in her chair. I know she's on the lookout for Clem, but what can she do? Beat him with her Vera Bradley?

"Mama, I… " Thoughts collide in my head—*not a victim* versus *run for your life.*

Mama leans close and whispers to me. "You're safe, Julianne. No one will hurt you here. Your daddy and I will keep you safe."

"Why is he here?"

"Probably the mandate." Patting my leg, but still searching the now crowded room, she says, "I'm sure he's just here because of the mandate. He's not here for you."

"Hmm."

Mama digs around in her purse for a moment, hands me a handkerchief, then turns her attention back to me. "Dry your face. As soon as this is over, we'll be back in the truck and back home."

"I don't think I can do this." Looking around, the main hall is so crowded now. So many people closing in and blocking lines of sight. People fill the rows behind me in groups of twos, threes, and fours. They fill the left side, too. So many people. "I can't. I just–"

"You have to, honey. You can and you will." Mama squeezes my hand, squishing my fingers. The pain, the sensation of bone pushing bone, breaks the panic rising in my throat. She pulls me in close, stroking my hair and squeezing my shoulders.

I take in a full breath, and the air in my lungs feels like salvation. "Way to get in my ooda loop."

"Get in your what?"

Sniffling, I dab the end of my nose with the handkerchief. "It's something Jacob used to say. Ooda. Loop. It has some complicated definition, lots of military jargon, but basically it means that you broke the reaction loop I was in. Thank you. You've got quite the grip."

"Mamas know things." She holds my hand—gently this time—rubbing her thumb across the top of my hand, soothing me as only she can.

After a few minutes, Daddy takes the seat next to Mama. His lips disappear into a thin line as he stares straight ahead. His jaw works. He must be grinding his teeth. Mama lets go of my hand and takes Daddy's instead, his tremor visible.

"Please take your seats," Shahin shouts over the crowd, then strides down the center aisle. He walks like this isn't just his area of concern. He fills the space like it belongs to him. Several soldiers follow him in, taking standing positions along the walls.

"Good afternoon. I appreciate you all taking time from your day to come here."

"Like we had a choice," a man from behind me says, loud enough for the entire room to hear.

Shahin clears his throat, allowing the shifting in seats to die down. When he speaks again, his voice is strong, reminding me of what I called Jacob's officer voice, an authoritative tone reserved for addressing soldiers under his command. "Yes, this meeting is mandatory because the updates we have for you are that important."

Just get on with it, I think, ready to bolt for the truck as soon as Shahin speaks his last word.

"As I don't want to waste your time, I'll dive—"

A woman seated in the back interrupts Shahin. "You already have!" The voice sounds like Mrs. Renaud. When I turn in my seat, I find her seated between her two adult sons, both grinning, easily amused.

Just as I turn to face Shahin, the sound of shuffling feet causes me to look back again. In a single-file line, the red-faced freaks enter the main hall and march, in step, down the center aisle. Today, all ten people wear BDEL T-Shirts along with their painted faces. In the fluorescent light, the red on their faces makes the whites of their eyes glow like white marbles on a red carpet.

BDEL. BDEL. *By dawns early light*. No apostrophe. Well, I certainly wouldn't describe this display as mild-mannered Methodists. The Way must be something far more intense.

Watching the display, I look through their line to find Clem seated on the left of the room. He's by himself. His wife isn't with him. She's probably at home baking pies and ironing Clem's dingy underwear. Clem's son Dave isn't here either. Dead or alive, he's still *whereabouts unknown.*

My breath catches in my throat when Clem glances in my direction. I look away. Eye contact with him will send me over the edge. Again. His presence makes the red-faced freaks almost comforting. At least they provide a proper distraction from the fact that one of my captors is sitting in the same room as me. Of course, I have no idea what the red-faced Way is planning for dawn's early light, so I don't know who to fear more—Clem or the unknown?

Shahin's voice breaks through my inner monologue. "Anyone who causes a disturbance during this meeting will be escorted out." The soldiers standing along the side walls step toward the audience, hovering just outside of the seating area, ready to pounce.

At the front, the freaks stand before the left side of the audience. Thank god, I'm on the right. Without saying a word to the residents seated there, each protester stands in front of one seated resident, glaring at the unfortunate soul with their white marble eyes.

"Sit or be detained," Shahin threatens.

A mother in the front left row grabs her two children by the arms and drags them out of their seats, retreating to chairs far away from the freaks. An older couple, probably both in their eighties, vacate their seats and rush into our row. More scared occupants scatter about the room, finding open seats where they can. Once the ten front row seats are empty, the freaks finally sit. In unison. *Fucking weirdos.*

Shahin glares at them. "This is your one free pass. Interrupt again, and you will be removed." He stares at the red, unmoved faces for a moment longer, then addresses us all. "My name, as many of you know, is Captain George Shahin of the 128th Military Police unit. Every soldier standing in this room today lives in Alabama. This is our home state, and we have been ordered by Governor Freidman to protect this land and the safety of its citizens. I myself have a personal connection to Bellefontaine, so your wellbeing is important to me. But do not mistake my kindness for weakness."

"Is denying us rations kind?" a man from the back yells.

Shahin glares in the direction of the interruption, and a stillness falls over the crowd. "This is still a community under martial law. I intend to enforce that law as long as I am in command here."

Shahin says nothing more to the interrupter or the freaks. Maybe it's best not to make outright enemies of anyone, but the entire scene rubs me as wrong. Shahin says he wants stabilization, but without recognized and practiced social contracts, how stable can we be? Denying food to the hungry and starving isn't cool. Kicking an old couple out of their seats isn't cool. Scaring mothers and children isn't cool.

We also don't like people who engage in secret conversations with known criminals behind buildings. Perhaps I should remind my old pal Georgie Shahin of that.

"Rest assured that the likelihood of future bombings is very low."

Shit. Did he say bombings? I've done it again. I let my mind wander and missed something important. Shahin was talking, but my mind was on the front row of freaks. "What was he saying?" I whisper to Mama.

"That Troy Cowart is dead, so we are much safer now."

I snap my focus back to Shahin and try to wipe my memory of Troy's long, stringy hair brushing my face as he pinned me to the ground.

"The investigations following the bridge bombing and market bombing, the murder of Sergeant William Roberts, and evidence found at the Knights' compound following the Army raid last summer, prove that Troy Cowart was the culprit in all of these heinous acts. Many of the Knights, although not directly involved, were found to have aided and abetted Mister Cowart in these crimes. The martial law order in effect here mandates intervention by any person who knows of or sees a crime in progress."

The stillness in the main hall just minutes ago is gone. As Shahin speaks, a restlessness builds behind me.

"For their compliance in Mister Cowart's crimes," Shahin continues, "Governor Friedman has warned that any future militia involvement will be punished to the greatest extent under the law."

"Being in a militia is our right," a woman yells, but Shahin presses on without acknowledging her.

"In the spirit of reconciliation, Governor Friedman deemed mercy to be best for all involved and the best path forward."

"No!" A man somewhere on the left side of the room calls out. I watch as a soldier steps forward, towering over the residents seated on the left side.

"In the spirit of reconciliation," Shahin repeats, saying the words slowly this time, "All who knew of Mister Cowart's intentions or gave him shelter after his crimes were given time served and probation." The buzz of hemming and hawing builds in the crowd, but Shahin speaks over them, his voice growing in volume and intensity. "Those citizens will pay restitution through community service. Their labor will help Bellefontaine recover from this period of unrest."

"Who made that decision?" Mrs. Renaud calls from the back. I turn toward her voice to see her standing—five-foot-nothing of piss and vinegar. Waving her cane for emphasis, she continues. "Those boys should've been charged by the feds not the state. It took more than one man to blow up that bridge. That was an act of terrorism!"

"Mrs. Renaud, you need to sit," Shahin orders.

"I'll sit when you answer my question."

"Please do not make me remove an old woman. That is not something I want to do, but I will." Shahin motions to a soldier near him, who in turn walks toward Mrs. Renaud's row.

"I'll sit. I'll sit. But you need to know that your granddaddy would be disappointed in you right now." Mrs. Renaud sits, all but disappearing behind the people sitting in front of her.

Shahin picks up where he left off, ignoring the old woman's chastising. "As I was saying, Troy Cowart was determined to be responsible for the violence and destruction previously thought to be the work of the Knights organization..."

Unbelievable. Friedman pinned it all on Troy. And because Troy died during the Army raid, this whole thing gets tied up in a shiny bow. My fingers curl into fists, yearning to punch something, someone. I'd like to start with CPT *Georgie* Shahin.

Shahin pauses and looks at me as if he can hear my thoughts. "We are still looking for Dave Richardson. He is wanted for questioning in the alleged abduction of Jules Martin Jones."

Alleged? Alleged! I'm sorry, what? I keep my voice calm and steady, but I can't keep silent. "Dave Richardson is guilty of my very real abduction and very real attempt on my life."

"Miss Jones, you must remain silent," Shahin says, a look of complete annoyance on his face.

"This is a town hall, not a lecture," I retort.

"You will have an opportunity to ask questions after the briefing."

"Dave only failed because I'm too stubborn to die."

A woman behind me busts out laughing at that comment. Shahin nods to the lead soldier on the right who in turn steps closer to me. The others in his line follow, closing the distance between themselves and the crowd.

Mama puts her hand on my knee, her silent plea for me to shut my mouth and keep it shut.

"I'm going to stand in the back," I say, and before Mama can protest, I'm on my feet and walking past the line of soldiers.

But I can't leave. Mama and Daddy are here. They're my ride home. They'd flip if I walked outside by myself. I don't even know if the soldiers will let me leave. Bewildered, I lean against the back wall. My fingernails dig into the soft skin of my palms as I stave off another wave of panic and the urge to tackle Shahin and Clem and beat the hell out of them both. Because I won't get probation. No, I'd end up in a padded cell on Brookley, with no hope of community service bullshit to atone for my sins.

I stand at the wall and try to focus on Shahin's stupid words. *Residency data collection will continue. This is for the safety of us all... blah blah blah. You must cooperate with the new procedures at all security checkpoints... blah blah blah. The travel ban is still in effect... blah blah blah. Rations and storm readiness and resource conservation and blah freaking blah.*

I cannot believe I thought Shahin might be good for this area, good for us. He just wants this over and done with so he can collect a medal and get on with his life. Well, CPT Shahin, CPT Fuck Stick, this is my life. My whole damn life. *Wanted for questioning.* I really need to punch him.

I slide down the wall, squatting with my arms folded over my bent knees. *Breathe. In one, two, three, four. Out one, two, three, four.* Breathe through the crisis. Don't act. *Just breathe.*

"The last item on the agenda today is the introduction of the Bellefontaine Stabilization Council. Now that we have neutralized the physical threats to Bellefontaine, it is time to build this community up again."

So, we're officially done with all the scary shit, huh? No more bombs or abductions? Just peace, love, and harmony from this day out. *What utter bullshit.*

"Prepare this town for the future. This group, made up of myself and devoted community stakeholders, will plan and coordinate Bellefontaine's recovery. From rebuilding the Fowl River Bridge, to making necessary repairs to communication systems, to increasing the availability of food and potable water, and to eventually rebuilding the local economy, the BSC will spearhead recovery efforts. It is important to me that your needs are addressed—"

Bullshit.

"So, I must be aware of your needs. The civilians serving on the BSC will serve as liaisons between you, the community, and me, representing government recovery efforts."

More bullshit.

"The civilian representatives selected are all long-time members of this community, geographically spread throughout the boundaries of Bellefontaine, and hold vested interests in Bellefontaine's recovery and future success. Father Monroe, Mister Martin, and Mister Richardson, would you please stand?"

I watch as my father stands. He turns and looks at me. His face is blank, his eyes stoic.

Shahin's voice carries over the whir of the fans and rustling in the crowd, "These men are ready to field your concerns and guide me to where recovery efforts are most needed. I've no doubt these three will provide me good council—"

"Bullshit!" The word flies from my mouth. "This is bullshit," I yell and move down the center aisle, right toward Shahin. Soldiers move toward me, but I don't stop. "Clem Richardson is a criminal."

Shahin attempts to stop my ranting. "Miss Jones—"

"You know it, I know it. Hell, even the red freaks know it."

Shahin motions for the soldiers to hold. "Miss Jones," he tries again in a cool tone.

"No," I fire back. "You had your chance to talk. It's my turn now. Clem wants all of us to live like those neanderthal Knights. Follow their fucked-up rules. But you want to put him in—"

"Miss Jones, if we can keep this civil—"

The red freaks begin to chant the word *repent*, over and over again, low at first, then building in volume until I have to shout over them.

"What does that even mean?" I shout at them, then redirect to Shahin. "You are putting a psycho back in a seat of power. What the hell is wrong with you? He wanted me dead. What about Billy? Did you know Billy Roberts? He was one of us, and The Knights killed him! Troy didn't act alone!"

In my peripheral, I see the freaks stand and unfurl a banner. *BY DAWNS EARLY LIGHT BLOOD WILL FLOW.* All caps. No punctuation. "Use a fucking apostrophe," I yell at them. The one nearest me flinches. *Good.*

"And what about last night?" I yell at Shahin. The soldiers force their way through the seated audience members, so I speak faster but to the crowd this time. "Did you all know they're running blackout drives? They caused someone to wreck their truck last night right by our garden. Where's the driver, Shahin? Is he dead?"

"Miss Jones, there's no such thing as a *blackout* drive."

"Semantics, Shahin." I turn back to the crowd. "If someone you know drives a red Nissan—"

More soldiers rush into the main hall, doubling the uniformed number in the room.

"That's my Rudy's truck," a woman to my right shouts, standing to face Shahin. "He didn't come home last night."

"Miss Jones, you will be silent." Shahin crosses to me.

He's close. Too close. Shahin grabs me by the shoulders, and I push against him, hard. But I'm trapped. I can't break free of his grip. I'm trapped, and I can't be trapped. Not again.

"Jules," Shahin says, a hard whisper in my ear. "You have to trust me. This is the best way."

"No. You're a liar."

"When did I lie to you?"

"Every word is a lie. I know it is. What happened last night? Where is the driver of that truck?"

Mama and Daddy appear at my side. They each take one of my arms.

"We're taking her home, Shahin," Daddy says. "Let go of her."

I feel Shahin's hand fall away from me, and Mama and Daddy guide me toward the foyer.

"We have to leave, Jules," Mama says. "Now."

"Outside. Get in the truck," Daddy tells me.

"No. We need to know. Don't you want to know?" I stare into Daddy's face and see a heartbreaking combination of pity, resignation, and fear.

"I'll ride in the back by myself," I tell him, turn, and march myself to the truck. Sitting on the hot steel of the truck bed, I glare at Daddy as he opens Mama's door for her. "Did you know?"

"About Clem?" Daddy asks.

"Yes, about Clem. Did you know?"

"No. I didn't know until just before the meeting started."

"Sure," I say. "Like I can trust anything anymore. Just take me home."

"What do you know about that truck, Julianne? The one in the ditch?"

"You better get going," I say to him. "Don't want to break curfew."

Daddy opens his door and hops behind the wheel of the truck.

As we pull away from the Community Center, a man exits the building. He's tall and rail thin. He pulls his baseball cap low, obscuring my view of his face. After a few minutes, he turns and walks toward the woods, and we turn onto DIP, heading home.

7

That man watched us leave. He watched me. Even though I couldn't see his eyes, I felt them on me. Now, I can't shake the feeling of being watched.

That's why I can't sleep. Not tonight. I tried. I fluffed my worn-out pillow, pulled the sheet up to my chin, kicked it to the floor, turned on my stomach, then my back. I chanted *Hail Marys* in my mind, made mental to-do lists that will never come to fruition, and even conjured a few of my favorite Jacob memories, but nothing worked.

All the while, I felt I was being watched. Am being watched.

An hour ago, rather than wake Cole with my insomnia Olympics, I relieved Garrett and Kate of their guard duty shift an hour ago. There's no point in them forcing their eyes open if mine refuse to close. Because I know I should be seeing something, someone, but I don't. All I have is this feeling.

So here I sit. On the pier. Awake. Alone.

Mobile Bay is quiet tonight. The water rises and falls with the grace of a ballerina. Her long arms lift and fall, fluid with the music of the soft waves. Above the black water, a million stars shine and wink at me. Over the last hour, two gave in to the darkness, their light extinguishing in an arc across the sky. The waning crescent moon glows on the water, and its reflection casts golden stripes on an inky tapestry. All of this should soothe me. It used to soothe me. It doesn't now. Because somewhere out there, too close to ignore, someone watches us. Watches me.

As a teenager, I sat on this same crab deck—lower than the boathouse and main deck behind me, so I was hidden. For hours, I'd marvel at the beauty of Mobile Bay at night. But not tonight. Tonight, I only see places where others can hide. Below the surface. In the shadows of neighboring piers. The expanse of water outside of the moon's streak is too dark to see any small vessel that may float my way. Even the boards I sit on create a dull anxiety in me, fraying my edges. *What if something is beneath me, floating in the water? Waiting for me to drop my guard.*

Monsters lying in wait.

"You're being a little paranoid," Matt told me earlier, after I returned home from the town hall meeting, so filled with fear and hurt that I barely formed the words for Matt. *Clem. He's on that committee with Daddy.* But that's not what Matt deemed paranoid. He understood why Clem in another seat of power upset me. What Matt didn't understand and still doesn't is why a strange man standing in a parking lot staring at me would cause me such fear.

Everything hurts. Fear and anger manifest in my joints and muscles. Stomach cramps, headache. Every one of my cells knows that meeting was wrong. Shahin is wrong. Use of blackout lights is wrong. Drivers disappearing is wrong. That strange man, something about him, is wrong. But my family refuses to admit any of that. Facts. All facts and they glossed over every single point I tried to make. In the garage before dinner, they told me to breathe and *calm yourself.*

"Jules, there's no way the guy you saw was Dave Richardson," Matt had said. "I know you're scared he's still alive, but there's no way he'd show up to the town hall with a bunch of MPs standing around. He's psychotic, but not stupid." After that comment, I kicked Matt out of the garage. I kicked them all out. *My sanctuary. My rules. My fear.*

At dinner, I went inside the main house, fixed my plate, and took it to the garage to eat. Alone. No one tried to stop me. I ate a few bites and saved the rest for Cole. When he came in from kicking a soccer ball in the yard with Jessie—an after-dinner pickup game—he scarfed down the cold, leftover fish and charred squash in four huge bites. Watching him fall fast asleep was my one pleasure of the day. At least I did that right. I looked out for my boy, making sure he had enough food in his belly to fuel his next growth spurt.

Lying on my cot in the dark, I closed my eyes and begged for sleep. Instead, my mind played the man in the parking lot on a loop. He exited the doors of the community center, pulled his ball cap down low on his face, and turned his body toward our truck. Again and again, I saw myself in the back of the truck, watching him watch me.

Because he was watching me, right? I'm not being paranoid about that. He watched us leave the lot. I felt his stare.

I still feel it.

In the garage before dinner and before I banished my family from *my space*, Mama said the man was too tall and too skinny to be Dave Richardson, but how good a look did Mama get? She was in the truck's cab. I had a much better view. I also know exactly how tall Dave was or *is*. He towered over me in his boat, in his shed, at his kitchen table. Even when he sat next to me, I had to lift my face to look him in the eyes.

But he wasn't skinny. Mama is right on that point. Dave was muscular. The Dave that abducted me carried me like a rag doll thrown over his shoulder. I remember thick muscles flexing under his T-Shirt. His gym-rat biceps bulged from too-tight sleeves.

The man today was tall like Dave, but so skinny. Is it possible to go from linebacker thick to beanstalk thin in a matter of months? Has he been starving in the shadows? Beefy guys like Dave turn doughy when the gym closes and the steroids and HGH run out. The man today wore baggy, worn cargo shorts and a T-Shirt that hung loose on boney, angular shoulders. His legs were thin—two toothpicks holding up a long torso and neck. The lower half of the man's face showed sallow cheeks.

But Dave could have lost dozens of pounds since I saw him last. What food is available to a man on the run at the end of the world? An occasional squirrel or blue crab? But if he's back, if he's been here at home with mommy and daddy, they'd have fattened up their prodigal son, even with reduced rations. A skinny son is a blight on any Southern mama. Is it possible that Dave would be in Bellefontaine, even seated in the community center, without his father's knowledge? I don't buy that.

Troy Cowart was skinny. And tall. When Troy stood before me in the garden, right before he shoved me to the ground, his tall frame cast a slim shadow over me. Could he be alive? No. That thought is paranoia. Troy is dead. Dead, dead, dead. Riddled with bullets according to Libby's many, many reports on the raid.

Maybe I am paranoid, but I have reason to be batshit crazy, afraid of every minor bump and slight noise. Isn't it perfectly normal for me to flinch with every splash of a trout or mullet? In the dark? Lurking somewhere beyond my sight?

With Shahin's behavior today, his lack of any plan other than to form a bullshit committee, only justifies my fear, and if my family can't understand why I feel this way, maybe I don't belong on this pier anymore. Maybe Cole and I should leave, go into hiding ourselves. Maybe we should flee through the woods, sneak past the checkpoints and blockades until we are miles and miles away from Bellefontaine, the Knights, the Richardsons, the National Guard with their careless tactics, and every single Martin.

That would serve Daddy right. How can I trust him if he works with Clem? I can't, and that thought sparks a wave of anguish through my body.

The water changes in front of me. Uniform, full waves—big for Mobile Bay—roll toward me, then beneath and beyond my hiding place. Row after row of ship waves roll in from the shipping channel. The waves' crests catch the moonlight. Peering further into the darkness, I can make out the enormous silhouette of a cargo ship. I try to make out any markings on the ship, but it's too far away. For months, the only ships of that size in Mobile Bay have been military vessels moving equipment in and out of Brookley Field. But this ship carries only containers, from what I can see. Could the port have reopened to commercial vessels without our knowledge?

A flash of movement startles me to the right. I hit the deck and hold tight to my rifle. I've never fired a gun while on guard duty. Cole is the only intruder I've ever caught red-handed, and I certainly wouldn't use this or any other gun on a child, not even when Cole came back for a second chance at robbing us. But I will use it tonight, if forced.

Peering across the deck and water to the neighboring pier, I find what has my heart pounding in my throat. Or rather, *who*. Someone is pulling themselves from a vessel below onto the deck. It can't be one of our neighbors. They took off as soon as reports of Clayton Van Cleave and his aerosol repellent poisoned half of Downtown and Midtown out of existence. And they haven't returned.

But someone crouches on their deck. Someone that doesn't belong there. *Please be a looter. Please be just another hungry mouth.* Laying on the hard boards, I prop up my chin just enough to see over the barrel of my rifle. The smells of metal and oil fill my nose as I watch the person. Man or woman has yet to be determined.

The boards beneath me shake. Vibrations that signal I'm not alone on this pier. My pier. My hiding place. I'm not alone. And whoever is out here with me is running. The pier rattles—back and forth and back and forth. I pull my legs in beneath me, rise to my knees, and take aim.

A blond-haired figure hits the floorboards. "Jules, it's me," a voice calls to me in a whisper. "It's Cole! Cole!"

I swing the rifle away from Cole and point it at our neighbor's pier. I can't see the intruder, but I hear a splash. "Cole, stay down," I order, my voice low despite my pulsing adrenaline. I creep into the shadows cast by the boathouse and whisper to Cole again. "Someone's over there," I whisper. "Don't move until I tell you it's clear."

Peering into the darkness, I spot a kayak moving against the current. The red plastic shines without the cover of shadows, and the silver-handled paddle flashes, betraying its owner in the moonlight. Just above the surface, I make out the roundness of a head and two hands guiding the kayak away from me. Away from the pier. Away from Cole.

"Cover your ears," I tell Cole and fire a single warning shot in the air. The shot bucks me backward, but my legs hold. For several minutes, I stand in the safety of the shadows and watch the kayak disappear down shore into the night. "Whoever that was, I hope they pissed themselves when they heard that shot." My bravado is a lie. My trembling hands tell the truth.

On the main deck, Cole lets out a nervous laugh. "Can I move yet?"

"Yes," I say, and put the safety back on. "Get down here and explain to me what you are doing out here." I sink down onto the boards, willing my heart rate to slow with deep, slow breaths, and place the rifle on the deck next to me. My ears ring from the shot.

Cole scampers down the stairs, surefooted as if in full light. "I woke up, and you were gone."

"Oh," I say.

"What are you doing out here? It's not your shift."

How does he know that? "I relieved Garrett and Kate."

"But Mister Martin says to stick to the schedule."

I turn to the boy who seems older every day than the day before, the longer I know him. "Cole, do you listen to the adults talking? I really don't want you to worry about those kinds of things. Guard schedules and what not. That worry is for adults, not kids."

"I'm old enough to know what's going on. And I haven't heard or seen anything I can't handle."

"Fine, I know you're not a little kid, but you're not an adult either." I look at him for a long moment, until he looks away, uncomfortable with eye contact. I guess in that way, he's a normal kid on the brink of full teenage-hood. "I guess I do treat you like a little kid sometimes."

"Like the other kids around here, Mallie, Lucy, and Miss Kate's boys. I ain't them."

"Yes, like that. And don't say ain't. You're better than that."

"Correcting how I talk is also annoying."

"Wow," I say, a bit proud that he feels comfortable enough with me to say what he thinks. "I'll stop if you use words worthy of you."

Cole expels a sound like a harumph—a scoffing sound of derision.

"I mean it! I will try. You know being responsible for another person is new to me. I will try to treat you like a kid your actual age. I will not stop nagging you about your vocabulary."

"Okay. So, here's your chance to treat me like I should be

treated." Cole glances at me, then down at his hands. "Why aren't you sleeping? Tonight is not your night to be out here."

"Stress, I guess. Just feeling a little anxious. I didn't want to wake you."

"Because of earlier? Something at the meeting?" Cole asks.

"Were you listening in on the adults when we got back?" I lean forward, craning my neck to get a better look at his expression.

"Not on purpose. But y'all were loud. Jessie and I were on the front porch, and we heard yelling."

"Oh. I'm sorry about that. I know that it must be hard to under—"

"You're doing that thing again. Treating me like a baby. I remember my parents saying that. 'It must be hard to hear us fighting,'" Cole says in a mocking tone. "It's only hard when I hear the yelling, but don't know what the yelling is about."

"Oh."

"So, tell me."

"Cole, I don't want to scare you."

"Who says you will?"

I draw my knees up and press my face against the roundness of my thighs. *Parents do difficult things.* Daddy's words echo in my mind, but I'm not in the mood to accept any advice from Daddy right now. He hasn't been forgiven. But for Cole, after everything he's lost, doesn't he deserve to know exactly what is happening here? In his new home? Would keeping secrets from him help? I draw in a breath and dive in. "Clem Richardson was at the meeting. Captain Shahin invited him to serve on the stabilization committee."

"With your dad?" Cole asks, surprise in his voice.

"Yes. I was surprised, too. I didn't handle it well."

"What'd'you do?"

"Freaked out. Lost it, screaming and yelling in front of the whole town. Well, most of the town. And I haven't spoken to Daddy since."

"Oh."

"The red-faced freaks were there, too. The Way. I'm afraid they're more dangerous than anyone is willing to admit. That acronym I keep seeing everywhere."

"That what? Acro… ?" Cole asks, trailing off with the word unfinished.

"Acronym. It means an abbreviation of a phrase into initials." I nudge his arm with mine. "We really need to get serious about your education."

"Don't change the subject."

"You asked." I stare at Cole until he looks away. "Fine. I keep seeing B-D-E-L written in all sorts of places. On their banners. Graffiti on old road signs. It stands for 'by dawn's early light.' I don't like the implication."

Cole looks at me, confused.

"Implication means—"

"I know what implication means. I do read, you know."

"I know. Sorry."

"I was confused by why that a-cro-nym scares you."

"Because I don't know what's coming at dawn or even when their dawn is. But mostly, I'm upset because my father agreed to work with Clem just like that." I snap my fingers and the sound slices into the still night. "After everything the Knights did to me, my own father is willing to work with them. So, that's what's got me out here instead of on my cot. I can't sleep because I'm worried."

"That's a lot," he says, shrinking into his body as he wraps his arms around his knees, and my regret is harsh and immediate.

"I'm sorry. I shouldn't have told you. I thought if you knew, you'd know what to keep an eye out for. Was I wrong? Was I wrong to tell you?"

"No." He shakes his head with the word.

"Tell me what you're thinking."

"What are you going to do?"

"I don't know."

"B.S."

I nudge Cole in the ribs, and a second of levity feels good.

"Jules, I know you have a plan or are at least making one. So, tell me what it is."

"Cole, I don't know. That's the truth. I don't know what the best option is."

"So, tell me the options."

Looking at his beautiful, unmarked face, I contemplate the question I need to ask him, then shove away my hesitation. "What would you think if we left?"

Cole sucks in a breath. "You and me, or all of us?"

"Just you and me."

Cole stares at the waves, and I wait for him to put his feelings into words.

"I like it here," he says, just above a whisper.

"I don't know if I can stay here if my father works with Clem. I feel so betrayed."

"I thought we weren't supposed to leave. Wasn't that an order?"

"We'd have to be careful, keep to the woods."

"Is that what you really want? To leave your family? Your parents are strict, but out there… "

"Oh, Cole, I'm sorry. I know you'd give anything to be with—"

"Stop feeling sorry for me."

"I'm sorry," I say quickly, and change course. "I don't want to leave my family, and I absolutely won't leave you, but I don't know how to sit by and watch Daddy work with Clem. Just hide here while the man who signed off on my death makes plans for my home."

"Then why don't *you* work with the group and Captain Shahin?"

"Shahin didn't ask me."

"Well, why don't you ask him? If it were me, I'd want to. If you're working with Shahin, then you know what's coming. I think knowing is better than not knowing."

"When did you get so smart?" I ask him.

"I've always been smart. A genius, really," he says, and moonlight reflects in his grin.

"Maybe I'll follow your advice, kid. Go see Shahin tomorrow." The thought of working with Clem Richardson feels like being covered by a million spiders, crawling and biting and suffocating. "Being in the know is better than not, right? Maybe I can convince Shahin that Clem is dangerous." I look out at the Bay, marveling at Cole's ability to challenge and calm me at the same time. *Maybe this is how a mother feels.*

Cole rocks on his haunches, expelling youthful energy. But he says nothing, just rocks and stares at the waves and stars and moon. "Is that a ship?" he asks, pointing off into the distance.

"Yeah. You must have the vision of an eagle if you can see it all the way out there. It passed by earlier. Cargo ship. I couldn't make out if it was military or not."

"What?" Cole says and hops to his feet. "See, if it were me, I'd have hopped in a kayak and gone after it."

"And that's why I still have to look out for you. Even geniuses do dumb things."

Cole sits back down. "Nothin' dumb about it. I'd paddle hard and fast, get a good look at it, then come back."

"Oh, okay. I didn't know you could paddle fast enough to catch up with a cargo ship three miles out."

"I'd paddle so fast, I'd just be a blur across the water. Like an airboat."

I laugh hard as Cole enacts paddling fast enough to hover above the water. Then I stop, aware of how loud my laughter is. "Shh," I tell Cole. "We're being too loud."

He stills and whispers, "Guard duty."

I wrap an arm around his shoulders. "That's right. Guard duty."

"You and me versus the world, right Jules?"

A sob builds in my throat, and I swallow hard against it. *This sweet boy. This little devil.* Tonight, when my emotions are so raw, my nerves frayed and splintered, is the night he names what we have. "Yes, Cole. You and me versus the world."

8

*Y**ou and me versus the world.*

I woke this morning feeling more like myself than I have in months, really since Jacob died and I retreated home. I searched for months for that woman—my old self—and thought she was gone forever. I was wrong. Cole's faith in me brought her back.

You and me versus the world. Cole's words echoed in my mind as I pulled on my khaki shorts and a tank top. Before leaving the garage with my hair tucked under an old baseball cap, I watched Cole sleep. His breathing was even with a slight rise and fall of his chest. I examined his beautiful face—blonde hair, pink lips, and long, blonde lashes curled below closed eyelids. I made him a silent promise. *I will not fail you. It's you and me versus the world, kid.*

Now, I'm paddling south in my red kayak with Matt trailing close behind me. I've heard of mothers who lift cars to free pinned children. Mothers who run into traffic to snatch up wayward children. Women whose fear disappears when catapulted into motherhood. My own mother was terrified to drive over bridges until Kate came along. That first baby sleeping in the back of her old station wagon gave her the ability to drive across the skyscraping Dauphin Island Bridge without hyperventilating. *So, maybe I can do this mothering thing. The proof of the pudding is in the eating, right? Well, my pudding is kayaking without fear, and this pudding is delicious.*

"You seem different. Not depressed." Matt's suspicious tone has been there since I demanded he kayak with me to the combat outpost.

"That's right," I say. "I have put up with too much bullshit over the last eighteen months. Now, I'm done."

"Just like that?"

"Yep. Head above water. I will no longer accept the bullshit of this life. I will not be everyone's *good girl* anymore."

"Were you ever?" Matt asks with a cackle.

"I damn sure tried to be. Or let it happen. I don't know, but I've accepted every limit put upon me since I came home. For what? None of it has kept us safe, so I'm done with being that woman."

"I'm not sure how accepting you've been, Jules."

"Well, I tried, and even the trying feels like a lie. I'm a fully grown-ass woman who's seen and done some shit. I've kept myself alive, I'm keeping Cole safe, and I'm reclaiming my life—"

"You are woman. Hear you roar."

"I'm starting to regret taking you along this morning."

"Like you gave me a choice." Matt sprays my back with water.

"Hey! Use that paddle for paddling, not splashing."

"Does Daddy know where we are?"

"Yes, I told him. But I didn't ask his permission."

"I bet he didn't like that."

"I don't care if he liked it or not. I told him what I was going to do, and I did it." I hear Matt chuckling behind me, so I stick my paddle in the water so that my forward motion stops.

"Shit, Jules, I almost crashed into you." Matt glares at me as my kayak rotates, and I get a good look at his shocked face.

"Laugh at me again, and I will do this by myself. After flipping your kayak."

"Then tell me what exactly we're doing. The last time you and I paddled to the outpost, you ended up abducted, locked in a shed, then dumped on Middle Bay Lighthouse to die."

"All that happened when we got back home, not at the outpost." I glide my paddle through the water, heading south along the shoreline again. "The reason the Knights lost during the raid was because I convinced an Army captain to be on my side."

"So, this has to do with Shahin and Clem? Jules, maybe you should stay out of things this time around."

"Impossible."

"No, it's not. This is not your business."

"Shahin putting *Clem the Criminal* in a seat of power is absolutely my business. Daddy being on the committee is my business. The third civilian member of this committee being a sauced old priest is my business. This is all my business. Yours too. And I told Cole I wouldn't hide anymore. That I'd do whatever I can to keep us safe."

"So, sticking your nose in is going to keep us safe? You know, Daddy can keep us informed."

"I don't trust that he will," I say.

"What the fuck, Jules? Now you don't trust Daddy?"

"Not when it comes to this. Daddy wants to protect us from harm, and I think he will sugarcoat or omit things if he thinks it will upset me. I'm not going to give him that choice. I don't trust Shahin to be transparent, and I don't trust Clem to do anything that's morally right, so yeah, I'm sticking my nose in. I'm getting a seat at the table."

"So, why am I here?"

"Safety in numbers. Now, try to look respectable. We're going to have to talk our way in."

"*Jesus Christ.*"

From the lagoon, I stare ahead at two MPs standing atop the old, wooden, raised deck they use as a lookout tower. They have rifles slung across their chests and binoculars pressed against their faces. I wave to them, putting on my best friendly face as I paddle closer.

As we drift around the last bend through the reeds, the lagoon glassy beneath us, an MP descends the lookout steps and walks toward the water's edge. He holds up one hand, the universal signal for *stop, come no further.*

"Hi," I call out to him, letting my kayak coast closer to the sloping bank. "I'm Jules Martin Jones. This is my brother Matt. Our dad owns this land."

The soldier's lips fall into a frown, and he stares at me. At least I think he's staring at me. The lenses on his sunglasses are so dark that he could have his eyes shut, and I wouldn't know it. He takes another step towards my kayak and me in it. I'm unarmed, save the paddle, but he reiterates his lethal prowess by tapping a finger too close to the trigger for my comfort.

I hold up both hands. "We're unarmed. Just need to speak to Captain Shahin."

"What is this regarding?" the soldier asks me, and his voice is higher pitched than his large body would suggest. I force a smirk to stand down.

"It's BSC business. My father's on the council and needs me to relay a message."

"He should've come here himself, then."

My kayak reaches the shore and teeters on the keel, the water too shallow for buoyancy. "May I get out of this? I'm going to tip over if I try to balance on the shore much longer."

The soldier gestures for me to exit the kayak, so I grab my flops and hop out, placing the paddle inside the hull and grabbing the safety rope just in case the boat drifts out into the alligator-infested water. In the lagoon and swamp, where the reeds form swirling passages, I am an above-water-only woman.

"Thank you," I say, barefoot in the grass. I drop my flops on the ground and slide into them. "My dad can't come today. He's ill."

"Give me the message, and I'll pass it along."

"No. I don't think I should do that. It's very important, so I don't want to risk any misinterpretation." A voice crackles through the radio clipped to the soldier's vest. I hear a garbled something, then the number six. I point to the radio. "That's Shahin, isn't it? Would you please let him know we're here?"

"Watch them," the soldier tells a fellow guard that has joined us on the bank, then steps away, talking low into his shoulder radio.

Matt sidles up beside me. "How did you know that's Shahin? I could barely hear anything."

"The call sign. The commander of a unit is always *Something Six*."

"I guess you do still speak Army."

"Yep." What I want to say is *do not question me. I'm in charge now.* But I don't. I will play the role of concerned and useful citizen until I get what I came for—a seat at the table. "And here he comes."

Between the few trees the Army didn't chop down when they first inhabited the outpost, Shahin walks toward us. His strides are casual rather than the top-dog posture he used at the town hall meeting yesterday. I guess he wants to play nice, too. We'll see how long that lasts.

"Miss Jones, Mister Martin," Shahin says by way of greeting.

"George, you can call me Jules. We don't have to be so formal." My tone is so kind, so sweet, I stifle a gag.

Shahin stares at me, incredulous and showing only mild interest.

"If I apologized for yesterday, would you accept it?"

"For causing such chaos and showing a level of disrespect and selfishness that I never thought you capable of?"

"Ouch. I guess I deserve that. Yes, I'm sorry for disrupting your meeting. I shouldn't have done that. I can't believe I was so triggered by Clem. I'm so embarrassed. Were you able to get things back on track after I left?"

"No."

"Oh," I say, and look at the ground for a moment. The top layer of soil is dry and gray, despite the recent rain. Looking up at Shahin, I do my best impression of a contrite woman. "I truly am sorry. I wish I could take it all back."

"Is there something I can do for you, Jules?" Shahin asks, reminiscent of our first encounter in the garden. Well, first encounter as adults with years of living to influence our thinking and plenty of baggage to lug around. Only this time, it's he who looks annoyed by my surprise visit, rather than me wanting to put as much space between military police members and Cole.

"I need… We need to speak with you. In private. Can we go to your office? I assume you've taken over Captain Johnson's quarters."

Shahin lets out a long stream of air, seeming to mull over my request. "Fine. Follow me."

Shahin does indeed occupy the same trailer that once belonged to Brandon Johnson. I feel the most awful déjà vu as I ascend the three stairs and enter the metal shed. Inside, the furniture is the same Army-issued brown metal, but Shahin has his things organized with military precision, unlike Johnson, who was more concerned with stopping violence than office organization.

The few papers on Shahin's desk are in two neat stacks—one in an "In" box, the other in an "out" box. A pencil tray holds two black ink pens and two mechanical pencils, all aligned perfectly. A laptop sits in the center of the desk. My eyes zoom in on it as Matt and I sit in the two folding chairs facing Shahin's desk with Shahin opposite us. I want to ask Shahin if he knows how Johnson is doing. Has he healed? Did he get home safely? Did he recover enough to remain in service or was he med-boarded out? But I don't. Shahin wouldn't know, and I have urgent matters for him to focus on.

"You have a laptop?" I ask Shahin. "Does that mean the internet is working again?"

"Not yet," he says. "Just sipper."

"Just what?" Matt asks.

"Sipper," I repeat. "S-I-P-R. It's the secret network the military uses, but it's not an open signal, so it's useless and unavailable to us civilians."

"Yes, but do you know what the acronym means?" Shahin asks, giving me a slight grin.

"I'd guess secret internet… protected… router."

"Close. So close."

I wait for Shahin to reveal the correct words, but he doesn't. Instead, he changes the subject. "So, what's this urgent message?"

"My father thinks it's a bad idea for Father Morgan to serve on the BSC, and I'd like to replace him." I feel Matt flinch at my lie. For my brother's sake, Shahin better not have seen it.

"Father Morgan seemed fine with the assignment, and he is a trusted leader in this community."

"He's… Well… Let's just say he really loves his communion wine." I look at Matt for backup.

"Oh, yeah. Just ask our mother," Matt says, securing his place in my good graces.

I nod, turning back to Shahin. "Between you and me and

Matt, I've seen him decline throughout this horrible situation. It's understandable at his age. He was actually set to retire before we all got stuck here. And I've heard the Archbishop fled Mobile, so there's no one to order a replacement priest. I want you to consider leaving him with the one job only he can do—saying Mass. He has enough stress to deal with without adding to his burdens."

"I hadn't thought of that." Shahin adjusts in his seat, casting a glance out a small window.

"Do you have somewhere you need to be?" Matt asks, and starts to rise. I pull him back into his seat. "Okay. I guess we're not leaving yet."

"George, I want to serve in Father Morgan's place."

"Are you forgetting your outburst yesterday? You know, that spectacle you just apologized for? How would it look if I put someone so fragile—"

"I'm not fragile."

"Someone still recovering—"

"I'm recovered."

"Someone who flew off the handle in front of the whole town."

I suck in a breath, staying my nerves and the urge to choke out the man sitting in front of me. "Yesterday caught me by surprise. First, I see you speaking with Clem Richardson in private. Then you put him in a seat of power, when just weeks ago he was in jail. I was in shock. You can understand that, can't you?"

"Mister Richardson has been cleared of any suspicion of criminal activity, so I—"

"Mister Richardson *is* the criminal activity in this area. It's not like being let off the hook changed his entire belief system."

"The investigation concluded that Mister Richardson was not integral to Troy Cowart's actions."

"What investigation? Clem was in charge. Can't you see that?

I saw it. He was the one getting them all riled up. He may not have been the one to leave me at the lighthouse, but he certainly would have approved."

"Miss Jones, what I see is a woman—you—way out of line, and a man—Mister Richardson—who wants to serve his community."

Matt speaks up, probably trying to lower the temperature. "George, I don't—"

"You will address me as Captain Shahin. Both of you." Shahin's eyes alight with anger, showing me a side of him I haven't seen before. "Do not make me reconsider accepting your apology."

"*Captain* Shahin, I am sorry," I begin again. "But please do not put us all at risk by taking guidance from Clem. He doesn't want what you want."

"And how do you know what I want?"

"I don't know for sure, but I'd assume you want peace. A return to normalcy. For us all to be safe. For your job here to end because we don't need martial law anymore."

"What makes you think Mr. Richardson doesn't want those same things?"

"Oh, I'm sure Clem wants martial law to end, but I'm worried about what he wants to come after the end. I saw inside the Knight compound. I saw how Clem governed the people living there. He and the Knights want a radical Bellefontaine, where the men lead and the women obey. Where anyone deemed an outsider goes away. Ever met a Black Knight? Neither have I. There's a lot of Creoles who live in Bellefontaine, but I didn't see a single one at my trial. And every single person there was chugging Clem's Kool-Aid."

"So, you believe that not only is Clem Richardson a criminal, but he's also racist and sexist?"

"That's what I *know*."

Shahin stands, his face void of any compassion. "Ms. Jones, Mr. Martin, this meeting is over. There will be no changes made to the BSC. The committee remains as I've arranged."

"Please don't do this. Don't ignore what's in front of your face."

"Right now, Miss Jones, what is in front of my face is a woman who shouldn't be pointing out supposed criminals when she harbors one."

"Excuse me?" I ask.

"You know exactly what, or rather, who, I'm talking about."

"No, I don't," I lie.

"Miss Jones, so much of your personal information is there for the taking, reading, knowing."

"Jules," Matt says. "I think we should go."

"Rank of your dead husband," Shahin continues, the blank expression replaced by one far more sinister. "Pay. Addresses. Number of *dependents*."

"Now, Jules." Matt grabs me by the arm, pulling me toward the door.

"He's not yours, *Miss Jones*," Shahin says, lowering his volume but somehow more threatening than before. "And if you don't start playing nice, he's mine."

I hear the trailer door slap shut as Matt drags me toward the water and our waiting kayaks.

"Move it, Jules, before that guy decides to take us both into custody."

"We haven't done anything wrong."

"Just once in your life, shut up and walk. Fast."

At the shore, Matt unties both of our kayaks and practically pushes me into mine. He shoves my kayak with me in it, away from the land. The nose of my vessel bends several reeds, as it floats into a thicket.

"Paddle, Jules," Matt tells me.

I watch Matt's jaw work just like Daddy's does when under stress or worried to the point of panic or anger. The image snaps me out of my stupor, and I pick up my paddle and push through the water, moving faster around the bends of the lagoon than I ever have, trying to keep up with Matt. When we reach the open water of Mobile Bay, he finally slows enough for me to coast the last few yards up next to him.

"What the fuck, Matt?" I ask, panting from exertion. "I can't believe you just dragged me out of there. What the hell has you so spooked? That wasn't the first time I've pissed off someone in uniform."

"I'm guessing you didn't see the picture on Shahin's desk?"

"Just the back of the frame."

"It was a picture of a little boy sitting next to a man in a golfcart."

"So?"

"The little boy looked a lot like Shahin. The man looked like an older version of Shahin, probably his dad."

"Okay?" I ask, confused as to why a picture of a boy and his dad scares Matt so much.

"The golfcart was decked out for a Mardi Gras Parade on Dauphin Island. The Knight emblem was hung across the front of the cart. I think Shahin's family is in the Knights."

"He's one of them?"

"Yep. And we're not."

9

Matt and I made it back to the pier in time for the bottom to fall out. The dark clouds that gathered while we paddled against time and nature seemed fitting. I fear Bellefontaine's darkest clouds are on the horizon, just waiting for the wind to pick up, blow our way, and release hell on all of us.

Matt, eager to spread the horrific news of Shahin's family belonging to the Knights—at least when it was a Mardi Gras society—ran through the pouring rain to the main house. I didn't. Matt can share the news all he wants. I will sit my butt on this swing until the weather clears. Maybe the rat-tat-tat on the tin roof will beat the unease out of my body. *Is sound therapy a thing?* If I had access to Shahin's satellite network connection, I could look it up. Google it, as we used to say. But I don't.

I keep going back to this state. The state of being in which every cell of my body screams, "Time to freak out!" I am so damn tired of freaking out. I want peace. I want boring. I want a string of nothing days and un-special nights. *Is that too much to ask, God?* Stop offering us *what we can handle* and decide once and for all that you've given us too much. Too many setbacks. Too many challenges. Too many awful situations to manage. I'm ready to do something good, but I fear I'm the only one. *How about it, Jesus? May I please have a reprieve?*

"What's the plan here, bud?" I ask. I wait for an answer, but all I hear is the pouring rain. "Fine. Ignore me." God is on my nerves today.

What are we supposed to do about the military unit that governs every aspect of our lives being led by a potential member of the crazed militia that tried to destroy our lives and end my life? The Knights killed Billy Roberts. They did. Does Shahin care about that?

Mama and Daddy probably heard this news and immediately started saying a Rosary. Well, we can do all the praying in the world, but that won't change the fact that George Shahin is on the wrong side of this. That appears to be true. The good captain is a Knight.

But maybe he isn't. Maybe Shahin's father was a member of the Knights way back when they were merely a Mardi Gras society. Just a bunch of drunk granddads and young professionals and blue-collar workers looking to escape into a little debauchery for an afternoon and evening. Maybe Shahin and his family cut ties with the Knights when the country blew up and their monthly dues went to buying guns and explosive components instead of beads and an open bar.

Why didn't I notice the photo? If I'd seen it, I would have asked about the photo. I would have looked Shahin in the eyes and got my answer, good or very, very bad.

"What the fuck, God?" Yelling that into the deluge feels good, but it accomplishes nothing. God isn't going to answer me because God has nothing to do with this.

That photo is another betrayal in a long line of betrayals. It's proof of how far gone this community and our country are. Months ago, when the enemy was a faceless terrorist group radicalizing a few individuals, I hitched my little, red wagon to the idea that this hatred was limited to the fringes of society, to just Liberty's Guard. I was sure the hatred hadn't infected the masses. I thought our leaders and institutions were still guided by better angels and that those angels—be they elected officials or warriors in US Military uniforms—would lead us to safety, would root out the hate, and save us all. But now, if the Alabama National Guard is being led by a militia member, is safety even possible? Who else in their ranks falls on the side of the militias who work to dismantle this country? How far up the chain does this go?

The wind shifts and the relentless rain turns sideways, right at me. I'm soaked in a matter of seconds. So much for staying out of the storm. That's hard to do when the storm insists on landing in your lap. I laugh at that thought and the perfect timing of the metaphor. Yes, the storm has landed on my lap. Again. It slaps me in the face. I fear it's all around me, threatening to draw me into its darkest clouds.

I draw my knees up to my chin and squeeze my arms around my shins, burying my face in the space where my knees touch my clavicles. The swing sways in the wind, back and forth and back and forth, forcing me to grab the chains on each end so I don't topple out and onto the soaked deck.

Then, just as quickly as the rain came, it slacks until at last, the drops cease, leaving a calm bay and me, soaked to the bone.

I can't avoid my family any longer. My stormy barrier between the boathouse and the yard is gone. When I turn to look toward the house, I see Mama and Daddy on the porch. Daddy waves me in, and against every impulse to drop my kayak back in the water and paddle away, I rise from the swing and slosh through the shallow puddles to the walkway.

As I approach the porch, Mama wipes down the patio furniture with a towel, which is a waste of time and effort. I'm wetter than any chair I'm about to sit in. I stretch my arms wide. "Can this wait a few minutes for me to change?"

"Fine," Mama says. "But change and come right back. You've avoided us for long enough."

———

"Mom, this is why I've been avoiding the both of you last night and today." I lean back in my chair and cross my arms, wanting to be anywhere in the world other than this porch right now. I may be in dry clothes, but I'm no more comfortable than I was soaking wet.

"Because you don't want to listen to our advice anymore," Mama responds.

"Because if you understood how betrayed I felt after that meeting yesterday, Daddy wouldn't have agreed to work with Clem. At the very least, he would have warned me before Shahin's announcement. But instead, you let me be blindsided. In public."

"Your father was blindsided—"

"Mama, I can speak for myself." Daddy leans forward, resting his elbows on his bent knees. "Shahin told me who the other council members were right before I sat down. I didn't know how to tell you. I didn't have time to tell you."

"Your father was still processing the information, Jules."

Daddy pats Mama on her knee, his polite way of telling her to be quiet and let him speak. "Your Mama's right. I was processing."

"So Shahin told you that Clem would be on the council, and you just said yeah, sure. That sounds like fun. Let's all hold hands and pretend we're friends."

Daddy's brow furrows. Whether out of frustration or guilt, I can't say. "Julianne, what was I supposed to do? Refuse? Then we would be left with Clem Richardson dictating what would become of all of us. Of this town. Do you want that?"

"Of course not."

"That's why I'm going along with this. Father Morgan is a fine priest, but I imagine he won't be very involved in planning or implementing next steps. Someone has to be on the council to keep the military and Clem in check."

"I understand that, Daddy. But why didn't you fight Shahin on appointing Clem in the first place?"

"That wasn't my decision. Shahin had decided on Clem long before he spoke with me at the meeting. Why he trusts Clem, I don't know."

"You don't know a lot."

Mama shoots me a lethal look, so I close my mouth.

Despite what Mama calls my sass mouth, Daddy continues, "We are not in charge here, Julianne. But if I remain on council, I can have some influence. I can keep us all safe from Clem."

"I don't know if that's true, Daddy."

"Julianne, of course it's true. If Daddy says he will keep us safe, he will. I don't want to hear you doubt him again."

A laugh forces my lips open. "You were quiet for as long as possible, huh, Mom?"

"I will choose to ignore that, Jules, because I know you are upset right now and not thinking clearly. But your father knows what his is doing."

Mama's faith and devotion to Daddy is impressive. Once upon a time, I thought I felt that way about Jacob. That I'd never doubt his ability to always take care of me. But now he's gone, and I must take care of myself. "I don't have to stay here. And maybe I shouldn't. Now that Shahin knows the truth about Cole, we might be better off leaving. You all would be safer if we left. Then Clem wouldn't have reason to go after you, after us."

"What do you mean he knows the truth about Cole?" Daddy asks.

"Matt didn't tell you that part?"

"What part?" Mama asks.

"Shahin knows Cole is the blond looter from months ago. He's holding that over my head. So, I either get on board with Clem's and Shahin's plan, or Cole gets arrested."

"He said that to you?" Mama looks to me then Daddy. "Cole hasn't stolen anything for months. Not since he's been in this family. And he's a child!"

Mama's words tug at my heart. The fact that she accepted the orphan boy as family so quickly surprised me, but it shouldn't have. If there is one thing Mama and Daddy can't deny, it is a child in need.

"Mama, I don't think Shahin cares about the needs of a single child. He made it pretty clear this morning that Cole is a means to an end."

"So, what's the end?" Daddy asks.

"You know what the end is, Daddy."

Daddy nods. "I suppose I do."

"Well, I don't. So, would one of you fill me in?"

Daddy takes a swig from his water jug, then sets it back on the plastic rattan side table. "Shahin doesn't aim to just keep Jules in line. He expects us all to fall in line. Including me in my role on the council." Daddy looks at me for confirmation.

"That's the impression I got. Shahin didn't say as much, but I think that is the best assumption to make."

"So, is your father just supposed to go along with whatever Shahin and Clem suggest? Just agree to everything no matter if they are doing what's right or something very, very wrong?" The pitch in Mama's voice rises, revealing her feelings on the matter and the depth of my latest mistake—thinking I could persuade Shahin to let me in the inner circle.

"Mama, there are two men in this county that people trust. For some, that man is Clem Richards. For others, it's Daddy. With Daddy's stamp of approval, the ones who trust him over Clem will go along with whatever they're told to do. I shouldn't have tried to talk to Shahin. I don't have influence over anyone. If anything, I proved today that I am a pawn, and Shahin played me well. I know that, so you two can skip the lecture."

"You are too old for lectures, Julianne."

"No, she's not." Mama cuts her gaze at Daddy. If she had the power to melt people with one look, Daddy would be a puddle.

Daddy exhales a slow breath. "Julianne, yes, you are too old for lectures. Hell, you're too old for me to tell you what to do at all. But I am asking you to leave this to me. Let me handle Shahin and Clem. Now that I know where Shahin's loyalties lie, his history with the Knights, I know what my job really is."

"To make sure all of Bellefontaine doesn't become one big, swampy Knight compound?" I ask him.

"Exactly." Daddy takes a handkerchief from his pocket and wipes sweat from his face. "And I'm asking you to stay. Don't run off. You and Cole belong here. If not for yourselves, stay for us. Your mama and I need you. We need to know where you are and that you're okay."

As much as I want to be my own woman and run my own life, I can't deny Daddy this request. I understand the position Shahin has put him in and can't say for sure I'd make a different decision.

"I'll stay," I tell him. "I'm okay. Really, I am. But I don't trust Shahin."

"None of us do. We can't," Mama says, looking fretful again.

"No, we can't." I turn my focus to Daddy. "Tell me what to do. How do we get rid of Shahin and the Knights for good?"

"I don't know if it's the other shoe," Matt says, barging through the garage door. "But it's definitely dropping."

"Come again?" I ask, ignorant to whatever has him in a tizzy. "And thanks for knocking."

Matt didn't knock. He never does. After meeting with Shahin yesterday, my nerves are shot, so I really need Matt to stop bulldozing his way into my space.

"No time for that. Shahin's at the gate. Jessie's letting him in. And before you freak out, I sent Cole to the end of the pier with Mama and Kate. Told him to hide in the boat and wait there until Shahin leaves."

I look out the garage window. In the distance, Daddy's 21-foot fishing boat hangs from the boathouse above the water. I can just make out a small figure on the railing near the boat. My stomach lurches as I watch Cole leap from the railing and into the boat. A woman, Kate I assume, pulls the boat cover in place, concealing Cole from view. *Thank you, dear sister.*

"What do you think Shahin wants?" I ask Matt.

"Probably something with Daddy, but it sounds like we're about to find out."

The crunching of large tires rolling over oyster shells filters into the garage. I breathe once, twice, and then the sound stops.

"Shall we?" I ask Matt and motion to the door, my game-face on.

Under the carport, I watch Shahin leap from the raised vehicle. His boots kick up dust when he lands hard in the crushed shells. He removes his helmet and sunglasses, then smiles at me like he's greeting a friend. "Afternoon, Miss Jones. Mr. Martin." He walks over to us with the posture of someone invited, someone welcome.

Matt eases toward the main house. "Daddy's inside. I'll get him for you."

"No need. I'm here for Jules."

This stops Matt. He turns to me, and I give him a reassuring smile. I let my expression drop before addressing CPT A-hole. "What can I do for you, Shahin?"

"It's nothing bad," Shahin says. "You can put away your fight face. I have a favor to ask of you."

"I didn't know I owed you a favor."

"Maybe favor is the wrong word." Shahin steps out of the sun and into the shade of the carport. With him closer, I see his expression change. "I have a duty assignment for you."

"I'm not your soldier, so I can't imagine why you would think you could assign me anything."

"Well." Shahin stretches his arms out wide. "Martial law. So, you are under my command."

I swear there is a glint in his eyes, like he relishes the idea of having me under his control. "My mistake. What do you need me to do?"

"That's more like it." Shahin smiles, then allows the muscles in his face to slacken. "I've decided that you are going to serve as secretary for the council. Take notes during our meetings, draft memorandums for distributions, make coffee." The tone with which he said the word *coffee* proves what an utter asshole George Shahin is. "You wanted to be involved, so I found you a role."

I swallow my disgust and the only word in my mouth—*unfuckingbelievable*—and return his smile. "That sounds like a wonderful opportunity."

"I'm so glad you agree," Shahin says, over the sound of Matt choking on whatever words he just apparently swallowed. "You okay there, friend?"

"Oh, yeah," Matt says, clearing his throat. "Just a little dust in the windpipe." He looks at me, raising one eyebrow ever so slightly. Our sibling telepathy comes through loud and clear. *You okay with this, Jules?*

I turn to Shahin and plaster a smile on my face. "I think this will be great for me. It's always good to have a purpose."

"I'm glad you feel that way. You and your father will meet with the council at the outpost tomorrow." Shahin pats Matt on the shoulder. "Matt can hold the Martins' place in the ration line while you're in the meeting. No need for the whole family to come to distribution. I know how leaving this place unattended makes you nervous."

"Of course," Matt says.

"Oh, and Miss Jones, I feel I must make myself clear. You will be a silent observer in this endeavor. Committee membership stands as previously established."

10

A *lion lifts itself.*
It will not lie down until it devours the prey,
And drinks the blood of the slain.
BDEL

"Jesus Christ," I say after reading the red writing.

Matt, standing next to me in the ration line—as ordered by Shahin—gestures to the red-faced freak wearing a sandwich board sign made of painted plywood and rope. "That's Old Testament. Pre-Jesus."

Matt's tone elicits a nervous laugh from me. "Since when do you know Bible verses?"

"Hey, some Catholics read the Bible."

I try my best cocked eyebrow look, but I've never had facial muscle control like Matt does. Instead, I just look surprised and a bit insane.

"I've told you, Jules. You're either born with the eyebrow or not."

"Fine. But I still can't picture you studying the Bible. If you start throwing out quotes for every possible situation, I'm going to punch you in the throat."

"Wow. Jules Jones, model Christian."

Ahead of us at the outpost gate, Daddy waves both arms at me, then gives me the universal gesture of "Get your butt over here." I nudge Matt and hand over the wagon to him. Hopefully, by the time Matt's through the line, the wagon will be filled with this week's supply of flour, rice, government cheese, and whatever else is on the menu.

"Daddy's waving me over. I guess my lifelong dream of being a bunch of men's beck-and-call-girl is starting."

"Good luck with that. I'll be here when you're done, just hanging out with the freaks and brushing up on my Old Testament."

I glance at the empty blue canvas wagon that used to haul beach towels, snacks, and coolers of cokes and beer. "We're getting so low on everything. Kate's afraid we're going to be eating wild onions and dandelion leaves pretty soon. I hope they have enough for everyone this week."

I leave Matt in line and walk to the gate. As I walk between the line of residents waiting for their weekly share of food, I notice each of the red-faced Freaks wears a homemade sandwich board sign, each with a different Bible verse painted in red letters. Stepping quickly past them, I avoid eye contact. I don't think I'll ever feel comfortable staring into white, dead eyes surrounded by beet juice.

"I'll escort you to the meeting now. The others have already arrived." A stocky MP motions for Daddy and me to walk through the gate, then walks along a worn path through several tents, frayed from months of wind and rain and yellowing in the sun.

"I hadn't noticed Father Morgan or Clem arrive," I tell the soldier. "We've been out there for at least a half hour."

"They arrived earlier," the soldier says with a clip in his voice.

I guess that's all the information the soldier feels like sharing today or is allowed to say. He does pick up his pace, forcing Daddy and me to half-walk, half-jog behind him.

The meeting hasn't even started, and I'm already on high alert. I don't like Clem having private time with Shahin. Not one damn bit. And I don't like feeling like we're late when we are very much on time. Again, my father is never late anywhere, anytime.

Trailing the soldier, we pass a group of MPs hunched over their rifles. Passing cans of spray paint between them, they paint their rifles in camouflage designs. "Cool guy bullshit," Jacob whispers in my mind's ear.

I double step to our guide. "Wouldn't y'all want your rifles to be as visible as possible. Intimidation and all?"

The soldier doesn't even glance in my direction. In fact, he seems to walk even faster.

"Could you slow down a bit? My legs aren't as long as yours." I glance behind me to see Daddy struggling to keep up. "Seriously. Slow down," I say and trip over an errant root. But the soldier makes no accommodation, only speeds by another group of MPs that look to be unfolding additional cots in an open-air tent.

Winded from our near sprint, we arrive at a tent I assume is a mess hall of sorts because the smell of boiled cabbage nearly knocks me to the ground. A buffet line for food service—empty, industrial chafing dishes sitting on top of folding tables—looms along the left side of the tent. Stacks of trays, canisters of silverware, and a tray of condiments rest on their own rectangular table near the buffet. I give the condiment tray a quick scan and find what my subconscious was searching for—a row of eight or nine bottles of Tabasco sauce. Jacob was right. The one constant of Army dining facilities is hot sauce. According to him, choking down Army food was easier if he drowned the boiled and reconstituted eggs, noodles, vegetables, or mystery meat with the red, spicy elixir. "Tabasco covers most culinary sins," Jacob told me more than once. I'm pretty sure those sins included my cooking. But he was always sweet with a thank-you and quick consumption.

The closer I walk to the back of the tent, the more I hear the rumble of a kitchen at work. I'm guessing somewhere behind the back canvas wall is a group of soldiers, aprons tied over their ACUs, stirring big pots of cabbage. Nothing but cabbage.

Rows of tables and chairs form plentiful seating, using every inch of the remaining space the tent provided. All are empty except for the last table in the last row. In the back right corner of the tent, Shahin sits next to Father Morgan. Clem Richardson's bald head shines from the seat opposite Shahin. Empty chairs remain on either side of him, but I notice a bottle of water at the empty seats on Clem's left and right, along with a yellow legal pad and pen at one seat. Surely, Shahin doesn't think I will sit next to Clem. I know I'm only here to help Shahin keep his enemies closer, but sitting next to Clem is too much. Being in the same room—tent—with the man is enough to earn me an award for trauma denial.

As Daddy and I approach the table, I notice condensation dripping down the water bottles and onto the hard plastic, uncovered tabletop. The promise of cold water is almost enough to make me sit next to Clem. Trauma be damned. Offer me some ice and I might climb in the asshole's lap. But there's no ice, and cold water isn't enough of a peace offering for me to buddy up to Clem.

I step aside so Daddy passes me to sit on Clem's far side. Leaving an empty chair between Clem and me, I feel the legs dig into the dirt an inch or so when I sit down. Clem's chair must be halfway to China if my weight is a strain on the flimsy chair. He outweighs me by a good fifty pounds.

While noticeably thinner, as are the rest of us who've endured the last eighteen months, Clem had further to go. *You are the Biggest Loser!* An image of Clem atop the podium of a decades-old reality show flashes in my mind, causing me to stifle a laugh. I reach across empty space to grab the water and catch the annoyed look on Shahin's face.

"I think there should be a bit of space between the council and the council's secretary. Don't you? I wouldn't want to join your conversation by accident."

This seems to appease Shahin.

"That pad of paper and pen are for you, also. After the meeting, I'll give your notes to one of my people to type up."

"No need to use their precious time on that. I'd be happy to type them. Just show me to a computer." I fix a pleasant expression on my face and hope Shahin buys my bullshit. I'm dying to search the net for information on the rest of the country. Even Libby doesn't know much of anything taking place outside of Mobile.

"No." With that curt response, Shahin turns his attention to Clem and Daddy. Father Morgan snaps out of whatever trance he's been in when Shahin clears his throat and taps the piece of paper placed in front of him. "Now, I have a few items on the agenda for today but would like to hear from you two first. What are your immediate needs?"

I jot down a note about writing up and distributing an agenda before the next meeting. That's a task I will question Shahin about later.

Clem urges Daddy to speak first. While Daddy speaks, I scribble notes.

Food shortages - suggestions for action?

Ration portions are shrinking.

Redfish population is down.

Unable to resist the bottle of water, I crack it open. Taking a small sip, I swallow it so it coats my throat in cool bliss. Even when the power is on or we have enough propane to run the generator for the fridge, cold water isn't a luxury we enjoy. But this water is cold. I feel it rush into my chest and cool my torso in a way I'd almost forgotten—a delightful chill blooming in my core. If I must be here in the role of Shahin's assistant rather than partner, and I do if I want Shahin to leave Cole alone, I'm going to enjoy the few perks of the position.

"Did you get all of that?" Shahin asks me. "I didn't even think to ask if you know shorthand."

Who knows shorthand anymore, CPT Dumbass? That's what I want to ask and the exact words I want to use, but I don't. "No, Captain Shahin. I don't know shorthand. I don't even know if that's a thing anymore. But I'm getting it all. No need to worry."

"Worrying is my job, Miss Jones." Shahin holds my gaze for a moment too long. I'm wondering if he is as psycho as Clem and sonny boy Dave put together.

Father Morgan, either incapable of reading the room or of making the awkwardness stop, slaps his liver-spotted hand on the table. "We need to figure out how to get people back in church. Never gonna fix this without divine guidance."

Oh, my lord, is he drunk? The cloud of fermented fruit that wafts across the table is more pungent than the cabbage boiling away behind the buffet line. Whatever is running through his bloodstream must be homemade and possibly toxic. He smells as if he's pickling himself.

"Perhaps that's a conversation you and Mister Martin should have later. We must remember we are here to serve all of Bellefontaine, not just the Catholics."

Well, that's the most sensible thing I've ever heard Shahin say. I write *Daddy and Fr. M to talk about bad Catholics*, underlining the word bad three times for emphasis. I'm tempted to doodle little devil horns around the word bad, but I don't.

"What are we going to do about the red-faced people?" Clem

asks, moving the conversation away from deficiencies and resources, eternal souls and empty church pews. "I think they've worn out their welcome."

"They're more of a nuisance than a problem," Shahin says without looking up from the typed page I assume is today's agenda.

"They are far more than a nuisance," Clem objects. "They are a disruption, and I am tired of fielding complaints over their presence at every gathering in Bellefontaine."

So, people still approach Clem as a trusted community leader. Noted.

Clem lets out a whistle of a sigh, then continues. "From what I've seen, they serve no purpose other than annoying and frightening people. And they've got a—"

Without glancing up from his written agenda, Shahin cuts Clem off. "They are non-violent protesters. That is their right."

"Rights? This is martial law. Rights are suspended. I remember that much from my law days."

"Mister Richardson, allowing the people one or two of their civil rights in a time like this does my soldiers a lot of good."

"How so?"

"For one, the people don't feel oppressed. We, my men and myself, are seen as peacekeepers instead of authoritarian oppressors."

Peacekeepers don't go boom in a heap of twisted metal on the road. Or end up lynched like Billy.

"Also, they appear to be some sort of religious group," Shahin says. "I really don't want to interfere with the right to religious freedom. I do that, and this peace we're experiencing goes downhill fast."

"Religious freedom, my ass," Clem says.

"Watch your language, Clemmy." Fr. Morgan disciplines Clem as if Clemmy is a little boy.

Clemmy. I scribble that on the page and underline it. Twice. No devil horns.

"Morgan," Clem says, clearly agitated, "I'm not one of your flock." Clem turns his gaze to Shahin. "You know they got a tent city going. Up north of the Holy T. With that abandoned cabin. You can see it from the water. Got one of their banners hanging from a couple of trees."

So, that's what that banner was. I thought it was just a cryptic advertisement like a billboard, but it's a marker telling The Way followers where to find them. With everything that's happened lately, I stopped fixating on that banner and what it meant and why the men chose that spot and moved on to fixating on the asshole sitting next to me and the one sitting across from me. But now I know why they chose that spot. It didn't occur to me earlier, but it does lead to something—an abandoned half-built fishing camp with a nice, big clearing.

"Jules and I saw the banner a week or so ago. While we were fishing around the abandoned piers over that way," Daddy says. "But I didn't see any tents."

"Have you been over there since then?" Clem asks Daddy.

"No."

"Well, it's a damn encampment now. I've got crab traps out there. Those abandoned pylons are good breeding grounds, especially for snagging soft shells in molting season, but don't y'all go spreading that around. When I went out there to lay my traps, all I saw was that banner. The next day, I go back to check the traps, and it looked like a druggie den. Must be twenty tents set up now. Shahin, you gotta shut that down. We can't have who knows who squatting in the woods. Trespassin' is a crime."

I choke down a laugh at Clem's hypocrisy and bury my face in the crook of my elbow. "So sorry. Dust in my throat." I take a sip from my water bottle to sell the fake coughing. To think Clem Richardson is concerned with criminal activity is indeed laughable. Maybe he's only comfortable with the crimes he commits himself.

I feel Shahin staring at me, so I pick up my pen and jot a couple of notes.

Who is The Way and what do they want?

The Way tent city?

Does The Way wash the paint off their faces in the bay? Does it look like blood in the water? (That one's just for me.)

"Does anyone own the land?" Shahin asks.

"I know the Roberts bought it a while back, but they're long gone. They all took off as soon as the violence started."

Not all Roberts. Not Billy Roberts. My murdered friend. Billy came back. He was serving his country and trying to bring some peace back here, to make it safe for all of us, but Clem and the Knights dubbed him a traitor. Billy's service was rewarded with an agonizing death and gruesome display of his beaten body. If Shahin wasn't sitting across from me, the temptation to use my pen as a shiv and drive it deep in Clem's neck might be too strong to ignore.

Daddy speaks up. "If we could get back on track. I think the only thing to be done about the protesters at this time is to figure out who *The Way* is and what their end goal is. They may be harmless. Plenty of people in Mobile were left homeless after the poisoning, so they may just be looking for temporary shelter."

"The rhetoric on their signs is getting more concerning. This morning—" I stop speaking when Shahin cuts his gaze at me. "Sorry. Won't happen again." I mime zipping my lips shut, then stare at my notebook while scribbling.

Secretary is not allowed to speak by order of CPT.

The men will do the speaking and deciding. The little lady will scribble.

Shahin leans forward to read my notes, but I put my pen down and fold my hands over the writing. He'll get his turn later.

"I will investigate The Way and this supposed encampment. If there is a reason for concern, I'll take action. Now, moving on." Shahin takes a long pull from his water bottle, replaces the top, and speaks while Clem fumes. I can feel the heat from his bloated body two seats away. "Our biggest concerns right now are rations and the budget. Prices are increasing across the country, but our budget has not. Also, charitable donations of money and supplies have all but dried up. I think people have tired of this situation. They've given what they can, so we need to figure out how families here can do with less."

"Less?" Daddy asks. "What about money and supplies from the state? Is Governor Freidman aware that commercial trucks are still avoiding this area? And even if Greer's suddenly had food on their shelves again, most everyone has been out of work this whole time. There are no jobs. There is no money."

"Yes, the governor is aware of our need, but emergency funds are running low. The state legislature refused to allot any more money to Mobile County, and now they're on summer break."

"Summer break?" The words fly out of my mouth. *Shit.*

"Miss Jones, if you cannot fulfill your duties here, I will find someone else to record our meetings."

I wave and frown an apology. *Just keep your mouth closed,* I tell myself. *Closed.* Not a peep. Being here is the only way I will know what is really going on, so I can't risk getting the boot. Even if I'm only here so Shahin can keep an eye on me.

"Miss Jones is right," Clem says, even though I in no way need or want his approval. "Why don't I give Alice a call? I'm sure you have a way for me to talk to her." Of course, Clem is on a first-name basis with the Governor who couldn't give two shits about Mobile County and never has but used her power to pardon her good buddy Clem. I am officially screwed.

"I've talked to her, Mister Richardson. I've tried to convince her to use her power to get more help down here, but she says she can't do a thing if the money just isn't there."

"So, what's the plan?" Daddy asks. "People are lined up for rations right now. Will this week's rations be cut?"

"No. Rations will remain the same."

"Then, I'm confused. If money is running out, we will have to revise distribution somehow." Daddy grips his water bottle and the crackling of plastic echoes in the cavernous, nearly empty tent.

"Ration portions will be the same. Distribution will change to every two weeks, instead of weekly."

"Do the people in line know that?" Daddy's tone is familiar to my ears, and it's not a happy one. I know he's itching to roll out one of his favorite dad lines, such as *God didn't make you stupid; you're doing that all on your own.*

Luckily, Fr. Morgan jumps in. "Are your soldiers informing residents today that they need to make this week's rations last two weeks?"

"It's best that they are told later. To avoid unnecessary upset or escalate tension in the line today." Shahin doesn't make eye contact with any of us with that line of crap.

"So, no, they don't know," Daddy says, his exacerbated tone replaced with one of disappointment.

Clem leans back in his chair, speaking low. "You made this decision without consulting the council, so when folks find out about your decision, you can blame it on us. Is that what you're planning to do, boy? Is that how this is going to play out?"

"No, that is not my plan. I am doing what I think is right. What I think will best keep the peace around here."

"I know you got a phone around here somewhere. One of those satellite doohickies." Clem stands, and his chair falls backward. "Right now. You and me are calling the governor."

"We're not done with our business—"

Clem cuts Shahin off. "Oh, we're done here. We either call the governor right now, or I go out to that line and tell everyone that their pants are gonna get a whole lot looser this week. And that cutting rations is all your idea."

Clem crosses behind me so close he brushes against my shoulders. The slight touch makes me cringe.

At the end of our row of tables, Clem looks at Shahin. "You got two seconds to be on your feet and leading me to a phone."

Shahin rises from his chair, his jaw clenched. He steps back and pushes his chair in. I glance at his hands and see his knuckles have gone white. Gripping the back of the chair, he exhales, then looks at Clem. "Fine. Maybe when you speak with Friedman, you'll understand that this is the only choice I have."

I turn in my seat to watch Clem and Shahin exit the tent. Before I can digest or comprehend the obvious power shift, the soldier that escorted Daddy and me here appears in the entrance. He calls over to us. "Time to go. Follow me."

I clutch my notebook and pen and to my chest as we walk across the outpost, back toward the gate. I lean in close to Daddy and whisper, "What was that? Did Shahin just let Clem order him around?"

Daddy's lips go tight, then he whispers, "Wait until we are on the other side of the gate."

"Do we tell them about the rations?"

"Who?" Daddy asks.

"The people waiting in line."

"No. Don't say a word. I don't want that crowd turning on us. I need to see what Shahin does next. And Clem."

At the gate, we're searched. Even Fr. Morgan empties his pockets. Our escort takes the pen and notepad from me, much to my disappointment. I'd hoped to use it to get back through the gate later to pump Shahin for details about the phone call. But I will have to come up with a different excuse to get back on Post.

Outside of the gate, it looks like the ration line is moving at a snail's pace.

"How'd it go?" Matt asks us when we join him in line.

"Not great," I say. "We'll explain when we're back at the house."

Just then, the line of freaks takes a sideways step toward the ration line. One red freak—a woman with long, blond twin braids—changes places with the freak nearest me. She pulls out a poster of some sort from behind her sandwich board sign. As she unfolds it and holds it flat for me to see, she glares at me. Refusing the urge to glare back, I lower my gaze and read the paper:

Whoever sheds man's blood,
By man his blood shall be shed.

11

EFFECTIVE IMMEDIATELY by order of the BELLE-FONTAINE STABILITY COUNCIL: This order contains immediate changes to ration distribution for the town of Bellefontaine:

1. Any person receiving rations must be a resident of Bellefontaine.
2. Residency will be verified at the distribution site.
3. Standard ration allocations per household are reduced from once weekly to once every two weeks.
4. Any person found to be involved in illegal trading, distribution, sales, or theft of rations will be detained and charged according to the Uniform Code of Military Justice.
5. No exceptions will be granted to this order.

The smoke was white at first, pale wisps against a bright blue sky. For several minutes, we thought it was just another burn pile. Those are common here. When the smoke turned gray, we told ourselves it was a bonfire or maybe meat fat flaring up over an open flame. That's common here, too.

When it turned black, blooming into dark clouds that churned and rose high above the trees, we knew there was a problem. Something big was on fire.

Although we didn't know where the smoke originated, we knew it was too close to ignore. Mama and Daddy ordered everyone inside, fearful of what the smoke may carry, except Matt and me. We covered our noses and mouths in bandanas and set out in the truck. Everyone agreed that we had to know where the fire was and if it was contained. After the actions of Liberty's Guard and then The Knights, ignoring disaster is no longer a luxury any of us have.

But in my most heinous nightmares, I wouldn't have dreamt this.

Now, standing in the back of the truck so I can see over the gathered crowd, I watch the last of the St. Phillip Neri rectory burn to the ground. There's nothing to be done, other than pray the embers don't jump to other structures. Perhaps prayers of gratitude should be said also, as the ground surrounding the charred residence seems too wet from recent rain to burn, at least not past the asphalt road and driveway.

But the sight of it. Crumbling, black heaps where walls once stood, statuary peeking from ash, and twisted, melted appliances tell the tale of a fire that burned white hot and fast. My hand flew to my mouth at the sight of Fr. Morgan's metal bedframe—the only recognizable piece of furniture I see.

"Did he make it out alive?" I ask Matt standing in the truck next to me.

He doesn't answer because he doesn't know. He only knows what I know, and I know nothing.

"Do you think this was intentional? An accident? Maybe he lit a candle and forgot about it."

Matt remains silent. When I turn my face to look at him, tears stream down his face from behind his sunglasses.

"This burned too fast to be that," a woman on the ground in front of us says.

"You saw it burn?"

"Start to finish. Almost the start." She turns to look up at me, revealing soot-covered cheeks and clothes. "I was inside the church when I heard a loud pop, like a big firecracker going off."

"You're the new organist's daughter, aren't you?" I ask.

"Yes. Fr. Morgan lets me practice on the piano in the church sometimes. I don't have one at home."

"Was he inside?"

"Yes."

I sit on the wheel well, unable to stand or look at the remnants of the rectory any longer. "Did he make it out?"

"Yes, he—" The young woman gestures to the right, her charcoal smudged arm flailing toward several military vehicles, then stomps away.

I want to call out to her to come back, to tell me everything she knows, but I don't. I saw a brokenness in her eyes, one that begged for isolation. Instead, I scan the crowd and then the soldiers milling about the fringes of the fire. Fr. Morgan isn't here. But Shahin is.

"Come with me," I tell Matt and hop down from the truck bed. "Captain Shahin," I call as I approach.

"I don't have time for chit chat, Miss Jones."

"I'm not here for conversation," I tell him, then lower my voice. "Where is Fr. Morgan? Is he alive?"

"He was taken to Brookley."

"Burns?"

"What do you think?"

"I'm just concerned, George. He's important to this parish. To my family. How bad are the burns?"

"I don't know, Miss Jones. I'm not a doctor."

"Do you know how it started? I spoke to a woman who said she heard a loud pop like a firecracker."

Shahin turns to me, glaring at me from behind his sunglasses. No, I can't see his eyes, but I feel them burning me as the flames burned Morgan. "The last thing I need right now is you starting rumors."

"It's not a rumor. She was in the church and heard the pop."

"Go home, Miss Jones. This is none of your concern."

"Is this related to the BSC and food rations? Is this retaliation?"

"That's ridiculous."

"Is it? Within a day of learning through your order that rations will be cut, a member of the BSC nearly dies in a house fire. Shouldn't we be suspicious?"

Shahin presses his lips together. I can hear his breathing and wish like hell I could also hear his thoughts. "Go home. I don't need a bunch of civilians interfering with my soldiers today."

"But you put civilians on the blame line for reduced rations."

"Miss Jones, I said go home. That is all I have to say to you or anyone else right now."

"Do you really expect us to not be scared? To not want to know who is responsible for this? If someone is willing to harm a priest, why wouldn't they come for my father? For me? For all of us involved?"

"You told me yourself that Morgan drank. He probably got good and stinking drunk and started the fire himself. As far as I know right now, this was a terrible accident. Or are you going to tell me the only explanation for this is some nefarious plot? Go home, Jules, or I will have you removed and detained. That is an order." Shahin turns from me and grabs a bullhorn from the hood of the nearest vehicle. "This area is to be cleared of all civilians. Any civilian who refuses to leave immediately will be arrested."

Matt tugs on my arm, but he doesn't have to say a word. We need to get home. Shahin isn't going to admit or even suggest that this may be related to rations, his dumb decisions, and that he dragged my family into his bullshit brand of leadership. If my suspicions are right, being out here makes us easy targets.

"Maybe it was an accident," Matt says once we are safely inside Daddy's truck.

"Maybe. But I can't shake this feeling that it was intentional."

"But setting fire to the rectory? Would anyone really do that?"

"Maybe. If they're scared or angry enough."

"It had to be an accident. Lots of things can start a house fire, and a building that old would burn fast. Hell, it could've been electrical. It's not like anyone's inspecting the wires now that they're working again."

"True."

Driving along DIP, we pass a steady stream of pedestrians walking toward the church, probably curious and hoping to view the damage. They will be disappointed when Shahin orders them to turn around and go home. No answers will be provided today. I wonder if Shahin will ever tell us what happened, and if he himself will ever know.

"Matt, how are we going to tell Mama? We don't even know how serious Morgan's injuries are."

"Hopefully, he just took in too much smoke."

"Burns. Shahin said burns."

"We just have to say the words. There was a fire, and Father got hurt. That's all we can tell her because that's all we know."

Matt turns onto Bay Aire Road.

"She will be devastated."

"Yes, she will—oh fuck!"

Matt slams on the breaks so hard my seatbelt digs into my sternum, knocking the breath out of me for a second.

"Where the hell did they come from?" Bracing on the dashboard, I stare ahead at a line of red-faced freaks, arm-in-arm, extending across the road, blocking our path. Two members of The Way step out of line and stretch out a banner.

For where you have envy and selfish ambition,
there you find disorder and every evil practice.
BDEL

"That fire was intentional." I lean my head out of the open widow and yell, "Get the hell—ow, Matt! Stop that."

Matt releases his power grip on my arm. "Shut up! Jules, I swear to God, you've got to think before you act. For fuck's sake."

"How else are we going to get by them?"

"Just cool it, alright?"

For several moments, we all remain still and silent. The Way stares at us with their creepy red masks and stupid banner. Matt and I stare at them. Then Matt puts the truck back into drive and creeps forward.

"Matt, what if they don't move? You can't run over them."

"They'll move, Jules. No one wants to get run over."

"They're not moving. This isn't some game of chicken in the Bay, Matt."

"They'll move."

"Matt, just go around them. In the ditch."

"Too steep."

Matt's face is decided. He's not going in the ditch and he's not hitting the breaks. He's just driving toward them. Creeping. Steady.

"Matt, stop. They're not moving, Matt. You're going to hit them."

"Shut the fuck up, Jules."

Matt accelerates, just a little, but it's enough to make me grip the oh-shit handle. When we are within a few feet of The Way, the line breaks and my relief is immediate. The banner falls to the ground in a shoosh of white and red-faced lunatics dash to either side of the road as our truck passes safely through the protest.

"Told ya," Matt says. "I've always had a knack with chicken."

"Screw you, Matt."

"No other way. Ha! I guess I'm also good for a pun."

"You're not funny."

"Fine, Jules. But we're home and safe. Get the gate, would you?"

I hop out of the truck and swing the gate open. As Matt pulls the truck through, I call to him. "Go on without me. I need to walk."

"Suit yourself. I'm going to tell Mama and Daddy what we just saw, including those freaks on the road. Do you want me to wait for you?"

"No. Just go on. But tell them we've got to do around-the-clock guard on both the pier and the back gate. I've got a feeling—"

"You and your feelings."

With that, Matt drives to the carport, leaving me to walk the long driveway alone, which is exactly what I need right now. Nothing's on fire. No crazed protesters block my path. We're home. We're safe. But I can't help but wonder, for how long? And right here, right now, after Matt's actions on the road, I wonder who's the actual lunatic? The Way or my damn brother? I think we're all past our limit.

12

W hile we slept, The Way ransacked our garden. They ripped the gate out of the ground and tossed it into the ditch. Greedy hands pulled up pepper plants and stripped beans from vines, leaving the supports broken. Squash lie on the ground, as if stomped on by boots. Yesterday rows of tender leaves promised a fall harvest of onions, carrots, and turnips. Today lies ruin. Cherry tomatoes dot the asphalt, scattered and crushed beneath footfalls and truck tires.

All because The Way deemed us unworthy of this bounty.

All because one Army captain pushed the people of Belle-fontaine past their breaking point.

All because we didn't protect the garden.

My eyes fill with tears as I stare at the banner stretched between two stakes driven into the fertile soil.

Their day of disaster is near,

and their doom rushes upon them.

BDEL

Another Bible verse, I presume. Words from an almighty being meant to bring comfort to the afflicted, but here those words are a threat. Or maybe an explanation.

So much red paint. Where do they get so much red paint?

Cole squeezes my hand. His kindness makes my tears fall. I am to blame for this. At least partly. I'm sure of that. The frightful woman two days ago with her threatening sign, displayed just for me as she glared at me with such menace, is proof enough that I am to blame. They're not just angry with the BSC. They hate me for much deeper, primal reasons. They must blame me for Troy Cowart's death. That's the only explanation that makes sense. Rations were simply a tipping point—the black cloud that finally burst.

"This is my fault." The words, the only ones I can muster, come out between heaves.

"You didn't do this." Cole looks up at me, his blue eyes wet with his own tears. "I don't know who did, but it wasn't—"

"Cole, go to the house and get whoever's awake."

I watch the boy take off on a sprint down Bay Aire Road. His speed impresses me. He will be there in no time. He will tell Daddy and Mama, Matt and Lauren, Kate and Garrett—whoever has awakened unaware of this devastation—that Garrett's beautiful garden is gone. *All gone.* He will tell them to come. *Quick. Come quick.* Then he will turn and run back here to make sure I am not alone for a second longer than necessary. Because the boy I know—I do know him, right?—gives of his whole heart. His loyalty. His kindness. His bravery. He knows no other way.

As Cole runs around the curve of Bay Aire Road and out of my sight, I turn back to the banner. Were their faces painted red while they stole from us? Did sweat streak through their disguises while they drove four-by-four posts into the ground to hang their cruel sign? I stare at the red lettering of the banner. Always red. No other color. And then the signatory line—*BDEL*. It's just past dawn now. I guess they got me good.

What time did they come? The three o'clock witching hour, perhaps? The perfect hour to let demons run free. Maybe they came just before twilight. Just after the last of Shahin's night patrols sped past with their ominous, green glow. As Cole and I, both unable to sleep, dressed in the dark, were they here? I bet as we tied our shoelaces, The Way hung their banner and popped cherry tomatoes in their fists and into their mouths. Then they smiled at this missive full of hate and violence, in the name of a false Christianity.

I finally know what that gnawing feeling in my gut has been pointing to all these weeks. The Way scares me more than the Knights ever did. They flaunt their radicalism as righteous. They've literally remained silent, letting their threatening posture, red faces, glaring eyes, and cryptic banners speak for them. They haven't left a single, real clue to what their intentions are. Until now. Until yesterday.

I want to tear it down, light a match, and burn it into oblivion just like the rectory burned. I can't do that until the others see, no matter how much I don't want them to see something like this. Not ever. But they must see it. All of Bellefontaine should see this, see what The Way did. They should see the garden in ruins. All our work for nothing. All that life-sustaining food destroyed not by a storm, not by an act of God, but by neighbors convinced that God is on their side. Would Bellefontaine care? After all, not one of us ever suggested sharing this bounty.

I want to run until my feet bleed with blisters. Maybe then I will feel properly punished for not seeing this coming. Yesterday, I saw what came from blind rage. Two days ago, that woman at the ration line showed me who The Way really is. She threatened to shed my blood.

Whoever sheds man's blood,

By man his blood shall be shed.

For what? What blood have I shed?

Again, that voice in my head tells me I know the answer. They blame me for Troy's death. If I hadn't stabbed him with my gig, I would have never been abducted. My abduction was the action that triggered the raid on the Knight compound. My actions led to Troy's eventual death.

Whoever sheds man's blood,

By man his blood shall be shed.

Another terrifying thought tears at my sanity, that tiny threshold of logic and intellect and hope I cling to. Do they intend to shed my blood, or did she signal to me that my family, my blood, will pay the price for my sins? If that is the aim, they are well on their way to success. First, they try to kill Morgan. They know how important that church and parish are to my family. And what an easy target Morgan turned out to be.

Next, by destroying the garden, they have thrust my family ever so close to starvation. With the reduction in rations, we planned to rely on the garden even more than before. Now, the garden is gone. An entire harvest and future harvest gone in a single night.

I hear the Gator's motor before I turn to see it. The open-air utility vehicle, like a golfcart with muscles, displays its passengers for all the world to see. Matt sits behind the wheel with Daddy, Mama, and Garrett filling the other seats. Cole rides in the small cargo bin with Jessie, her red hair flowing wildly in the wind.

"Their doom?" Mama asks as she climbs out of the Gator, her gaze locked on the banner. "Whose doom? Ours?" Tears stream down her cheeks, and she swipes them away with an angry, shaking hand. "Why would they do this?" Every line on her face shows how deep her hurt is.

I should go to her, wrap her in my arms, tell her everything will be fine, but I don't believe that for a second. Only a catastrophe would force a woman like Mama away from her house in her nightgown, robe, and slippers. My mother doesn't show that disheveled side of herself to the world unless the world has fallen apart. But this garden is our lifeline in dystopia. *Was*. It was our lifeline.

Mama stomps toward the garden. She pulls her robe tight around her nightgown. "This wasn't a protest. This is pure hatred." She brings her hands up to her face, disbelief and sorrow in her eyes.

Daddy tries to comfort her, but she pushes him away. "How are we supposed to feed all of us now?"

"We'll fish more. Use the rations sparingly. It will be like the early days before the rations started. Before the garden." Daddy reaches for Mama again, and this time, she allows him to hold her.

Garrett, shocked silent until now, steps carefully along one uprooted row of squash. "We'll replant. I'll see what I can salvage. Cultivate any cuttings that are worth saving. I can have it back by spring."

"I'll leave." Cole's declaration surprises all of us. Six faces stare at him, but he stands resolute. "The Army doesn't count me for the rations. Y'all don't need another person to feed. Not now."

Jessie grabs Cole's arm. Her eyes flare as hot as the red in her hair. "You are not leaving." She turns to Matt. "Daddy, tell him he's not leaving." Then my sweet, fearless niece turns to me. "Aunt Jules, please. Tell him he can't leave." The look in her eyes and the cry in her voice suggest she thinks I might send Cole away.

"Jessie, Cole, no one is leaving." I meet Cole's gaze. "You are part of this family, remember?"

Cole's announcement seems to have shaken Mama out of her initial horror. "No one is leaving. And everyone will help to get this cleaned up. Garrett—"

"No, Mama. Not yet." I walk to where the gate used to stand, a flimsy deterrent to anyone with a truck and a wench. "Shahin has to see this. The garden is a crime scene. The Way, whoever they are, must be held accountable."

Garrett points toward the outpost lying a short distance away. "Then go get him. I can't wait long to gather anything I can use to plant. If it rains—" Garrett looks to the sky, worry across his face.

"It's not safe anymore." I say this to myself mostly, but everyone hears me.

"Not safe?" Daddy asks. "The garden? We'll reinforce the fencing."

Time to come clean. Tell them all what I should have told them last night. Tell them why I couldn't sleep and woke Cole by accident. Why we came to garden so early, with first light barely peeking over the horizon. "It's not safe because this wasn't about food. It was about me, and what I did. I haven't paid for my crime yet. I doubt The Way ever really cared about the rations being cut. They just used that as an excuse to act."

"You've paid plenty," Mama says, the sorrow in her voice replaced with annoyance. "And what crime?"

"They had a message for me at the last ration line. After we met with Shahin and the council. A woman had a message for me."

Daddy drops Mama's hand and steps closer to me, his face alight with a mix of fear and frustration. "A message? Why didn't you tell me?"

"Because I hoped I was being paranoid."

"What did it say, Jules?" Matt asks me. "When did one of them give you a message? I was right there with you."

"You were in front of me. And it wasn't like that."

"Dammit, Jules, just spit it out." Hearing Mama swear slaps me in the face.

"A woman, one of the red faces, she switched places with the person standing closest to me. She pulled a folded poster from behind her plywood sign. She held it open for me to read it."

"What did it say?" Cole asks, easing up beside me.

I take in a gulp of air. For a moment, my lungs and throat refuse to give sound to the words. Such awful words. "Whoever sheds man's blood, by man his blood shall be shed."

"Not again," Cole whispers.

"No," I tell him, far louder than intended. "No, they will not harm me, not like that. We will go to Shahin. Daddy, you and me. We will convince him that they mean to harm me. Like they harmed Fr. Morgan. That they may be trying to hurt me through all of you. He has to do something. He can't let these crazy people run around doing whatever they want. We will get him to arrest them. Once he sees that banner and the damage they've done here. He has to do something! He has to know that the rectory fire and this was done by them." I take Cole by his shoulders and stare into those blue eyes of his. "Cole, I promise. No one will take me from you. No one."

Cole looks around. His eyes turn frantic as he stares into the trees and thick shrubs surrounding the garden and further, the swamp. For the first time since I met him, he looks truly scared.

"We need to go home." His voice is low and flat.

"We will," I tell him. "Just as soon as I talk to Shahin."

"No. Now. We need to go home now. Back to the garage."

Mama looks at Cole, then scans the woods herself. "Cole, honey, do you see something? Someone?" she asks, her voice deliberate.

"Not yet," he answers. "But I have this feeling. There are too many places to hide out here. I know because I've used them all. Now, Jules. We have to go now."

For all the times Cole has seemed older than he is, older sometimes than all of us, right now his face, his whole body, is that of a child. A young, frightened child.

———

"That's what I'd do," Mama had whispered to me. "If he were mine." Then she hugged me and climbed into the passenger seat of the Gator. Mama and Daddy went straight to the outpost to speak to Shahin, while the rest of us jogged home. Cole's "bad feeling" had our feet moving faster than usual.

At home, with the smaller kids all within earshot, Kate and Lauren exercised control when we told them about the garden. It wasn't until later, when I watched Kate pace back and forth in the boathouse, that I saw how upset she was. Even from my spot at the kitchen window, I saw her arms gesturing wildly. Feeding us wasn't only about the availability of food. Mama and Kate plan meals and portions, cook what we have, and prepare and store what can be saved for later. Lately, as portions shrank, I've seen worry and regret in Kate's eyes. I hope she knows none of us blames her for our stomach pangs.

We all have a hand in this, our survival. Garrett oversees the garden. Matt and I fish and trap what we can in the Bay, swamp, and woods. Daddy ensures the outhouse, pier, fencing, and generators remain in good working order—regardless of the current state of the power grid. Lauren homeschools the kids—a job I don't envy in the least. Before and after school lessons, the kids have chores and help the adults with pulling weeds in the garden, emptying crab traps, replacing rotting wood on the pier, repairing fence boards, and more. Mallie, too young to help with such tasks, has the mighty job of bringing joy into our daily lives with her giggles and kisses, which she doles out with generosity, unaware that she is essential to our survival. But with less food— the garden in tatters—all our roles grow more difficult with each growl of hunger.

Matt and I wait until Kate appears calm, at least from this distance, before joining them on the pier. As our footsteps shake the pier, Kate turns to face us.

"Jules!" Kate rushes to me when she sees me. She hugs me

like she hasn't seen me in ten years. Then she nudges me backward and holds me by the shoulders. "We will get all of us through this. No red-faced freak is going to hurt my baby sister."

This is the Kate I like, not only love. I smile at her, and for the first time today, I feel like I can breathe. Maybe Kate squeezed me hard enough to expel some of the anxiety that locked my shoulders and strangled me as soon as Cole and I walked up to the garden this morning.

I turn toward the open water, letting the breeze bathe my face with its warm touch. Off in the distance, where the Bay meets the Gulf of Mexico, thin clouds gather. They will be here by late afternoon, by then black and heavy with rain, ready to cool us off. "Garrett, when do you want to go back to the garden? We will all pitch in to collect any salvageable plants. Anything that can be used to seed a new garden."

"I've been thinking about that," Garrett, still in the swing, says. "I think we need to move the garden. That location is too exposed and too far away for us to guard at night."

"Garrett's going to talk to Mama and Daddy when they get back." Kate sits next to Garrett and places her hand on his knee. "So, I think we should gather what we can, like the poles for the beans and anything that can still be eaten—"

Garrett interrupts Kate with a smile. "Woman, will you let me talk?"

That earns a laugh from Matt. "My sisters aren't good at letting other people speak."

I sit next to Matt and nudge him in the ribs. "And we get that honestly. From Mama." I wink at Kate, and she nods her head in agreement. I should be twisted with unease right now. Knowing the immense loss of the garden and the weeks of backbreaking work ahead of us, should have me in a ball of twitching muscles and hyper breaths. Let alone the knowledge that a cult thinks it's their divine duty to kill me. But I'm not. Because nothing feels more natural than being out here on the pier swings, trading jabs with my siblings. This is safety. If the outside world just left us alone, we could survive this new world just fine, until the time comes for us to separate again. Matt and Lauren back to Mobile. Garrett and Kate back to the land Garrett's family has farmed for generations. Cole and me, where? I haven't let myself plan that yet.

"Jules, why were you out in the garden so early, anyway?" Kate's tone is curious rather than accusatory.

"When I realized that neither Cole nor I were sleeping after our guard shift, I figured we'd do something useful with the extra hour. Get some work done before the heat comes."

"What was keeping Cole up?"

"I'm not sure. I'm afraid he was picking up on my worry. Either that or I woke him up fumbling around the garage."

"You didn't tell him?"

"About that crazy woman at the ration line? No. But he knows now. I've never seen him truly scared until today." My declaration hangs heavy in the air. What can be said about the most feral among us worrying over mortality. "Maybe the best thing I can do for him is get to work. Set new traps, fish, whatever we can do to make up for food lost in the garden. He knows where all the wild blackberries are around here. Maybe they haven't all been picked yet."

"Seeing you push forward would be good for him." Kate offers me a closed-mouth smile, one that reaches her eyes for the briefest moment.

Garrett speaks up, surprising me with his tenderness. "You two can help me in the garden, too. Maybe it would be good to show Cole you're not afraid to be there, even if it is only to move the garden closer to home."

"Where are you thinking of planting now?" I ask.

"The backyard. It's nearly a half-acre. Not as big as the garden now, but it will be behind the big gate where we can keep an eye on it twenty-four-seven."

"The kids will lose their play space," Kate says.

"Look around," Matt says, stretching his arms out wide. "This whole place is play space."

I smile at Matt and a flash of memory of our childhood here bursts in my mind. Matt chases Kate and me around the front yard. The game is Mud Monster, our favorite made-up, low-tide amusement on summer days. The trees are safe zones, but we can't stay at one too long because that is deemed cheating. We run from tree to tree, with the Mud Monster—Matt covered in black clay from the sandbars—fast on our heels. If he tags one of us, the other wins. After several rounds, black streaks stinking of sulfur cover our arms, faces, and backs. *Can we please go back to that, God?*

"Hopefully, I can save a few of the tomato plants," Garrett says, pushing the happy childhood memory from my mind. "Tomatoes grow fast, so we can have those again in a month."

Kate perks up at the idea of tomatoes. "I can do a lot with those. Thanks, honey."

A year and a half ago, I couldn't watch Kate swoon over Garrett without feeling a jealous rage course through my veins. Grieving Jacob tainted every aspect of my life. A part of me hated her for having a husband, a hand to hold when she's scared, a body to sleep next to, a partner to confide in. Now, I'm grateful she has him. He's not my cup of tea, but he loves her and she him. That's clear.

"Heads up," Garrett says, nodding beyond Matt and me to the water behind us.

An Army boat speeds toward our pier. "That's coming our way." I stand and walk to the crab pier steps. The others join me at the railing that separates the main deck from the lower crab deck. No one says a word as we watch the boat with four MPs riding in it pull into the shallows that surround the pier.

Matt calls out to them. "You need something?"

One soldier reaches out from the boat and grabs hold of a pylon attached to the crab deck. He holds the boat to the pier while another, a female with dark hair pulled into a bun, speaks. Fly-aways and curls blown loose surround her round face. "We're here to notify you of a storm approaching. Cat One. Voluntary evacuation."

Her words are the gut punch none of us need right now. "How long do we have?" I ask.

"Should make landfall in forty-eight hours."

"Where?" Matt asks.

"Biloxi."

Shit. *East is beast.* I know we're all thinking it. The eastern side of a hurricane is always the worse side. We need to prepare for the worst. "Do you have information on the evacuation?"

"No POV's," she says. "Shuttles will take anyone who wants to evacuate from the intersection of DIP and Laurendine Road to Mobile starting in—"

"Mobile?" I ask. "The city? Is that safe?"

"Ma'am," the soldier says, "I'm just here to give you the headline."

"But we need more information than that," Matt says, sharing my concern.

The soldier checks her watch, then looks back up at us. "Thirty-six hours. Last shuttle leaves at oh-nine-hundred Friday morning." She motions to the boat's driver to move on, and he obeys, without another word.

Just like that, any time we thought we had to salvage the garden, fish and hunt for food, or get cuttings planted and in the greenhouse for germination, ends. No loud alarm. No suspenseful count down. Just a boat and a soldier and we're done.

13

As soon as the MPs speed away, a stiff wake following them, we begin storm preparations, deciding to divide and conquer. I doubt I'm the only one with one thought drumming in my mind—evacuation to Mobile.

I don't know who, if anyone, lives there anymore. If people have returned, I don't know the conditions. Is life back to normal with police, emergency services, shops, and restaurants? Or is it a large ghost town? Shahin has to give us more information than what that MP told us—show up at a designated time and hop on a bus to an undisclosed location. That is batshit crazy. No way in hell I'm doing that.

In the garage, I crank the radio until my forearm burns with the effort, then set it on the worktable. Every few minutes as I gather supplies, I crank the radio, waiting for Libby's voice to break through the static. I know as soon as Libby hears of the approaching hurricane, she will broadcast what she knows. Finally, as I pull a plastic tub of old quilts from a top shelf, her voice comes through the small speaker. I drop the bin, letting it smack against the ground and hop off the ladder, giving her my full attention.

Good afternoon, my darlings. Unfortunately, I am not bringing you good news this afternoon. What we have all dreaded and tried to prevent through prayer is heading our way.

I grab my notebook and pen; the notebook I use to write Jacob the letters I cannot send. I know the family will have questions, and I don't want to forget a single detail.

I have just received a report regarding the latest storm update. This seems to be an evolving situation, so I will tell you what I know as of this afternoon.

"Get on with it, Libby," I say out loud as Cole comes through the door. I put one finger to my lips and point to the radio, then to a stool.

Cole sits, his eyes bright with adrenaline. Even a child his age knows the dangers of a hurricane. Every child on the Gulf Coast knows the meaning of the word hurricane, even before they can properly pronounce it.

The powers that be have named this storm Isadora. So, Hurricane Isadora is currently a category one storm with winds of eighty-eight miles per hour and is moving steadily northwest at eleven miles per hour. From what I understand, this storm formed in the Gulf. As warm as the water has been this summer, I'm not surprised. She also seems to be gaining strength.

I scribble the name Isadora and current speed. Winds at eighty-eight and gaining strength. Only eight more miles an hour, and this will be a category two. I was hoping this was barely a hurricane, but I was wrong.

The bad news continues as Isadora has enough open and hot water in front of her to intensify quickly. So, please do not ignore my warnings or be fooled into thinking this storm isn't going to be dangerous. I expect we will experience category two, possible three, winds.

Well, that answers my next question. Isadora is going to suck up as much hot air and water as she can before coming onshore with all the rage of a scorned woman on crystal meth. The difference between a weak Cat-1 with seventy-five miles an hour gusts and a storm with gas in the tank rolling in at 100-plus miles an hour is significant. That can be the difference between minor roof damage and the whole damn building coming down.

Isadora currently sits north of the Yucatan Peninsula, approximately 450 miles south of Mobile. Expected landfall is Friday evening along the Mississippi coast. I know none of us enjoy hurricanes, but especially not in the dark. I expect conditions to deteriorate quickly on Friday, so you only have a day and half to get ready for this.

A day and a half? While Libby does her best to convince the storm-weathered residents of Bellefontaine to take this threat seriously, I write a list of what needs to be done in thirty-six hours. We need to drag in the kayaks and all fishing equipment, get the boat to dry storage, pull in the crab traps, boil any crabs in the traps, boil water—gallons and gallons of water—gather up all towels, blankets, and anything else that can soak up water, move anything of value to higher shelves in the garage and pantry, take all buckets, baskets, and empty boxes to the garden for Garrett… what else? I stare at Cole's face for answers.

"What?" he asks. "Stop staring at me."

"Sorry. Just thinking. Your face helps me concentrate."

"Well, I don't like it."

"Shhh. She's talking evac now."

I've been told that the Army will take those who wish to evacuate to Mobile, specifically the Temple downtown. I do not know what condition the city of Mobile is in as a whole, but I do know the Temple is an immovable fortress. At the very least those thick, concrete walls should stand up to the winds as they have for nearly a century of storms. However, I don't remember The Temple being that big on the inside, so I cannot promise it will be a comfortable place to ride out the storm.

The Temple? I've always wondered what the interior of the odd monolith in the middle of downtown looks like. To me, the building has always been steeped in mystery. Guarded by two giant sphinxes, the entire building is made of concrete, sloping skyward at least four stories high. And that name—the Temple? Odd considering it's not a church. No one goes there for worship, just wedding receptions, galas, fundraising events, and the like.

Pay close attention to this: the last evacuation shuttle will leave no later than 9 a.m. Friday. If you are not at the St. Phillip Community Center by then, you will have to ride out this storm here. And I have no idea if anyone will be available to rescue you if you get yourself in trouble.

Is there anyone to save evacuees if the Temple takes on damage? A darkness seems to envelop me for a moment. Should we evacuate? Should we stay? But what if this storm intensifies? None of us should be here if that happens, but I know Daddy won't leave for a category one storm, and I won't leave him here by himself.

Stop it. No freaking out. Cole doesn't need to see me freak out. And freaking out is what I would have done a month ago, a year ago. Not now. This version of myself, this me, doesn't freak out. She doesn't panic. She acts. So shut up your bitching and listen to Libby.

Isadora, my darlings, has her eye on Biloxi. Some may say this is a good thing for us, although I never like being grateful for someone else's trouble. Biloxi is going to take a direct hit. That means, you guessed it, we will get the east side of the storm. As the eye rolls over Biloxi, those strong east winds will pommel us. That's what concerns me the most. That's why we have to prepare, get somewhere safe, make sure you and your loved ones are safe. Property can be replaced, but none of you, not a single one, my darlings, are replaceable.

Maybe a few of us, Libby, considering what The Way has put

us through over the last few days. I'm starting to think Shahin should be replaced as his decision-making leaves a lot to be desired. Just as I return my focus to Libby, the channel turns to static, so I switch off the radio and look at my hurried notes.

"Now who's staring at who?" I ask Cole, looking up from my notes.

"What do you need me to do?"

"Gather every bucket, basket, empty box you can find. We're going to need them in the garden. I'm going to check with Garrett to see if he's ready for us to go over there." Exiting the garage, I nearly run into Daddy. The look on his face is dead serious. "Everybody inside. Now."

Cole and I set off in different directions to gather the family. Matt is halfway down the pier, dragging a kayak alongside the walkway in the water below. Jessie follows close behind him, her arms full of fishing poles. Garrett and Kate have the grill going, boiling big metal pots of well water. Lauren, Lucy, Kate's boys, and little Mallie are gathering random plastic toys and balls from the yard—harmless, kiddie objects that, with the right amount of wind, become projectiles.

"I'm ready to go through the garden, if anyone's available to help," Garrett says as soon as everyone is accounted for and standing around the granite kitchen island. "I've got to get clippings before this storm washes it all away."

"Yes," Mama says. She purses her lips as if all she can manage without screaming is that one word.

"What's wrong?" I ask. "I mean, other than the obvious of a hurricane on its way."

Daddy squeezes Mama's shoulders—something he does when she is angry to the point of crying—then looks at all of us. "You can do whatever you have time for in the garden because no one from the Army will be going there today or tomorrow."

"No one?" Garrett says. "They're going to do nothing about us getting robbed?"

"They have to pass the garden to evacuate," I say. Disbelief over this level of negligence makes my brain swoosh back and forth. I grip the countertop, then look at Garrett. "We can save the banner as proof."

"Do y'all have an old digital camera?" Kate asks Mama and Daddy. "One that can be charged?"

Disappointment blooms in Mama's expression. "I think I got rid of those once we all had cameras in our phones."

"Maybe we can charge a phone." I don't know if any of our phones will hold a charge or even work if powered up. The photos showing damage would sit in the phone's memory until all of this is over. By then, it may be too late to punish anyone.

"We don't have time for that," Daddy says, and our family meeting dissolves into a flurry of objections, so loud that I can't distinguish who's yelling which protest. The Martin clan, whether born into it or wed into it, has a strong sense of justice. The idea of letting the perpetrators off scot-free is unfathomable. But all this noise isn't going to help.

"Daddy's right," I shout over the arguing. "He's right!" That silences all of us, but now six sets of eyes glare at me. "Daddy's right. We have a hurricane heading toward us. We've got to get ready. And we've got to collect what we can from the garden. As far as Shahin and the MPs, I have an idea that will do the trick."

———

Two hours later, the entire family, from Daddy down to Mallie, are at the garden. Fortunately, after helping me secure the garage for the storm, Cole made fast work of gathering containers.

The others did the same with their tasks. The main house is as secure as we can make it. Without storm shutters or plywood—I'd love to borrow a few sandwich boards from The Way—the house is what it is. Daddy keeps telling me not to worry and that the windows are hurricane-proof, but I'm struggling with believing anything will be as expected. Matt drove the boat to the Fowl River Marina. Lauren met him there with the truck and trailer. The boat now sits in the driveway, covered by a tarp and bungee cords. I'm worried about that, too. The kayaks and all the fishing gear are secured in the garage, and Kate, Mama, and Garrett cooked and stored what little perishable food we have and stacked jugs on top of jugs of drinkable water in the pantry. When all that was done, Cole filled the back of the truck with empty planters, boxes, and even Kate's good gumbo pot.

After pouring two precious gallons of gasoline into Jacob's old SUV, the truck started on the third try. I was afraid it had sat in the driveway unused for too long. But, for my plan to work, we need Daddy's truck, the Gator, and Jacob's truck. Being back in the gray, vinyl driver's seat, I breathed around the tennis ball-sized lump of anxiety in my throat. Then, I opened my eyes and executed a perfect three-point turn and exited the safety of our driveway.

At the garden, I parked in front of Daddy's truck, which was parked in front of the Gator. The three vehicles sat in a row with noses to bumpers. I hope it will be the barricade we need.

The plan is pretty simple: park the cars across the road to block any military vehicles trying to leave the outpost. Next, gather up anything useful for after the storm in the new garden. Last, when we spot a military vehicle exiting the outpost gate, all thirteen of us line up across the street on foot, in front of the trucks and Gator—a barricade with a human element. And unlike The Way's little display two days ago, the Humvees will have more than just bodies and a banner to roll over.

"Like human shields?" Kate had protested earlier.

"Yes," I said. "You'll be holding Mallie to make sure she

doesn't run toward the Army vehicles." I looked around the kitchen to my family. "This will work. Soldiers are decent people. They won't try to smash through the trucks, especially with people standing in front of them." I held Daddy's gaze with mine. "We won't do it unless we all agree."

One by one, each Martin agreed to the plan—the only way we could think of to force Shahin to lay eyes on the destruction of our property and the hateful, threatening banner hung above the broken garden gate. Perhaps more of a miracle than Jacob's truck starting was getting all of us to agree on something, but we did.

I assigned myself as lookout and am now positioned in the tall grass near the intersection of Bay Aire Road and the outpost road. There is only one way out of the outpost by car, truck, or armored vehicle, and that is to take a left from the outpost road onto Bay Aire Road, right beside the garden. The swamp's long fingers wind through the woods, forming creeks, lagoons, and deep sink-holes. Leave the road and you won't get far without a small ATV, canoe, or kayak, unless you want to risk going on foot. That option promises snakes, gigantic spiders, bobcats, and alligators. So, I know for a bunch of soldiers to leave in a quick, safe manner, they'll be in big, clunky vehicles that must drive right down this road.

Crouching in my lookout and peering between the reeds and dandelions, I see a tan vehicle approach the outpost gate. Two waiting MPs hop into the vehicle. *Guess they're done with guard duty.* "Here they come," I call to my parents and siblings. "Get in position!" I hightail it to my spot in line, directly in front of Jacob's rear, left tire.

"That didn't take long," I say, smiling at Matt out of nervousness. I hope I'm not putting too much faith in the humanity of the 128th Military Police Brigade. I lean forward and call to Garrett down the line, "Did y'all finish in the garden?"

He gives me a thumbs up, then faces forward, chest puffed up, holding Kate's hand.

A column of Army vehicles comes into full view. The lead Humvee pauses at the stop sign then turns left, toward us and our vehicles. I hold my breath at the sight, then exhale pure relief when the lead Humvee slows to stop, forcing the vehicles behind it to stop.

"Thank, God." I whisper, but loud enough for Cole to hear. He smirks at me, as if to say, *What the hell, Jules? I thought you were sure they'd stop!*

The driver of the Humvee leans his head out the open driver's side window. "Clear those vehicles. We need to pass."

"No." I call back. On cue, we join hands. I hear the crack of a radio, and a few seconds later, CPT Shahin hops out of the second vehicle.

"Martins, you're going to clear this road now," Shahin says, walking toward us.

"Not until you see what they've done," I say.

Ignoring me, Shahin looks at Daddy. "Mister Martin, I told you this cannot be our priority today. I don't like what happened to your garden, but we have a hurricane headed this way and people to get to safety. You all need to get to safety."

"Not until you see what they've done," I say again.

Shahin shoots me an annoyed look. "Move. These. Vehicles."

"Look at what they did." I point to the banner.

I see Shahin flinch when he looks at the banner with its red, threatening words. "Fine. I looked."

"Shahin," I say, careful to make my voice strong and sure, rather than exasperated. "Take thirty seconds to look at the broken gate, the destroyed plants. That was all food. Food that was going to keep us from starving. The Way stole it all. And you will punish them after this hurricane blows over. You will. That is your duty."

Two soldiers approach, one with sergeant stripes and the other wearing specialist rank. "Sir," the sergeant says, "we need to get moving. We have three stops to make."

My face contorts, and Shahin sees my curiosity. "We have to check on several elderly residents on our way to the shelter who cannot transport themselves. I'm not a monster, you know."

"Prove that by looking at what they did. All I ask you to do today is look."

Shahin expels an angry breath and walks to the broken gate. With his back to us and his hands on his hips, he scans the garden from right to left. Then he turns back to me. "Happy?"

I grab the notebook and pen I threw on Jacob's backseat before we left the house. "Thank you," I tell Shahin, then turn to the two enlisted men. "May I have your names?"

They both look a bit confused but offer their names.

"Sergeant Stanstead," says one.

"Specialist Burch," says the other.

"Thank you," I say to them then address Shahin. "I've got their names as witnesses, Shahin. You can't ignore this."

Shahin takes a step toward me, and in a loud, hissing voice, says, "I'd think you'd avoid this place if what you claim happened last year with Troy Cowart is true." Shahin's eyes burn with hatred. He directs his next order to my family. "Move. The damn. Vehicles" He takes a step toward the Humvees, but stops and looks at Matt. "Is that redhead yours?"

"Yes, she's mine," Matt says, apprehension in his voice.

"I hear she has quite the arm." There's that flat, menacing tone from Shahin again. My arms turn to gooseflesh despite the thick heat. *What is wrong with that man? Does he take issue with how Jessie defended me against Troy Cowart's assault on me? He seems to know what happened but doesn't believe Troy attacked me.*

Shahin climbs into his vehicle and waves an arm at the

convoy behind him. The engines roar to life, and I fear they won't give us time to move out of their way. Daddy must have the same concern. He yanks open the truck door. "Everybody load up!" The kids pile into the back of Daddy's truck with the cuttings from the garden gathered into a few containers. Matt and Garrett pull the banner, stakes and all, and toss them across Jacob's backseat. Once everyone loads in, one by one and as fast as we can maneuver without rolling into the steep ditch, we clear the road, forming our own convoy home.

14

"You're going to the shelter," I tell Cole, who woke up today with an attitude to rival any full-blown teenager or enraged toddler.

"No, I'm not."

"You are my responsibility. I am the adult. You are the child."

"There you go again." Cole pulls on a tennis shoe and stomps his heel into it.

"You know what I mean. As the legal adult in this situation, I am responsible for your safety. Have you ever ridden out a hurricane before? It gets pretty scary."

"Yes, when I was an actual child."

"A big hurricane? Because we don't really know how bad it's about to get."

"No, not a big one. We went to my grandma's for that."

"Your grandma? I didn't think you had any—"

"She died when I was seven. But she had a brick house which was way better than our trailer. According to my dad."

"Oh… okay," I say, and the relief I feel at knowing Cole's grandmother is dead and will not show up one day to take Cole away from me is immediately replaced with guilt. What kind of person is relieved to know a child has no blood relations left on this earth? I am a monster. "I don't mean you're a child. I didn't mean that."

"Yes, you did."

"No, I didn't. If I know you're at the shelter, that's one less 'thing I have to worry about over the next twenty-four hours. The last bus leaves in an hour, and I want you on it. Please let me be selfish."

"That's what you're good at."

"Excuse me? Cole, we do not have time to argue about this. We've got about fifteen minutes to get you packed and in the truck, or all of you are going to miss the bus."

Cole stands, and I swear he somehow makes himself appear taller. With balled fists, he glares at me. "You talk about safety a lot, but you're the one getting yourself in trouble. Do you know how long I lived in those woods alone?"

"Not exactly, no."

"Long enough to learn how to survive!"

I brace against his tone as I fold a T-shirt and place it in the small stack of his clothes. "Cole, do not yell at me."

"Well, you don't seem to hear me when I talk normal, so I gotta yell."

I give up on folding his laundry and turn to him. "I'm listening. Please. Just breathe—"

"Stop it with the just breathe crap. I am breathing. If I wasn't breathing, I'd be dead on the floor." Cole huffs in and out several mocking breaths.

"What has gotten into you? Are you going to make me pack for you? Where's your book?" I grab for his backpack, but he snatches it away from me and holds the empty bag to his chest. "Cole!"

"I'm not going."

"Yes, you are."

"No."

"Yes, you're… Oh, good lord, I am not playing some back-and-forth, yes-no game with you. Get packed."

Cole raises his face to look at me, and I see tears in his eyes. "I'm not going without you. I'm… you need me. You're not safe on your own."

Finally, a bit of truth, and the gut punch hits hard. "Cole, I will be fine. Daddy doesn't want to leave the house unguarded, which I get, so I'm staying with him. I won't be alone."

As if on cue, Matt busts through the garage door.

"Jesus Christ, Matt," I snap, turning to him. "Can you please knock for once in your life?"

"Love you, too, sis."

That's when I notice his eyes alight with stress. "What's wrong?"

"Lauren and I discussed it, and we want Jessie to ride out the storm here."

"Matt, I was just telling Cole he has to go to the shelter. Now, you want me to send him off but keep Jessie here? I don't need to worry about Jessie and try to keep Daddy from going out in the middle of the storm if the pier starts breaking apart. You know he's going to try. He's done it before."

My memory flashes to Mama bracing against the wind on the front porch, screaming at Daddy to get back inside the house. Mama's shoulder-length hair whipped around in the gray wind. I was seven, maybe eight years old, with Matt on one side and Kate on the other as we pressed our faces to the windows, searching for Daddy. Before going out in the storm, he'd said something about boards and the pier. When he finally emerged from the wind, soaked to the bone with his clothes sticking to him, I cried with relief and decided then and there that my father was a complete and total badass and needed me to watch out for him.

"I'm staying," Matt says, then knocks on the table. "Jules, are you listening to me?"

"Yes. Of course." Matt doesn't need to know that my brain still wanders off at the most inappropriate times.

"Lauren's going to help Kate with all her kids. We don't want Jessie around Shahin after what he said at the garden. There's something wrong with that guy. I'm pretty sure he threatened her yesterday, which is insane."

"I thought the same thing. As soon as he said it."

"It was a threat, wasn't it? Or at least his way of telling us he knows what Jessie did in the garden last year, and he can twist it around if he needs to."

"She stopped Troy from attacking me. That should impress him, but that would require Shahin to be a good person."

"What if he knew Troy? What if some of the Knights have convinced him that she hurt Troy for no reason?"

The fear in Matt's eyes is more than I can take today. The storm, the garden, Cole, Shahin being a gigantic ass, it's all too much. Matt changed in the best of ways when Lauren had Jessie. It was as if instant maturity and selflessness overtook him. Anything and everything his girls want; Matt will work to the bone to provide. Now, he's questioning his ability to keep Jessie safe.

"I get it," I say. "Stay here. With us. We'll have ourselves a little hurricane party." I look away from Matt for a second and catch a searing glare from Cole. "You, too, Cole. Stop looking at me like that and go to the house and help everyone load up." Cole looks at me, relief spread across his face, then nods, and heads out the door.

With Cole out of earshot, I look at Matt. "It's probably a good thing to keep Cole away from Shahin, too. I hadn't thought about that. This parenting shit is way harder than I thought it'd be."

"Definitely not for the weak."

———

Saying goodbye to Mama, Kate, Garrett, Lauren, and the littles left an immediate tightening in my chest and stomach. I know they will be back in a day or two, but the idea of us being separated at all, for any amount of time, feels strange. And I know they are only going twenty or so miles away, but they might as well be going to another planet.

As I watched Kate wave from the driver's seat of Jacob's SUV, I questioned if we were doing the right thing by splitting the family up. Putting their lives in the hands of an Army that I don't trust anymore. Because I don't trust Shahin. And if I can't trust him, I can't trust any of them.

Part of me wishes we all could have gone, but that suggestion got nowhere with Daddy. I get it. Leaving the house vacant for any amount of time puts us all at risk. Looting after a storm is a concern in the best of times, much less when there are so many have-nots in Bellefontaine. Losing fishing equipment or the boat would be a death sentence to us, now that we can't depend on the garden or rations to feed us.

I can't express my doubts to Matt or Daddy because they watched most everyone they love roll down the driveway. My brother and father need to believe they did the right thing and that every Martin in the Temple tonight will be safe from the storm and that we will keep the house safe in their absence. But I worry about the other storms, the black clouds that hang over my head all the time, just out of reach.

Mostly, I worry about the storm that may be waiting for them in The Temple. The danger that lurks in the fragments of the Knights. The danger in CPT Shahin. Because he is dangerous. I feel that now. But I can't show that. Not on my face. So, I swallow every bit of doubt until my stomach aches with it, and I pray my face doesn't give me away.

A part of me wants to sprint down the driveway after my family. Wave my arms and yell until they stop the car. *Turn back!* Come back to where the people are trustworthy and love you. Come back, and we'll take our chances with Isadora. But I don't. Instead, I follow Daddy and Matt around the side of the house, scanning the flower beds for projectiles. I check Mama's greenhouse to make sure Garrett moved all the seedlings and Mama's orchids inside the main house. The greenhouse, with its light wood frame and plastic sheeting for windows, isn't long for this world. We expect it to blow down within the first band of high wind.

We also expect the crab pier to go. Daddy built it as one solid piece that sits atop pylons driven to extend only a foot above our typical highest tide. Perhaps it will make it through the first band, only to choke, drown, then drift off its moorings during the second. We hope it will thrash in the coming rough water until resting on the shore, somewhere along Dead Man's Beach—that vacant, undeveloped strip of shoreline just to the north of the house. If it lands there, we can tow it back like we've done before.

After we double checked everything on the exterior of the property, I take one last walk to the front yard. Standing in the grass, I feel the breeze become wind, changing as if just for me. "She's coming," the wind whispers, and I look out at the gray water before me. From north to south, the water is choppy, churning in preparation for what's to come. Almost in the microsecond of a blink, I see what's coming for us. To the south, blowing straight up the middle of the bay is a dark, threatening wall of water.

15

A black curtain moves across a stage. As the curtain closes, the background scenery disappears. I watch the wall of water—this curtain, this line of demarcation—block the light. Black in its density and mass, the wall inches closer.

Daddy squeezes my shoulder, and I flinch. So mesmerized by the oncoming rain, I didn't hear him approach. "Time to get inside," he says.

"I'll be there in a minute."

Daddy walks away, up the hill and into the house through the front door. When I glance behind me, I see Matt, Cole, and Jessie standing at the windows. They must be watching the sheet of rain, too. I turn back to the water, noticing that the wind is carrying mist now, and it dampens my face, arms, and legs. Alone on the hill, I say a silent prayer.

God, if you're listening, please let this pass quickly. Make Isadora fall apart as she travels onshore. Make her lose her anger. Mercy, God. I beg for mercy.

Prayer is soothing, right? It's supposed to be. That's what I've been told my whole life. Give it to God, the nuns of my elementary education told me. Give your troubles to Mary, Mama's said, at least once a day for her entire life.

Before the others left for the shelter, Kate took me aside. Urgency filled her eyes and voice. "Okay, Jules, remember to pray to Saint Medard. He will hear you."

My puzzled expression told Kate that I couldn't remember something I never knew. After rolling her eyes so far into the back of her head I thought she may spit them out of her mouth, Kate explained. "Saint Medard of Noyon is the patron saint for protection against bad storms. Once, as a child, he was protected from terrible rain by an eagle. The eagle hovered above him with his wings outstretched until the rain subsided, and he was safe."

"Oh. Cool," I told her, nodding at her telling of the legend. "I mean I hope to God the birds are smart enough to get out of town for this, but I'll keep Medard in mind."

"For god's sake, Jules. Learn your saints. They're here to help." With that, she hopped behind the wheel of Jacob's SUV.

This knowledge and prayer are supposed to bring me comfort. Kate told me about St. Medard as if praying to him was the shield we all needed and would use. Without question. And standing on the front slope, watching the monstrous wonder that is a hurricane creep into the bay, I do pray. For a moment, my faith, my hope rises. Then, I twist the doorknob and walk inside.

Jessie has Monopoly, the traditional hurricane-waiting game for the Martin family, set up for us, ready to play on the glass-top table. She smiles at me when I sit in the one empty chair at the table, next to Matt and across from Cole. "Dad said the car is your favorite, so I put that one down for you." Jessie points to the GO square on the board, as she counts out everyone's money—$1500 worth of colorful bills. "I appointed myself to be the banker, as you and Dad have been out of school so long, I doubt you remember simple math." She tosses her hair back in a mad cackle.

"Comin' out hot, I see." I smirk at Jessie. "Remember, little girl, your dad and I have been playing this game for decades. We know all the tricks." I pick up my stack of bills and feel years of stormy days and nights in the paper.

"Cole," Jessie looks across the table at him. "You sure about the rules?"

"I read them over. I should be good." He's arranged his money in neat stacks along his edge of the board.

"Have you never played Monopoly?" I ask. Cole's face shows a slight sting as answer to my question. "Oh, no. I'm sorry. I guess you were a bit young—"

"It's fine, Jules," Cole says, mercifully ending my babbling and attempt at an apology. The look on his face tells me to shut my mouth and play, and that is exactly what I need to do.

If only I could lift the rock in my chest. I was fine outside. But as soon as I walked in, saw the game set up on the table and Daddy pacing in front of the radio, which spits out only static, the dread from the driveway fluttered, then settled with a thud in my chest.

"Has Libby come on at all?" I ask Daddy over my shoulder.

"No," he says, now fiddling with the antennae.

"She may have evacuated, Jules," Matt says, moving the dice around in his hand. "We still haven't figured out exactly where she is broadcasting from."

"True," I say. "If she's on Fowl River, I hope she left. Flooding can get really bad there."

Maybe that's what has my nerves on end. Maybe I'm worried for Libby, and I'm mistaking that concern for worry for my family. Libby, as far as I know, doesn't know me, but I consider her my friend. A very important friend. It's funny how the one-sided relationships we have with media and celebrities become so integral to our lives. And that's what Libby is to me. She is integral, critical.

She's been silent for nearly twenty-four hours now. That's not like my friend to be silent for so long.

That must be what's bothering me. I'm worried for Libby, not a hurricane. Because I know hurricanes, even bad ones. Horrible, destructive storms that ravish everything in their paths. I've lived through all of that. The straight-line winds that seem to never end, leaving everything from cars to cows stranded in trees. I've seen waterspouts spin off the water and onto land. I remember my grandfather's house decades ago, when I was little and none of us knew we only had a few more summers to jump off his pier into the bay below. A hurricane blew through with wind so strong that all it left of his house was the foundation and a toilet. No walls, no roof, nothing but that toilet bolted to a concrete slab. I'm not scared of hurricanes because I know them.

So, this feeling must be over Libby. If she's silent, if she's not there, wherever that *there* may be, she may be in trouble. And whether she's safe or not, we're going to go through this without her. What else would be the source of this dread? After all, the silver lining of a hurricane is that whatever else is plaguing your life presses pause as the hurricane rolls through.

"Aunt Jules," Jessie says, "It's your turn."

I pick up the dice and am about to roll for my first turn when Matt interrupts me. "It's here," he says, and nods toward the windows.

All of us look out and see the wall of rain swallow the pier.

16

Normally, days of build-up precede hurricanes. Local and national media share the exact wind speed, how fast or slow the storm will move, and projections for the time of landfall and the height of the storm surge. Interstates jam with evacuees while grocery store shelves are picked clean by those who chose to stay. That's what I'm used to.

As a kid, once the official hunker-down time hit, I'd watch Mama and Daddy pace in front of the windows, staring at the water and the clouds. They'd pour themselves a drink while I waited until Mama finally let us break into the storm snacks. Then more hours of waiting came before the deluge of rain and wind— the sound that always scared me. But, for the most part, the storms came and went as expected. We knew what to expect because of the meteorologists. Their adrenaline energized every update as the public's fascination with natural disasters encouraged around the clock coverage.

But we have no media. No meteorologists. No *'round the clock coverage*.

About an hour ago, it occurred to me that Bellefontaine doesn't have tornado sirens. Through all the years I've lived here, I have never heard an emergency siren. Sure, we've got brass bells on the ends of the piers to ring and ring and ring when a jubilee happens, but nothing to warn people when their house may pull a Dorothy Gale. Under normal circumstances, an ear-piercing cell phone alarm would signal a tornado warning or flash flood in times of severe weather. "A siren in your pocket," I recall one meteorologist saying years ago regarding sirens versus cell phones for weather alerts. I'd really love a siren blaring from a telephone pole right now. Or, not blaring. Because if I knew to listen out for a siren, I would find comfort in the absence of the sound. But we don't have sirens on poles, and we don't have working cell phones, so we don't have sirens in our pockets.

We should have Libby, but she hasn't broadcast from her secret location all day and all night. Nothing but static from the radio for hours. So, we stopped cranking the handle and left the radio dormant.

At least an hour ago, when the wind grew so strong and the house seemed to take in big gulps of air, then blow out a breath that pressed against my inner ears, I feared a tornado was about to rip the roof off the house. I made Cole and Jessie move away from the windows. The wind got louder. We probably insulted Isadora for not being shit-your-pants scared, so she had to show out more. That's when all of us, even Daddy and Matt, decided the guest bathroom, the only room in this house without a window, was our safe space, our panic room for the duration of the storm. By that time, the front wall of windows that frames our view of the Bay became a glimpse into Hell, if only it were light enough outside to see the demons.

But we can hear them.

Right now, in the bathroom, I hear the windows shake. The rain pounds on the glass. The wind howls as it whips, unimpeded, across the bay and around and against the house. No thicket or forest to break its terror. No barrier at all. Just the house, the water, the wind, and our palpable, collective fear.

When we first huddled in here, I ordered Jessie and Cole into the bathtub, plopping pillows and blankets in their laps. "Wrap these around you," I told them, and was met with distressed looks. "If debris starts flying around us, a blanket is better than no protection at all. Be ready to cover your heads with those pillows." They both fell asleep in the long, dark night; preteens can block out anything, if annoyed enough. We adults stayed awake, chatting in distracted whispers while we listened to the wind. Because how can I be expected to sleep when Isadora is trying to get inside this house like a band of witches high on meth?

———

We all fell silent for a long while. We listened to the storm, each of us, I assume, inside their own game of "what if?" Now my body vibrates as the wind shakes the walls and floor.

"How about a Rosary?" I ask and cannot believe I'm the one to suggest it. I guess there really aren't any atheists in foxholes. Not that I'm an atheist or in a foxhole, but I will broker a truce with the Holy Trinity and all the angels and saints because this—Isadora and the wind and the constant rain that sounds like gunfire—is not okay.

Daddy begins *The Apostle's Creed* and I force my mind to focus on the words.

Block everything else out. All that exists are the words.

We say the Rosary twice, for good measure and because I swear the wind got louder during the first round. As we muttered the final prayer, a noise comes from the front of the house that sounds like Mardi Gras beads whipping against the windows.

Matt stands and moves to one of the jack-and-jill doors.

"What are you doing?" I ask him.

"Going to check on the windows."

"You're an idiot."

"If the glass is cracking, wouldn't you like to know?" he says, and opens the door.

I tuck my head between my bent knees and wait through a long, breathless minute for the storm to carry Matt away.

"I can't tell if the water has reached the house or if the wind is spraying the water on the windows," Matt says, returning to the bathroom and his place between the toilet and the tub. "It's too dark to tell, but that sound is water hitting the windows."

"Sideways rain?" I ask him, full of naïve hope and foolish optimism.

"No. I mean, yes, it's still raining, but I could see well enough to know that it's water, bay water, not rain. It's like a giant is throwing buckets of bay water at the windows. It's splashing up on the windows."

Deep breath in. Deep breath out. Repeat. Panic crying right now does no one any good even if the windows are going to bust, rushing high tide into the house, and drowning us all.

"Should we move to the second story of the garage? If the windows burst—"

"Julianne," Daddy says, reaching across the darkness to grab my hand. "Those windows are rated for 150-mile-per-hour winds. The wind's not that strong. They will hold."

"But the door," I squeak out.

"The door will hold."

"Okay, Daddy," I say. More than anything I want to curl up in his lap and cling to him as I did through many thunderstorms as a child when the wind's whistle hurt my ears, the lightning was too close, and the thunder shook the house. Instead, I squeeze his hand. "You can stop reading my mind now."

"Uncle," he says.

"Huh?" I ask, letting go of his hand.

"When did you get such a grip?" Daddy asks me.

"Oh," I say and force a slight laugh, grateful for the darkness that hides the tears running down my cheeks.

———

I must have dozed off for a while because I wake with a jolt. An eeriness surrounds me, like I've missed something important. Then, I know what's different. The world is silent. No wind thrashing trees around us. No rain hitting the windows or hammering the roof. Just quiet.

I look at Matt and Daddy and gesture toward the door. Grabbing towel rods and countertops, whatever provides the right amount of leverage to pull our bent legs and backs straight again, we stand. Being upright feels strange and unsteady. Daddy opens one of the doors and steps out of the bathroom. Following him into the front room, I gaze out the windows and see light creeping above the horizon. A gray glow of sky above a charcoal bay.

In the living room, I see that the windows held, just like Daddy said they would. Almost morning, the water still kicks with white-topped waves rare to Mobile Bay. But the air feels calm. The house feels solid. *Safe. We're safe.* I let go of the breath I'd been holding for hours and with it comes nervous laughter and fresh tears.

Matt wraps one of his thick arms around me, squeezing the life out of my shoulders. "Scared shitless, huh?"

"Yep," I say and swipe at my wet cheeks.

"Should we wake the dynamic duo in there?" he asks.

"No. Let them sleep." I walk to the windows and look outside. Opening the front door, a warm breeze hits my face. On the front porch I look left up shore, and smile when I see that my corner of the world looks damaged, but repairable. Straight ahead, the last five feet of our yard is submerged. Further, the raised walkway sits just above the surface.

Looking right, I see something I've never seen before. "What is that?" I ask Matt and Daddy, now on the porch as well. I point south at a wall of black clouds extending from the water up and up, hundreds of feet into a blue sky.

"That's an eye wall," Daddy says. "We took a direct hit."

"Jesus Christ," I say, and Daddy doesn't chastise me or correct me. He gets it. If there were ever a time to invoke a higher power, it's now when we are inside a dome, hedged in by the full strength and fervor of nature. The bleak reality of our situation is clear. We must face it all again. The eye of a hurricane is intermission. Act II will devastate. "I've never stood in the center of the eye before." I can't think of anything else to say. Staring at that wall of clouds churning and pushing toward us, robs me of better words.

"Shit!" Matt says, leaping off the porch. "The pier!"

Daddy and I both look at the pier and see a section of our neighbor's walkway—an eight-foot length of planks held together by screws and two-by-fours—slamming into our pier. One of our pylons already leans as the battering waves push the wayward section into our walkway. Waves splash against our walkway, and as the light increases, we see our walkway bowing.

"It's gonna come apart if we don't free that section," Daddy says, rushing down the front slope to the pier.

"Daddy, stop!" I say, but my objections are useless. He and Matt wade through the flood waters then run along the walkway, down the pier.

By the time I shuffle down the wet, grassy slope, nearly slipping several times, I stand at the water's edge. Daddy and Matt are at the midway point of our walkway, with Matt on his belly trying to turn the floating section so that the four-foot end will go between our pylons instead of hammering into them like an eight-foot-wide battering ram.

"Go get something to turn this," Daddy yells at me.

I push back up the slope, kicking off my flops for more secure footing. In the kitchen, I run—almost literally—into Cole.

"What's happening?" Cole asks, concern in his eyes at seeing the panic in mine.

"The neighbor's pier lost a section and now that section is pounding into our pylons and is going to bring down the whole pier if Matt can't get it turned." Cole sprints toward the door, but I catch the tail of his T-Shirt. "Where are you going?"

"To help!"

"The hell you are." I pull him back from the door. "If you want to help, go to the garage and grab the flounder gigs."

I watch Cole rush out the back door, then look back at Daddy and Matt. Now, both of them are on their bellies, trying to get the damn thing to turn. Waves crash against the pier, spray soaking both of them. "Turn dammit!" I yell, as if the blasted section can hear me and will obey. After a quick scan of the kitchen, I glimpse the broom hanging on its hook on the pantry door. I grab it and a long handle net and run.

The pier is wet, and I slide several inches forward when my feet hit the first wet board. Rushing to Daddy, I hand him the broom and Matt the net. Laying on my belly, I ask, "What do I do?"

Daddy pants out the answer. "Grab the end and try to pull it toward you while Matt and I push the other end out."

When I plunge my hands into the water, I'm surprised that it's cool, as if Isadora pulled the cooler, deep water to the surface and pushed it to the shore. For a second, I wonder what else the storm has wrenched from the deep and made swim into our waters, but I banish the thought as my fingers find purchase on the first board of the section. With everything I have, I pull the floating dock to me, grunting against the strength of the current.

Turning the section proves difficult with the waves still churning, even in the calm of the eye. Still tugging, my fingers slip free of the boards, and I feel a splinter dig into my skin. Ignoring the pain, I grab for the board again and miss when a wave knocks the section skyward, nearly smacking me in the face with soaked wood. I scoot on my belly to extend my reach and hook my toes against the opposite edge of our walkway. Reaching as far as I can, I grab the section, slipping my fingers between two boards, and yank it toward me. For a second, I think the force of my tugging is going to pull me into the water, but luckily, thankfully, I come down hard on our pier, still holding on, still on top of the pier, not under it.

As I hold the section of pier against the current, I hear the sounds of Matt's and Daddy's efforts, both using the long handles to push the length of the section away from our pylons. Finally, with one final shove, resulting in Daddy dropping the broom into the water, the section turns and speeds through the pylons below us. The sliver of space between the walkway boards gives me a glimpse of our victory and utter relief. Until I look south. The eye wall is so much closer.

"We need to get inside," I say, pointing at the approaching wall of clouds. Hurricane Isadora, round two, will be on us in minutes.

Rushing back into the house, I look around the open kitchen and living room combo. No Cole. I head to the guest bathroom and find only a groggy Jessie.

"Have you seen Cole?" I ask her.

"No," she says and stretches out her legs to the length of the bathtub.

"The wind's gonna pick up again soon, so get what you need,

then get back in here. You've only got a few minutes. Do not go outside." With that, I leave Jessie in the bathroom.

"Cole!" I call for him as I cut through the guest bedroom back to the living room. "Have y'all seen Cole?" Daddy and Matt both shake their heads.

Daddy moves toward the bathroom. "Is he not in the bathroom?"

"No. I sent him to get my gig, but that was a while ago, before I got back out to the pier." I rush out the back door to the garage. Swinging the door wide, I call into the dim space, "Cole!" Irritation fills my body.

No response.

"Cole!" I call up the stairs to Matt and Lauren's apartment. "Cole!"

No response.

When I find this boy, I'm going to let him know that disappearing in the middle of a damn hurricane is far from funny.

I turn back to my workspace. Nothing. He's simply nowhere. I step closer to the worktable, peering behind it, one last desperate look. Then, I see it. There's something here that shouldn't be here. It's out of place because it's not mine. At the worktable, I lean over a piece of fabric, nothing more than a remnant, spread out on the table. I run my fingertips along the weave and read the words written in red.

The righteous will rejoice when he sees the vengeance;
He will wash his feet in the blood of the wicked.
BDEL

17

"Cole!" A gust catches the door to the main house when I rip it open. "Cole!" Fighting against the wind, I struggle to pull the door closed behind me.

"He's not in here," Matt says, meeting me in the hallway.

Terror grips my throat, and I force the fabric into Matt's hand. "What's this?" Matt unfurls the fabric, then reads it. "Fuck."

I push past Matt and yank open the hall closet. Four rifles stare back at me as another whip of wind shakes the house. I snatch one rifle from the rack. "Are these loaded?"

From the kitchen, Jessie and Daddy hear me. They appear in the hallway, both wearing their concern and surprise.

"Cole is missing," I tell them. "They've taken him."

"Who?" Daddy asks.

"The Way. Those red-faced—" I fumble for a word other than fuckers. "People. Those people took my boy."

My hands tremble as I check the safety of the rifle, then pull the lever back and check the chamber. Empty.

"Julianne," Daddy says, his voice steady, annoyingly steady. "Put that back on the rack."

"No. I can't go unarmed. I'm not stupid."

"You can't go after Cole. Not right now."

"I have to!" I step into the closet again, scanning the slim shelves that line each side. "Which ammo goes with this one?" The chamber's empty and a gun without ammo is as useless as a hook without bait. That shiny silver tip may look serious, but all it will do is prick a finger. I need to do a hell of a lot more than prick those asshole's fingers. Matt places a hand on my shoulder, making me flinch. He takes the rifle from me.

"Give that back," I demand. "I'm going."

"Jules, you can't go out in this. It's suicide. And you don't even know where they've taken him."

I grab Matt by his shoulders. "I know where they are. I do. Clem told us at the meeting. They have some kind of encampment up shore." I turn to Daddy. "Remember? Clem said that. He wanted Shahin to have them removed. So, that's where they are. It's two, three miles max."

"Julianne, no one is riding out this storm in a bunch of tents."

"It's a place to start!" I push away from all of them and walk to the windows, staring down the storm that stands between me and my kid. "Why don't any of you realize that we have to get him back now? Not later. Now!"

The Bay is black with rage again, churning and pommeling, threatening to wash out the land. With every wave crashing over the rocks, my heart pounds faster. It thunders in my ears. All the panic I've forced down, swallowing every bitter bite, threatens to explode out of me. They will never allow me to leave if I'm acting as crazed as I feel, so I force my breathing to level out.

Daddy stands beside me. "Julianne, why do you think The Way took Cole?"

"Is Cole here?" I snap. "No, he's not. Matt," I look across the room at my brother. "Show Daddy what I found." Matt hands the fabric to Daddy. "See? I went to the garage to get Cole. He wasn't there. He's nowhere. But that was on the worktable. They left that for me to find." My lips tremble with the words, threatening to release the sob pushing against my chest and throat.

Jessie walks closer and reads the message in red. "What does that mean?" Her voice sounds small and scared.

"It's a threat disguised as a Bible verse. Killing Cole will be their vengeance." I force down a cry again. There will be a time for tears. A time to curl up in a ball and curse the world for being such a hateful place, but that time is not now. If I break, Matt and Daddy will see me as too weak to rescue Cole. What they don't understand is that I have never felt stronger than at this moment. I could tear down a mountain rock by rock if I had to, if those rocks lead me to Cole. "They have my boy. *My boy.* I will get him back. I will—"

A horrendous cracking sound fills the house. But it's not inside the house. *Outside.* A splintering, shredding sound that grows louder every second. The sound of smashing glass and wood fracturing fills my ears. Time seems to stop as the destruction builds to a crescendo, then stops with a thud so violent it shakes the floor under our feet.

We all turn toward the noise, or rather where it came from. Matt rushes to the dining room off the kitchen, but my feet are glued to my spot. Frozen in time and space until the air around me changes. The storm is now inside the house.

"To the bathroom. Now!" I shove Daddy and Jessie toward the guest bathroom. As we rush past the doorway to the dining room, I see a long, thick branch of an oak tree draped across what used to be Mama's formal dining table. The table is cracked in half, like Aslan's stone table after he defied the White Witch of Narnia. I grab Matt's arm and drag him to the bathroom with us, wondering what sacrifice Cole will be forced to endure.

From the bathroom, I hear the rain. The door rattles on its hinges as the wind blows through the gaping hole of the dining room and into the guest bedroom.

Regroup, I tell myself. It's just a bad squall. Just a really awful band. Let the band pass us by, then go. I'll go. I will not let Cole suffer for long. I will find him and make those red-faced mother-fuckers pay for taking him. For threatening his life. God help them if they hurt him.

Crouched in my corner, I feel their eyes on me. Jessie, Daddy, and Matt—I know they are all watching me. "I'll stay put. For now." My words are clipped and my tone harsh, but I can't find any kindness or compassion right now. All I know is anger. How can they do this to a child? Why did they drag him into this?

The wind howls again, as if reminding me of why I'm in this stupid bathroom and not out searching for Cole. "I should have grabbed the gig myself."

"What?" Matt asks.

"To help you with the pier. I told Cole to get the gigs from the garage. That was the only reason he was out there. He was taken because I didn't get the gigs myself." A sob escapes my throat, my defenses too weak to swallow it down again.

Matt squeezes my hand. "You did nothing wrong. All you've done is love that boy."

Matt's kind words do nothing to quell my guilt or fear. They do nothing to stop my tears from flooding my eyes. They prob-ably make me cry even harder.

"Maybe another Rosary," Matt suggests.

"Go for it." I force the words around my sobs, but don't join in the spoken prayers. I can't. I listen to them recite words upon words, rolling off their tongues by muscle memory alone. Instead, I pray in silence, and my prayers are my own.

God, you've given us enough. You took Jacob. You took Billy. Maybe it was their time. Maybe your grand plan will one day make sense. But you will not take Cole. This is not his time. He is still a child. He hasn't had enough time to do everything that precious boy will do, is capable of doing. So, you will not take him. Got it? You. Will. Not. Take. Him.

———

I wake with a jolt. I fell asleep. How could I have fallen asleep? What mother would sleep while her child was missing? But, of course, I'm not a real mother. I'm just some woman who's supposed to care for a child but is careless and has probably gotten him killed. My foolish love for him will be his end.

I glance around the bathroom but see little other than the shapes of three people. The only light is the glowing sliver seeping beneath the door. Light from the guest bedroom and kitchen and beyond, signaling the day beneath the door. I sit still and listen to their breathing. Jessie's soft purr, Matt's heavy mouth-breathing, and Daddy's snore, which sounds like a definite case of sleep apnea. *How did I sleep through that?*

Guilt twists my stomach as the word *sleep* runs through my mind. Selfish, selfish woman. Cole is out there terrified with those maniacs, and I slept. Slept! How long was I asleep? How long has Cole been gone?

Wanting to run from the guilt, I stand and creep to the door. Twisting the handle a millimeter at a time, I pull when I feel the latch loosen. Opening the door just enough to slip through and out of the bathroom, I close the door behind me.

The living room is chaos, filthy with debris.. The dining room is in shambles. The gaping hole in the dining room wall allowed the storm to roam freely inside. From the dining room, through the kitchen, to the living room, everything is wet. Debris—leaves, grass, twigs, even small branches from a Japanese magnolia— litter the space. I run my hand across the granite countertop and feel dirt and sand.

But the storm—wretched Isadora—has lost her bluster.

Looking out the front windows, which are all intact, all I see is rain. The last band in Isadora's terrible onslaught doesn't pack a punch, more like a limp slap from a wet glove. It's nearly over now. The wind is light. The water is still high and cloudy with dirt, but Isadora's out of steam. No more white-capped waves. No more threats to the pier or the land. Just rain.

No more cause for me to stay.

Returning to the hall closet, I grab the lever-action rifle. I prefer this one because I know how to load it and the kickback isn't bad on my shoulder, which will keep my aim true. Do I like guns? No. Do I know how to use one? Yes. Jacob taught me. I check the safety. It's on. Looking into the chamber, I can see a few rounds. I grab a box of ammo, hoping the caliber and size is what I need. From the weight of the box—much lighter than I'd prefer—I know we're running low on ammo. I can't afford to waste a single bullet. From the backside of the door, I snatch a rifle strap off the hook. Then, I rush out of the house.

In the garage, I grab my backpack. The memory of escaping Savannah just days after Jacob's death threatens to fill my body with panic. I banish the memory, shoving it into the box in my mind filled with all the horrors of the last two years. I snatch the first aid kit from the shelf along with a baseball cap and shove both in my bag with the ammo. Just as I pull the rifle strap over my head and lace my arms through my backpack straps, I hear the garage doorknob turn.

Spinning around, I freeze when a flash of red hair appears in the widening doorway. Jessie.

"Jesus Christ, Jessie. You scared me."

"Are you going after him?"

"Yes, and before you try to stop me, know that—" I stop speaking when Jessie raises her hands and jingles two sets of keys.

"Do you want the Gator or the truck? I would take the truck as it's faster and will keep you dry."

Tears threaten to spill from my eyes.

"No need for tears. They're just keys."

I walk to her and take the truck keys from her, sliding them into my pocket.

Jessie pulls me into a hug, wrapping her arms tight around me. "If it were me, I'd go."

"I'll be careful, sweet girl. I promise."

She breaks the hug and steps back. "I guess I can't talk you into letting me go with you?"

"Not a chance."

"Fine. Then you better get a move on. I don't know how long Grandpa and Dad will be asleep. You'll want to get a good head start on them."

Jessie walks out of the garage, then jogs down the driveway, dodging fallen branches and puddles as she does. As I climb in the truck, she looks back, about halfway to the gate. I curse the loud engine when I turn the key, then roll along the driveway, crunching over branches and checking the rearview mirror for Matt and Daddy. When I pull through the open gate, I pause and look back.

That girl, my niece, may be the bravest among us. She's definitely the best of us all. I blow her a kiss and pull away.

18

My mind won't focus on specific prayers, so I keep repeating two words—be alive.

Be alive. Be alive. Be alive.

I press my foot down on the accelerator, mashing it into the floor.

Be alive.

Roll down the window to clear away the fog on the windshield that blurs my vision.

Be alive.

Skirt around the pools of water that cover large swathes of my lane.

Be alive.

Curse the tears that roll down my cheeks and prove that I'm ill-equipped to keep Cole safe.

God dammit, be alive.

I cringe at the water-logged plot of land that used to be our garden—wrecked first by The Way, then drowned by Isadora.

Were their faces painted red while they took Cole?

I can't believe I was so stupid, so careless to let Cole out of my sight for even a second. I should have known that we were never safe. Will never be safe. Not here. Not even in the middle of a hurricane. Which sounds ridiculous, but I can handle hurricanes. I know how to stay safe during a hurricane. It's these people that I can't predict. The Way doesn't operate like normal people. Religious zealots never do. I should have expected them to operate on the outskirts of what any sane person would deem reckless. Of course, the freaks risk their own safety to fulfill a mission for their higher power.

And I do mean *their* higher power. My higher power, the one I'm currently angry with, would never tell me to abduct a child.

Cole is with them. At least, I hope he's still with them. That's a weird thing to hope for, but the alternative is too awful to imagine. I hope The Way only abducted him and don't plan to do to him what the Knights did to Billy.

I slam on the brakes, fling the truck door open, and wretch onto the road. My vomit splashes up on the footboard of the truck, but at least there's nothing left in my stomach now to come up when I find them. Because I will find them.

Vomiting doesn't, however, rid my mind of Billy Roberts' body hanging on the end of our pier. What if that is the plan? What if The Way intends on beating Cole to death like the Knights did Billy? What if they've already fastened the noose around his neck and are just waiting for the perfect time to string him up on the end of our pier? Maybe they're waiting to know that the pier survived the storm.

It did, but will Cole?

Be alive. Be alive. "Be alive," I scream to the windshield as I turn onto Dauphin Island Parkway and immediately slam on the brakes again. The tires screech while I hope against hope that the brakes don't lock up. The bed of the truck lifts as the truck stops inches from a pecan tree laying across the road. Isadora ripped it out of the ground, roots intact, and repurposed it into a barricade. *What a bitch.*

Behind the wheel, I sit for several moments, shaking and trying to breathe. *Be alive* changes to *just breathe*. Because I am no good to Cole if I slam into a tree.

"Calm the fuck down, Jules." Jacob's voice sounds in my ears, so loudly I look at the passenger seat to see if he's here with me.

"Don't tell me to calm down," I tell him, and I feel a smile tease my face. "You know I hate that." I listen for him to answer but receive silence in response. That breaks my heart—less so now than a year ago—but it also brings me back to center. Grief over Jacob is familiar. Freaking out over the idea that I have caused Cole's death isn't. "Thank you," I say to him, without knowing if he can hear me or not.

"So, what would Jacob do?" I ask out loud to no one. "He'd probably tell me to stop talking to myself." I grimace at my own dumb joke, then put the truck in reverse.

Getting around this tree is not optional, so I back up several feet, then push the stiff gear shift back into drive. The tree is mature, so its trunk stretches across most of the pavement. I bite my lip as I place my foot on the accelerator and give it a gentle tap. Turning the wheel hard, I roll around the thick trunk, then gas it over some of the smaller, thinner branches. With two wheels on the pavement and two on the slope of the ditch, I give it a bit more gas to get around the tree and safely back on the road.

"Thank you again," I tell Jacob, knowing now that he is with me. I won't slide into a ditch if he directs me where to drive.

A bit more clear-headed, I take in the destruction around and in front of me. What looks like a hundred-yard-wide path has been cut through the woods and road-side homes of DIP. Tornado. Only a tornado could have leveled so many trees and homes in such a distinct line. Slowing to almost a crawl as the path opens on either side of the road, I see the scar Isadora left behind her. Hurricanes harm everything and everyone in their way, but this is different. This is flat. Demolished. Crude piles of nothingness to the left as far as I can see, and a clear view of the Bay to the right. A clear view that shouldn't be there.

An unwelcome sob catches in my throat. *What if Cole was in this?* Just as panic threatens to infest every cell of my body, I see a couple emerging from the remains of a building. The man tosses away what looks to be a sheet of plywood as he and a woman crawl out of the rubble. I stop the truck and lock eyes with her. Her face is red from crying, not paint. She looks around, presumably viewing the destruction for the first time, and falls into her partner's chest.

They survived. A tornado thrashed their home, but they survived. Maybe Cole did too.

No. No *maybe*. No *wishing*. He survived. Dammit, Cole is alive, and I will find him.

Beyond the scar, broken branches, debris from weak sheds, and remnants of plastic toys and backyard gardens litter both sides of the road. I catch a green flash of plastic—a children's slide, maybe—caught in a thicket of broken, twisted branches. Soon enough, every yard along DIP will have two piles in it. One will be the burn pile of small debris and animal carcasses. The other, residents will place on the side of the road, waiting for county debris removal. But that won't happen this time—debris removal by some government service. There are no county services that I know of, just National Guard troops and martial law. Will they remove damage? Will the released Knight criminals don orange vests and load piles of tree limbs and soiled sheetrock into military dump trucks? More than likely, the piles will remain long enough for nature to claim and cover them. The remnants of so many homes buried under honeysuckle vines and relentless kudzu.

The sun breaks free of the last of Isadora's clouds, and my mind drifts to what I should be doing today—putting on my rattiest clothes and closed-toes shoes with thick soles, ones that rusted nails can't punch through. I should be tying a bandana around my face, covering my nose and easing the nauseating effect of the dead birds, rats, and fish that will dot every yard up and down the shoreline. Instead, I'm searching for my kid because a bunch of radicalized, so-called Christians abducted a child in the middle of a hurricane. Rage burns hot on my cheeks as I picture them lying in wait for Cole.

But the rage turns into shock when I reach Holy T. The rectory is nothing more than a black stain in green grass. Isadora blew away all that was left after the fire.

I turn into the Community Center parking lot. The lot is full of cars and trucks—the vehicles left behind by evacuees. That's not surprising. In fact, the cars and trucks were why I chose this location as a parking spot. No one will notice Daddy's truck as out of place if I leave it here. I figure from here I have a few hundred yards to hike to the encampment, but I didn't expect the lot to be covered in shingles from the church and huge, twisted pieces of aluminum that until yesterday, formed the Community Center roof.

"Oh, thank goodness," I say, when I spot Jacob's SUV, appearing unharmed between two cars, both buried under aluminum sheets. I have a feeling Cole and I will need Jacob's old Xterra soon. After everything Cole has been through in Bellefontaine, I can't imagine he wants to spend his whole life here. Jacob's truck may well be our way to a new life.

I back out of the lot, fearing roofing nails will puncture my tires. If we have to make a fast getaway, which I expect we will, I can't risk a flat tire slowing us down. Instead, I drive just past the church to an old dirt road that used to lead to teenaged bonfires and hookup spots. As I turn down the rugged road, I dismiss the memory of first laying eyes on Troy Cowart at a high school bonfire here. I don't need that memory, only the memory of where an abandoned fishing camp lies.

Several yards down the road, I stop. The swamp that runs through most of Bellefontaine from north to south is high from the storm. What should be a land bridge to the fishing camp is now submerged, and I can't tell by how many feet of water. As I look closely at the swell, I see ripples of a current. Too deep to cross without risk of getting stuck in flood waters. Luckily, trees hide the truck from the dirt road, with nature narrowing the path and blocking my view of DIP behind me. If I can't see the road, the road can't see the truck. The same goes for anyone traveling along the parkway. I execute an ass-backwards three-point-turn that almost ends with my tires in the encroaching swamp. I want the truck pointed toward our escape route.

If I remember correctly, this road leads to a big clearing, about fifty yards in diameter and about fifty feet from the shore. The shell of a cottage stands in the middle of the clearing. As a teenager, I heard that the landowner cleared the pine trees and shrubs that grow wild around here, intending to build a fishing camp, but went bankrupt shortly after laying a foundation and building the basic structure. The remains of an abandoned dream were left to Mother Nature and local teens—a roof, four walls, one door, and two windows that faced trees and glimpses of water. The owner didn't even have money to lay a proper floor, leaving it wall-to-wall concrete.

The bankruptcy was theorized to be everything from embezzlement by the ex-wife, robbing the man of his riches, to the wife cheating, to betting it all on the Iron Bowl one year. Somehow word got out and local teens found it—the perfect location for underage drinking and speakers blasting music, as not a soul lived within earshot or view of the spot. What would have been an idyllic leisure spot for any fishing enthusiast became the perfect hideaway for teens.

Now, it's Cole's prison.

I never fully believed the story of the bankrupt owner because why would someone clear land for a fishing camp but leave the view of the Bay obstructed by trees? If it was embezzlement, couldn't he get his money back through restitution? I'm not a lawyer, so I have no idea. And no one could confirm which Iron Bowl or whether the owner was an Alabama or Auburn fan.

None of that matters now because Cole is there. He's the only reason this clearing and cabin are of any importance to me now. But Clem said the Roberts purchased it "a while back." I think that's what he said. Maybe they made something out of the lot.

Maybe I'm not looking for a clearing at all. As a teenager, it was a clearing and a shell of a cabin. The Roberts could have built a new house with outbuildings, a deck, and an Olympic-sized pool for all I know.

But Clem said it was a clearing. He would know, right? I shake my head to clear all these jumbled what-ifs. It doesn't work, but I grab my pack and rifle and hop out of the truck anyway and stand there debating whether to lock the doors of the truck or not. I decide not and shove the keys into the deepest pocket of my cargo shorts. Better to have every advantage during our escape rather than to fumble with a locked door. And Cole may be hurt. We'll need every second to pull this off.

I step off the road and into the woods and immediately wish I had bug spray. Isadora did nothing to wash the mosquitoes away. One little demon lands on my arm. When I slap it dead with my hand, the nasty fucker leaves a big blood splotch on my skin. It was full, which means it must have fed on someone else recently.

I'm not alone in these woods.

I follow alongside the road through the woods, keeping shrubs and trees between the road and me. I can't risk being seen before I find the camp. Every few steps, I stop to listen for voices. At first, I hear nothing but the cracking of twigs and rustling of leaves—

the forest settling after being assaulted. But, after several yards, waves washing onshore sound in my ears, albeit faintly. This stretch of shoreline still has a little beach left, thanks to its lack of development. I wonder how much Isadora left.

I keep marching through the woods, trying to step lightly, trying to keep the spindly pine branches from slapping me in the face or snagging my clothes. A long, thorny vine snags my tank top, and I nearly cry out when an inch-long thorn slices across the top of my hand. I bite my lip to silence my urge to scream, then blow on the scrape to ease the sting. Moving forward, I see nothing but the road to my left and trees, kudzu, vines, and shrubs to my right.

Ahead, the road curves left, but I remember that it curves back right a ways down, so I take the chance and cut across the forest in what I hope is a straight line.

"You've never been good at land navigation," Jacob whispers to me. He's back, at least his voice in my head is back. "Did you suddenly develop a sense of direction?"

"Then help me. Criticism alone is not helpful." I feel like we've had this quibble a hundred times. Probably because we did. On every road trip, change of duty station move, or simple hike in the woods, I would make a wrong turn, landing us in the middle of nowhere, at least nowhere close to where we needed to be. Just as I'm about to turn back and go back to the road, the trees open up. But not to the clearing. They open up to a gradual slope of grass leading to water and the slimmest beach in the world.

The water must be receding.

Fuck. I can't be that far off. They've got to be out here. I stop and steady my breathing, winded from adrenaline and the hike. Listening beyond the waves, I hear… nothing. No voices. No footsteps or milling about. Nothing but damn nature. I feel panic rising as I turn in a circle, trying to see anything that would point me to the camp, to Cole. I remember the trunk of a water oak used to lie across the sand, extending back into the forest, but I don't see it now.

That means nothing. It's been years, and an old rotting tree could have been removed or covered with sand or, plain and simple, eroded away. It doesn't mean I'm in the wrong spot. When I turn again, wanting more than anything to scream Cole's name, I spot something—a torn piece of fabric stuck to the trunk of a pine tree.

Without thinking or considering how many eyes may be on me right now, I sprint to the tree. That's when I notice a smaller scrap of fabric on another trunk about eight feet away. When I lift the bigger piece to examine it, I see a faded B and the rudimentary paint strokes that left the letter. *BDEL.*

My mind flashes to kayaking with Daddy, seeing two men hammering a banner into these trees, and the concern that washed over Daddy's face. If only we'd acted then. We should have forced Shahin to banish them from Bellefontaine. But if onlys are worthless. Right now, all that matters is that this is the right spot. It must be. What matters is that Cole is near.

Turning, I see a narrow path cut into the vegetation and leading away from the beach. It's nearly hidden with storm debris, but it's definitely a path and absolutely manmade.

My adrenaline surges and I dash for the path, sprinting past branches that lash my bare arms. My brain is yelling, "Quiet! Quiet!" but I ignore it because I can't give these assholes time to get away. I can't give them time to run. If this is a foot race, I will be faster.

My rifle hits me in the ribs as I hurdle a fallen tree, but I ignore that pain as well. Nothing on or in my body matters until Cole is home safely. Not even the ankle I just twisted in a divot. *Fuck! That hurt.* I jog-limp further along the path, until finally, it opens up to the clearing where nothing remains but a collapsed cabin.

No tents. No campfire or benches. No red-faced freaks deserving of every bullet in my rifle. Nothing.

"Cole," I scream out, unconcerned now if anyone hears me. My heart twists as I run to the pile of rubble. The walls are gone, ripped from the foundation. Looking left and right, I see what must be framing boards scattered about the clearing. Large shards of glass litter the ground—windows. Pieces of the roof tangle in the tree branches above.

I tear into the scant rubble left on the foundation. A nail rips into my hand when I yank part of a window frame from the pile.

"Cole, Cole," I yell. "Are you in here? Can you hear me?"

Be alive. Be alive. My mantra from earlier returns as I wipe my bloody hand against my shorts and lift my shirt to swipe away tears and sweat from my face. How could anyone survive this? What if he were swept away with the cottage? *No, no, no.* If he's under the rubble, I will find him, and he will be alive. That's all I ask—for him to be breathing. I can fix anything as long as there is air in his lungs.

Because if not, I will never forgive myself. I told him I'd keep him safe. Me. I did that. I alone dragged him into my world. Then I sent him to the garage without me.

No Cole. He isn't here. There's no sign of him in the rubble or the surrounding area. Other than the remnants of the banner, there's no evidence anyone was ever here.

I sit exhausted in the dirt, every muscle spent. Frustration overtakes my weakened body and drains my last bit of strength. I lay back, head in the dirt, and let the tears stream down both sides of my face, dripping into my ears and hair. I let go, but the letting go of my emotions isn't a surrender. It will be just a reprieve. "Where are you, my sweet, clever boy?"

After I cry every tear in me, I stand. If nothing else good comes from today, at least Cole was not in that cabin when it collapsed. I will say that until I convince myself that it's true.

I stride across the clearing—now more of a debris field—my head on a swivel, as if I may find him hiding in the surrounding shrubs and trees. But there's nothing. If The Way left anything when they packed camp, it was blown away by the hurricane. By the bend of the tree trunks—every tree bows northward—I assume that any evidence of the freaks' former settlement is a mile up shore. At least.

I clinch my jaw as my next terrifying thought takes hold. *I don't know where he is.* I know nothing, no clue or hint of where Cole is being held. I was so sure that he would be here that I didn't allow my brain to imagine any other possibility.

My plan was reckless, sure, but it was simple. And simple is good, right? Find the clearing, sneak into camp while everyone else was sleeping or distracted, find and free Cole, shoot anyone who gets in our way, and with Cole, run like hell to the truck. Yes, there are several points of failure with my plan—storm debris making the clearing impossible to find, The Way being awake and alert when I found them, finding Cole chained to a tree with no way to free him—but I never considered that the camp would be abandoned. That Cole wouldn't be here.

My hand throbs. Remembering the first aid kit, I grab my pack. Opening it, I realize the one critical item I didn't bring— water. Thirst is an overpowering bitch, and my throat is dry as sheetrock dust from all the yelling, hiking, and thrashing.

"Water, water everywhere, not a drop to drink," I chant as I pour a tiny splash of rubbing alcohol on the scrape. "Fuckity, fuck!" I shake my hand with the stinging of the alcohol on the open wound. As I wrap my hand with gauze, I pick up the chant again. "Water, water—" *Stop it.* I don't even like that poem.

But I survived the last crisis that unearthed that particular Honors English class recitation to the front of my brain. I survived being abandoned at the lighthouse. The poem had run through my mind then, too, and I lived. I didn't have drinking water then either, just miles and miles of brackish water mocking me for its inability to be digested. Well, fuck off, brackish bay water. You too, swamp water. I'll win this day. Just like I won then. I will find my kid and not die of thirst in the process.

But first things first—get the hell out of these woods. Cole's not here, so I shouldn't be here either. I sling my pack and rifle onto my shoulders and hike down the road, chancing the knee-deep flood waters because the quickest route from point A to point B is a straight line.

In the truck, I pull onto DIP toward Bay Aire Road, driving one-handed. Pain pulses in my hand if I grip the steering wheel with it, so I won't do that again. Lucky for me, I hurt my lefthand, which according to Jacob is purely decorative, as I am that righthanded. At the Holy T, I perform a rolling stop and, glancing right, spot two Humvees and two yellow school buses. *Shit*. I press the accelerator, smashing it into the floorboard.

Those Humvees carry military police, and if one sees me out and about, they may give chase. There's no way Daddy's truck can outrun anything less than twenty years old. If I'm stopped for suspicious behavior—being out so soon after the storm and going past Holy T would be just that—they will detain me. Who cares that Bellefontaine just took a direct hit from a powerful storm? Who cares that hundreds of evacuated residents will need help with their vehicles, most of which are covered in debris? I've gotten to know Shahin well enough to know that what he cares about is his own ego. He would enjoy taking me into custody and probably inflate my infraction into an act of terrorism against Mobile, the state, and the entire country. And is Shahin really bringing the evacuees back so soon? With all the downed trees, powerlines, and swollen waterways, is that safe?

A tiny voice in my head tells me I should go to the parking lot to help Mama and the others get home, but I tell that voice to shut it. Mama has Lauren, Kate, and Garrett to help her, if they are on those buses. Cole only has me. The problem with that is I don't know where to look for him. I only know where he isn't—at home or the freaks' former camp in the woods. But what if Clem lied? What if they were never there to begin with?

Every few yards, I check for Humvees in the rearview mirror. Nothing. Maybe they didn't see me. Maybe they did and didn't care. Maybe they saw me, recognized the truck, and will pay us a visit later, demanding to take everyone into custody. Hopefully, by then, I will be long gone, searching for Cole. My stop at home will only be long enough to change into dry shoes, properly bandage my hand, and decide where to look next. I look down at my shredding shirt and bloody shorts and press the accelerator hard again. Mama doesn't need to see me like this.

A glimmer of hope occurs to me. Two buses. I saw only two buses. That means the soldiers have to go back for the other evacuees. They will have orders to return to The Temple to retrieve the remaining residents. Thank you, sweet baby Jesus. That means they don't have time to worry about me right now. That means I have time. As for Mama, and any delay she might cause me, the Martins may not even be on the buses I saw. I say another prayer for that to be true. I just need time. I need time to figure out where to look. And I need to stop wasting the time I have.

Time! That's it. The Way only had a small window of time during the eye to grab Cole, make off with him, and get to a safe place before Isadora's second act ravaged Bellefontaine. That means they had to be riding out the storm somewhere close to our home—a lot closer than their camp in north Bellefontaine. They obviously didn't ride out the storm there. There was no trace of them. So, they must have packed up and moved well before the storm hit.

The familiar sound of chainsaws fills my ears through the open truck window. Up ahead, two men in a pickup tow a sizeable chunk of the fallen pecan tree off the road. *Just in time.* I smile and wave at them as I slow the truck to a crawl and maneuver around them. Once past, I speed to my next place to search, splashing through the remaining puddles until I reach the outpost gate.

The gate is locked, but that only means I'll go on foot. I park the truck near the gate and gaze at the muddy ground surrounding it. The fence erected to keep all of us out is high, but not so high it can't be climbed. I fit the rifle and strap across my body and take a good look around. Out of the truck, I don't see any spying eyes or immediate threat, so I creep over to the fence. As I survey the fence, looking for the best place to scale it, I notice a break in the chain metal. It's been cut.

Peeling back the chain links, my hand blooms in heat and pain. *Ignore it*, I tell myself. *Pain doesn't matter*. Crawling through the opening leaves my knees and shins covered in mud. *Filth doesn't matter*. Once inside the fence, I crouch low to the ground and listen. I hear the Bay. Water rolls in and out of the lagoon. Birds return from their hiding places. Vegetation shifts in the breeze and strains against their altered forms, reshaped by Isadora. What I don't hear are signs of human life.

Still, I must search. I must be thorough. No stone left unturned.

Sticking near the well-worn paths, I pass vacant plot after vacant plot where white Army tents were pulled up before the storm. I approach the dining facility tent, left for some reason to take on Isadora's full strength. The storm left it in tatters with poles bent and the canvas ripped at the seams. Behind the tent stand two large metal shipping containers. A creak sounds from that direction. I creep toward it and see one of the giant metal doors swaying ever so slowly on its hinges.

My breath quickens as I ready the rifle. I can do this. Just like Jacob taught me. It's a simple procedure—clearing a room. Just line up by the door, out of sight to anyone inside. Lead with the rifle. Quick, sure steps. Only I'm not a four-man stack like we had on Family Day back at Ft. Stewart. Lifeless mannequins don't await me inside the container. If anyone is in there, they are alive and very much a threat.

I hold my breath as I snap around the open door and take one long stride into the container. My breath comes out heavy, expelling air from my lungs. There's no one here. But someone was here. Several someones if I had to guess.

The container looks like it had rations inside it. *Had*. Not has. Like our garden, the container has been looted. The floor is covered with cardboard scraps and grains of rice. Rice sticks to the discarded packing tape. Plastic straps, probably used to restrain the goods during shipping were cut and hang limp, allowing contents to pour onto the ground. Whoever did this must have grabbed what they could carry and left the rest. They also left a shoe.

A single shoe, tucked between a crate and the thick metal wall, peeks out at me. The leather toe is decorated with hand-drawn fishhooks. They're the same fishhooks Jessie doodles in her school notebook while Lauren prattles on about geography and literature during their lessons. The very fishhooks Jessie drew on Cole's tennis shoes, hand-me-downs of Daddy's, after we discovered they wear nearly the same size and we all agreed that Cole is going to be much taller than any of the Martins before we know it.

I pick up the shoe and hold it to my chest. He was here. Cole was in this container. He left this for me to find it, for me to keep looking for him. He will get the chance to outgrow this shoe if it kills me.

I conduct a quick search of the rest of the outpost, even climbing to the top of the lookout tower deck to scan the surrounding area. That proves fruitless. Between the storm and the fact that The Way is more than likely on foot, I don't see a single trace of them or which direction they headed after looting the shipping container.

But I'll not feel defeated. Cole left me a clue, and I found it. I will find another.

Back in the truck, I place the shoe on the passenger side seat and inch home, scanning the ditches and tree line for any sign of

The Way. When I arrive at our gate, Matt, in the Gator, heads toward me, halfway between the house and me. When he sees me, he shakes his head and reverses the ATV back up the driveway. I park next to the Gator and hop down from the cab. Matt looks past me to the passenger seat and his face changes from pissed to disappointed the moment he discovers it empty. Cole's not there.

Jessie flings open the door to the house and runs outside. She looks at me with such hope that my heart breaks for the umpteenth time today. "He wasn't there, at their camp," I tell her, then turn to Matt. "No one was there. But someone did ride out the storm on the outpost." I reach over the driver's seat and grab Cole's shoe. "I found this in one of the shipping containers. I think Cole left it for me."

Matt nods, then leans into the truck and comes out holding my rifle.

"Matt, I'm going to need that," I say.

"Not right now, you don't." Holding tight to the rifle, Matt strides toward the house.

"Matt, I'm going back out. I have to go look for him!"

Matt spins toward me. "Where, Jules? Where are you going to look? Where are you even going to *start*?"

"What is wrong with you?"

Matt steps back, keeping the rifle out of my reach. "What's wrong with me? What's wrong with you, Jules? We agreed that we would find Cole after the storm. *We.* Not you alone. You know, I was sure this time was one time too many."

"Too many what?"

"One time too many that you go off with some half-baked plan. I was convinced that this would be the one to get you killed. Do you know how awful that feels?"

"Possibly as awful as I feel knowing Cole is out there, maybe hurt or worse. That he was taken by a bunch of psychopaths because of me!"

"Dammit, Jules." Matt exhales like he's trying to banish rage from his lungs.

"Does Cole only matter to me? Because he's not Martin blood, he's not our…" This time I gesture between the two of us, with the shoe I still clutch in my hand. "*Our* family. Tell me now so I know where we stand."

"Of course, that's not true," Matt says.

Jessie stands beside me and links her arm through the crook of my elbow. "He matters to me. We will find him, Aunt Jules."

I look into her majestic green eyes, emerald like the Gulf waters. "How are you so calm?"

"Because I know we will find him." Jessie makes the statement as if it is scientific and measurable. As if the faith she has in our abilities to locate Cole before the worst happens is all the proof she needs. "You found that." Jessie motions to the shoe.

"I envy your confidence," I tell her.

"I'm very enviable," she says, smiling.

Matt opens the door and turns to me. "A shipping container, huh?"

"Yes. Looks like it was full of rations before they got there. Whoever was in there ripped open the crates and boxes and took what they could carry."

"Why would Shahin leave a shipping container full of food to be washed away in a hurricane?"

"Maybe he didn't have time or the means to move it before the storm. Those things weigh tons."

"Or he doesn't care if all of our rations are ruined." Matt pulls the door open, then pauses again. "Would you please come in so we can make an actual plan? We can at least narrow down places to look."

I cross my arms, considering his plea.

"Jules, this is more than you can do alone. I've been wracking my brain about the Richardsons, Troy Cowart, Shahin—they may be more connected than we think."

That makes me follow him inside.

While I was gone, it looks like Matt, Jessie, and Daddy have removed most of the debris from the kitchen and living room. On instinct, I look into the dining room. The tree limb remains, as does the gaping hole it created.

"I'm sorry I wasn't here to help with cleanup," I say, then glance over the giant map of Bellefontaine spread out over the kitchen island. "What's this?"

"A map," Matt says in his *what do you think* tone.

"I know that. I mean, why do y'all have it out?"

"Daddy and I were trying to figure out where The Way is. We both figured they wouldn't be at the fishing camp, not during a storm that strong."

Irritation prickles my skin and teeth. "Yes, yes. Y'all are so much smarter than me. But I couldn't just sit around and wait for a better plan. Not while Cole is missing, and you were sleeping." That last part comes out more accusatory than I intended.

"Well, maybe if you got some sleep, you could think clearly."

"I'm fine."

"That bloody gauze says differently."

I look at my hand and walk to the pantry, digging out another first aid kit. After a year and a half of living like pioneers, it's depleted, but I snag the last gauze strip and a roll of medical tape that has a few inches left on the spool. I'm careful to use only what I absolutely need. Hurricane recovery always leads to injuries.

"So," Matt says, pointing to the map, "I don't think they left Bellefontaine, even with the Army abandoning their posts during the storm. They seem very attached to this place."

"Okay," I say and look around the room. "Where's Daddy?"

"He's out front checking on the pier. Trying to clean up what he can before Mama gets home."

"They should be here soon. I saw Humvees and buses pulling onto Laurendine Road when I was on my way back."

"You didn't wait to see if they were on the buses?"

"I was kind beyond the Holy T. I didn't want to take my chances."

"I get that." Matt turns his focus to the map again. "I figure with how the weirdos have grown in number recently, that they would move to a bigger space. I don't know if we'll be looking for tents—now that the storm has passed—or if they'll take over an abandoned property. But I think we should start with any large, vacant buildings. The ones we know were left to squatters. Hell, that might be where they're recruiting members."

I look at the map and my heart sinks at the vastness of Belle-fontaine. This is one of those places people come to disappear, to leave the crowded, visible world of a city. Here, the mass amount of undeveloped land with dense forests stretching miles beyond the few roads provide plenty of nooks and crannies. Even the houses here offer little visual access to the surrounding properties. No developer cleared acres of land to plop one hundred cookie cutter houses on tiny plots and ordain it a subdivision. Lots here are cleared only enough to fit a house. For the most part, the yards are big and mostly wooded, so much so that the trees provide natural property lines. No fencing needed.

Finding Cole will be like rooting out a singular, healthy cell in a cancerous, grapefruit-sized tumor.

"Okay, so where should I start?" I ask, overwhelmed by the task.

"Not you. *We.* I think we start on the road first. Left onto DIP will take us past the non-denominational church, Bailey's Corner, Greer's, that old Family Dollar and liquor store. Those have been vacant for months after the looters took everything of worth.

There's a couple of shuttered mom-and-pop restaurants we can check." Matt points to a dot on the map. "This is that RV park close to the marina. I don't think they'd go there because too many people still live there. But those people probably evacuated. At least I hope they did. Then, of course, there's the marina. I'd bet my last dollar Mrs. Renaud didn't evacuate. We can ask her if she's seen anything."

I flinch at the mention of the Renauds and the memory of my last conversation with the family matron. Mrs. Renaud wasn't thrilled to speak with me, and I was abducted within days of that conversation. I wonder if she regretted being so rude to me while all of Bellefontaine except for my family took me for dead. I didn't exactly have a chance to ask her during the town hall meeting. I was too busy worrying about Clem and blackout lights. I should have been worried about The Way.

"She'll talk to you, Jules. She's a cantankerous old lady, but we're looking for an abducted child. If she's seen anything strange, she'll tell us."

"Okay," I say, mentally searching for a third or fourth wind. Now that I've stopped moving, my muscles and bones beg for sleep.

"From the marina, we can look across the river. It wouldn't surprise me if they paddled across and are holed up in St. Rose of Lima Church."

"Do you think they would hide in a Catholic Church? Doesn't seem their speed."

"I think they'd plant their flag there and claim it for themselves. Save it from us cannibals."

I offer Matt a half-smile at his reference to the frequent accusation of Catholics being cannibals because we "eat" the body of Christ during communion. That's true only if Jesus was made of dry, unleavened bread.

"Wait," I say, remembering what got me into the house in the first place. "You said you think the Richardsons and Troy and the Knights are more connected to Shahin than we know. What did you mean?"

"Think about it. These freaks show up in the middle of martial law, and Shahin does nothing about it?"

"So you're thinking what I've been thinking? That The Way is just the Knights rebranded? In the meeting, Shahin said that he wants people to feel like they have some rights left. The right to peacefully protest," I say.

"And you believe him?"

"I believe most of what comes out of his mouth is horseshit, but he didn't seem concerned about The Way at all. Which makes me think he knows that The Way is just the Knights two-point-o."

"Exactly. And Clem Richardson? He's not the type of guy that's going to be happy about someone else having influence over what he considers his town, unless he's in on it."

"But Clem's the one who told us where their encampment was."

"You don't think that man would set a trap for you? I think this abduction has been planned for a while and the hurricane provided opportunity but also put a wrench in their plans. So, they moved. They're not going to harm a hair on that boy's head 'cause he's just bait."

That thought has occurred to me every minute since Cole went missing. "But what will they do to him when they get me to bite?"

"They won't see us because we're not storming into wherever they are half-cocked. Right?"

"Fine." I consider everything Matt's said, and one aspect still nags at me. "But how would Shahin be connected to this?"

"I don't know how, but I know he is. You know my gut is seldom wrong. Shahin told you if you didn't get in line, he would take Cole. *Take him.* That's what he said. Not arrest him. Not throw his butt in jail. Take him. And now that's happened."

"God, I hope you're wrong." My head swims and I feel my body wobble.

"Jules?"

Gripping the granite countertop, I force my posture straight again. "I'm fine."

"No, you're not. When was the last time you ate anything?"

"Yesterday. I'm fine, really. It's just all of this." I gesture toward the map as if looking at the layout of the land I've known my entire life would suddenly be overwhelming. By the look on Matt's face, I know he doesn't buy it.

"You're not fine. You need food and sleep. And probably two gallons of water."

"I'm fine, Matt."

Matt walks to the opposite side of the island and grabs a full water jug. "Here. Drink this. Every drop." He digs through the pantry looking for anything not ruined in the storm. He comes out with a jar of last year's green beans. With his meaty grip, he twists the sealed jar open. "It's better than nothing. I think it's going to be a few days before we have any protein around here. At least until the fish come back."

I slip a single green bean into my mouth and chew. "Needs salt," I say through chews.

"Don't talk with food in your mouth," he says and watches me eat a few more. "Next, you need sleep."

"No. I can't."

"You're no good like this. Your eyes won't focus. You reek of exhaustion and a little bit of swamp mud."

"Matt, what if it were Jessie missing?"

"I'd hope you'd shake some sense into me. How about two hours, or even just one? Lay down for one hour. I'll get us ready to go, then we will search everywhere we can think of."

"One hour?"

"One hour. I'll wake you up in one hour. I promise."

20

I hop off my cot, shove my feet into my shoes, and am out the door before deciding what I will do to Matt if he let me sleep more than an hour. I rush to the driveway, out from under the cover of the carport and look up to the sky. Nothing but blue. So blue with the sun so bright, I have to shield my eyes from the glare. At the sound of the back door opening and closing, I turn. *Matt.*

"How long did you let me sleep?" I ask him with more than a little irritation in my voice.

"Only an hour, so you can drop that tone now. Your anger won't help us find Cole."

"My anger will keep me awake until we do."

"Then, let's go."

I follow Matt to the truck and climb into the passenger side. Neither Matt nor I trust me to drive right now.

"I wonder if they've fed Cole?" I ask Matt as we drive down Bay Aire Road, a jar of green beans in my hands, courtesy of Matt and his immense concern that I am starving to death. To my surprise, I'm glad he brought them. I guess stopping my freak-out long enough allowed my body to function and let me know it needs fuel. I unscrew the lid and pop three wet beans into my mouth. "Probably not," I say around chewing. "They probably filled their bellies with stolen rations and made him watch."

With that realization—that Cole most likely has not been given any food—the beans sour in my mouth. I replace the lid and place the jar at my feet. Matt marks the action with a glance at the jar but doesn't argue with me.

We follow Matt's course as he laid out earlier, driving to each landmark and abandoned business. We find several of the aged and weathered buildings wide open, doors unlocked. Doors missing altogether.

At the Family Dollar, fresh tire tracks in mud look promising until I'm met at the front door by a frazzled-looking woman with a shotgun. When I peer around her, I see two other women on palettes on the floor and two small children, all filthy. They look hungry. Desperately hungry. I know the crazed stare of severe hunger, and it hits me in the gut every time I see it. I offer the woman the jar of green beans. She offers to "Blow my fucking head off." I get back in the truck, and Matt speeds away.

"Where to now?" I ask Matt, knowing we're running out of road soon. "Unless the National Guard built the bridge back without telling anyone, DIP's going to end soon."

"I want to check on the marina. See if I can get the boat back in the water."

"Oh," I say, but nothing more. I swallow my true feelings, which are anger and dismay at the idea of multitasking while my kid is missing. Because screaming at Matt that "My kid is fucking missing," would drain me of energy I can't afford to waste.

"Don't sound so disappointed. We're far from giving up. We're going to want the boat to search Fowl River."

Relief washes over me. "Good thinking. My head is all over the place."

"And in one place only."

Every tree we pass is bent from the storm, as if mid-bow. All in the same direction. "Do you think the trees will bounce back from this one?"

"Probably. Maybe. I haven't really thought about it. And I'm far from an expert on trees."

"Cole searched for me when I was missing." My voice sounds far away, disconnected from my body. "Mama told me you both searched for me around the clock. Never gave up on me."

"That's when I started to see in Cole what you saw. While we were searching for you. I saw how much he loved you already."

"Yeah. He's pretty special." I can't believe my body can still produce tears after my breakdown at the clearing, but with the words come fresh ones, rolling from my eyes, over my cheeks and jaw to my neck. In this moment, I let them fall unimpeded.

"That kid kills me." A half-smile blooms on Matt's face. "Sometimes I can see the child in him. Like he still needs people. Adult people. But other times, like when we were searching for you, I don't think he needed me at all. I think he'd have been out here looking for you whether I was with him or not."

"He's pretty fearless in a crisis," I say around sobs, choking out the words. "I'm afraid that's going to get him killed."

"Don't say that, Jules. I know you're worried, and damn, I'm worried, too. But I've got to believe that his fearlessness will keep him alive."

"He's pretty stubborn, too." The thought of all the intricacies of Cole's personality brings a smile to my mind, even if I'm too tired for the smile to reach my face.

"It's like you two do share DNA."

"Hey, being stubborn is a good trait to have when your life is in question." I sniff up the snot dripping from my nose and look inside the glove box for anything to wipe my face. "I guess any old napkins left in here were confiscated for the outhouse a long time ago." I slam the glove box closed—the only way to get the ancient thing to close—and use the hem of my shirt to dry my eyes and nose. "I hope he is as stubborn as I am. I stayed alive at the lighthouse out of pure stubbornness."

"Cheers to being pig-headed." Matt gives me a smirk, then turns left into the marina parking lot.

My breath catches when I see a Ford F-150 parked where Mrs. Renaud's trailer typically sits. "Where is she? Her trailer usually sits right there."

"Maybe her sons insisted she ride out the storm somewhere else. And maybe the old bird actually agreed." Matt opens his door and hops out.

Following his lead, I climb out of my side, looking right and left. The marina is never this quiet or this empty. The absence of people makes me feel exposed. And exposed is an unwelcome feeling that creeps up my arms and prickles the skin on my neck.

"Did yer Daddy send you to check on me?"

Matt and I both snap around at the voice.

"Hey, Mrs. Renaud." Matt eases into playing a charming Southern man with little, if any, effort. "You know we couldn't stand not knowing if you survived the storm." He strides over to her and hugs her. I follow him, but let him take the lead with Mrs. Renaud, remembering how tense our last conversation was and the way it ended. And there's no way I'm hugging her. She'd probably prefer to whack me with her cane rather than embrace me.

"You all know it'll take more than a damn hurricane to bring me down." She leans on her cane and nods. "I'd say we faired pretty well, 'cept for that corner of the shop roof." With her cane, she points to where the wind has peeled up a corner of the aluminum roof. But, unlike the community center, most of the roof held. "How 'bout y'all's place?"

"A big tree branch left a hole in the dining room and wrecked Mama's table. She's not going to be too happy about that." Matt shoves his hands in his pockets, displaying that tried-and-true Southern male posture of appearing at ease while the world goes up in flames around him.

"She wasn't there?"

"No, Ma'am," Matt says.

Mrs. Renaud pulls a hand-rolled cigarette from her pocket and slips it between her thin, creased lips. "You gotta light?"

Matt shakes his head. "No, ma'am. I don't smoke."

"Dang it."

"Sorry," Matt says, and continues. "Mama, Lauren, and Kate's crew evacuated. We didn't want to chance it with Mallie being so little still. Kate's boys and Lucy aren't much bigger, so it was best that they all went inland."

"Yeah, that's smart. My boys used to wail throughout hurricanes. I think the changes in air pressure hurt their ears."

"Mrs. Renaud," I ask, "are you here by yourself?"

"Well, I's wondering when you were going to speak. Never knew you to be so quiet." Mrs. Renaud gives me a skeptical look, one completely opposite from the saccharine she's been giving Matt. "'Course maybe you said all you need to say at that town hall meetin'. I thoroughly enjoyed watching you tearing into that Shahin."

"Mrs. Renaud, would you like me to start Daddy's truck for you? It's old enough that it still has a cigarette lighter. I bet it still works."

"Yes." Mrs. Renaud hightails it to the truck, moving faster on her cane than I've ever seen her move in the decades I've known her.

Matt tosses me the keys. "Hold on. Let Jules start the truck for you."

Luckily, the truck starts on the first try. I punch in the knob, wait a few seconds, then pull it out, revealing glowing orange, lava-hot coils. As Mrs. Renaud presses the end of her cigarette to the coils and sucks in smoke, I exchange a look of relief with Matt. Like me, he probably feared our visit would take a nasty turn if we couldn't get nicotine in the old bag.

Mrs. Renaud takes a long drag and exhales, smoke encircling her small frame and drifting inside the truck. "You know, Jules, I'm starting to like you a lot better."

I give her a smile, the only one I have.

"Now, what do you need?" She looks at me with this question, not Matt. "Go on and ask. I know you need somethin'."

"I need to know if you've seen Cole or saw anyone poking around here last night."

"I thought you got that boy under control," Mrs. Renaud chastises.

"Yes, ma'am. I did. But The Way took him last night."

"The who did what?" Mrs. Renaud chokes on her inhale of smoke, bending at the waist until she catches her breath.

"The Way. That's what those red-faced freaks call themselves. While the eye was passing over us, I sent him out to the garage for a gig—"

"We were trying to dislodge the neighbors' loose pier sections from ours," Matt says, interrupting me.

"Yes. I sent him out to the garage, but he didn't come back. When I went to look for him, he wasn't there, but I found a message from The Way on my worktable."

"Message?"

"Just a scrap of fabric with a threatening message painted on it."

"And you think that means they took the boy?"

"Well, yes." I cannot believe I'm going to have to convince people of what I know to be true.

"The day before the storm hit," Matt says, stepping closer to Mrs. Renaud. "They ransacked our garden. They left a threatening banner then, too."

Mrs. Renaud cuts me a lethal look. "You bringing trouble around again, aren't you?"

"I'm not bringing trouble. I'm trying to find Cole. He's only a child, and he's missing. They have him, and I don't know what they will do to him if I don't get him back."

Matt puts his hand on the old lady's shoulder. "If you saw anything, anything at all. We've got to get him back before they hurt him."

"They wouldn't hurt a kid, would they?" The innocence in Mrs. Renaud's eyes betrays her many years.

"I'm afraid they will. Matt and I also think they torched the rectory, so who knows what all they're capable of?"

"Well, I didn't ride out the storm here last night. The boys wouldn't let me, even though I'd have been just fine. Water didn't get in the shop, which is where I would've been. So, no. I didn't see anything. But I have noticed something." The old woman drops her cigarette and crushes it with the sole of her shoe. She leaves the butt on the ground and limps toward the back of the shop. Pointing with her cane, she says, "You see that rack of row boats? There should be four. Now, there's only three. I let locals use those boats to fish, so long as they bring back a few filets for me. Now I only got three boats. The one missing has a trolling motor, so I really need that one back. I'm also missin' two oars."

"Was the fourth boat here yesterday?" I ask.

"As sure as shit, it was. I secured those boats myself before the storm hit. Had the boys move the rack to behind the shop, away from the water where they usually sit, so they wouldn't drift away if the water came in too much. Those boats keep me and my boys fed."

"Thank you, Mrs. Renaud. That's what we needed to know." I lose all sense for a moment and lean in to hug her, but Mrs. Renaud raises one hand and takes an awkward step back, something akin to avoiding the plague.

"I don't like you that much."

"Of course."

I watch as she digs another hand-rolled cigarette from her shirt pocket. "If you want to show your appreciation, you'll crank that trunk again."

Mrs. Renaud leans inside, eager for nicotine. As I crank the truck and punch in the cigarette lighter, I ponder a question. Holding the hot coils to the end of her cigarette, curiosity creeps into my mind and out of my mouth.

"Mrs. Renaud, where are you getting the tobacco for your cigarettes? Is there a blacker black market around here that most of us don't know of? I've never seen anyone peddling tobacco at market days."

Mrs. Renaud straightens, pulling away from me in one short, sharp motion. She exhales and with her cigarette pinched between two fingers, she points at me, nearly grazing my shoulder with the burning tip. "Girly, you need to learn when to keep your mouth shut, when to ask questions, and what answers you deserve."

The curse in her eyes sets my pulse galloping. "Matt, let's go," I say, pulling the truck door closed. "I'll drive."

Before I can put the truck in gear, I hear the *thwomp, thwomp* of a helicopter. Craning my neck, I see a soldier toss a stack of white paper from the open door. The pages float in the air, mimicking the helicopter blades as they spin to the ground. *Shit.*

I leave the truck running in park as I hop out and grab a flyer that lands on the hood. Reading the familiar font—Arial 12, the font of choice for military missives and Unabomber manifestos— my adrenaline rises with each word. I don't know what I expected to learn, but Shahin doled out quite a surprise with this order. And I'm certain he won't make any friends with it. From the corner of my eye, I see Matt and Mrs. Renaud pick up flyers from the ground.

"Effective immediately. By order of Governor Freidman, blah,

blah, blah," I read aloud, scanning through the bullshit to get to the meat. "To provide security, the rule-of-law, and community peace, each household of Bellefontaine, Alabama, is allowed only two firearms. Acceptable firearms include handguns, revolvers, shotguns, lever-action rifles, bolt-action rifles, break-action rifles, and air rifles."

"What the hell?" Matt asks.

"Possession of any other type of firearm will be cause for arrest and detainment." I look up from the page. "I guess the gov's whole *2-A or die* is a thing of the past."

Mrs. Renaud hobbles closer to us, waving the flyer gripped in her boney hand. "As if we don't have enough to clean up around here, they gotta add to the mess with this. I'll tell you one thing, I'll be shocked as a thunderclap if either of my boys turn over one of their guns. We still got rights."

"Be careful about all that, Mrs. Renaud," Matt says. "I don't think we have rights at all now. Not as long as we're under martial law."

"Well, we'll see about that."

Matt stares at the page like it contains the secrets of the universe. "Bellefontaine residents," he reads, "must turn in any forbidden firearm and/or firearms in excess of two per household no later than forty-eight hours from the date of issue of this order as listed…"

Mrs. Renaud inhales from her cigarette held between her lips and talks around it. A constant cloud of smoke streams out of her mouth with her words. "Two guns per household? What is Shahin thinking? Nobody around here is going to turn over their guns. Has he forgotten we're in Alabama?"

"And that we've just been through a hurricane and have better things to do other than—" Matt pauses as he looks at the flyer in his hand, then looks back at me. "Turn in our extra guns at the church?"

"I saw that. Does he mean St. Philip's? Are we supposed to pile them on the altar?" I fold my copy and shove it in my pocket. "Garrett's going to shit when he sees this. Most of the guns in the closet belong to him. Garrett's got thousands of dollars in those guns."

"Maybe they got back while we've been out and already saw the flyer."

"I hope so. I really don't want to witness Garrett's head explode when he does see this."

Matt folds the flyer, making neat creases in the paper with his stubby fingernails. "Let's go."

"Mrs. Renaud," I say, turning to her. "Do you need a ride home?"

"Nah. Got one of the boys' trucks. I can still drive, you know."

She might as well have flipped me the bird with that last comment. I nod and open the driver's side door.

"Good luck finding your boy," Mrs. Renaud tells me, her expression softening. "He's a sweet kid. Doesn't deserve to be caught up with those red bastards."

Matt and I roll out of the marina lot, and I floor it as soon as the tires hit asphalt.

"I need to get the boat hooked up and come back to get it back in the water," Matt tells me.

"So, you're thinking what I'm thinking? That they stole that boat and took Cole upriver?"

"You know of anyone else crazy enough to go out in a hurricane?"

"Not off the top of my head. At least not anyone alive." Troy Cowart's ugly, pock-scarred face hovers in my mind.

"Exactly. They've moved somewhere off Fowl River. It'll be a lot easier to see anything from the water."

Matt's right. We need the boat. Not only would we have to

drive miles out of the way to search the south side of the Fowl River community in the truck due to the Knights having blown out Fowl River Bridge, but the vegetation throughout the community is too thick to see anything from the road. A good majority of homes are so hidden by trees that you only know anyone lives there by the driveway markers and mailboxes. Some driveways don't even have that. To know who's living on the river and what's happening there, you have to be on the water.

"We'll need whatever gas…" Matt's words become background noise as I contemplate Fowl River. No river is a straight shot, but this particular river has so many narrow creeks and offshoots. It will take hours, maybe days to search them all.

"Do that while I get the boat hooked up. Jules?" Matt's voice is louder now than whatever he said before my name. "Are you listening?"

"Yes. Yes. Sorry. Gas. Something about gas."

"We need the gas containers. At least two. Three, if we've got them. You need to load them while I get the boat and trailer hooked up. Once we're loaded, we can go back to the marina and get the boat in the water. I'll drive it to the pier. You take the truck home, then meet me at the end of the pier."

"That's wasting time. I can just park the truck and hop in the boat with you."

"I don't want to leave Daddy and Jessie without the truck. If something happens, I don't want them stranded."

"You mean if these assholes return to the house, knowing we'll be out looking for Cole." With that, the scope of the danger facing my family plays out in my mind like a cruel horror film. Red faces, Jessie and Daddy hogtied, Mama, Mallie, Kate, Lucy, the boys, Garrett, Lauren… no one is safe as long as The Way is out there.

21

"Jules and I are taking two rifles and leaving two for you," Matt says, handing one rifle to Daddy. "We have a couple of days before we have to decide to turn these in—"

"We're turning them in, son. Just like the order says."

Matt ignores Daddy and hands a rifle to Jessie. "Okay, baby girl," Matt says to his daughter. "You remember how to use this right? Do not. I repeat, do not flip that safety off until you are ready to shoot. I've loaded three rounds for you, so make each shot count."

"I know how to shoot, Dad," Jessie says, as if she's headed to the range for target practice rather than possibly having to defend the house against marauders or worse—people who don't care if she dies, as long as I die shortly after her.

"We're taking you to the marina," Daddy says and moves toward the back door, rifle in hand. "Julianne, how much gas did you load in the boat?"

"Two cans, leaving y'all two."

"Load a third. I don't want y'all running out of gas out there, and it may take a long time for you to find Cole."

"Wait." Matt closes the gun closet, and when we turn to face him, he doesn't budge. "I already told you the plan," he tells Daddy. "You and Jessie are staying here. I want you here when everyone else returns."

"And we will be," Daddy says. "All this back and forth you and Jules are planning is wasting time. You need to start your search now." Daddy's eyes are bright with intensity, and in them I see now how much he's grown to love Cole.

"Coming with us leaves the house unattended." Matt stands close to the wall and motions toward the living room. "You're staying here."

Jessie steps toward her dad. "If the bad guys come while we're out, wouldn't it be better for us not to be here? If we see anything suspicious, we won't even turn down the driveway. We can go to the church and warn the others. Get the soldiers to help us."

"She's got a point," I say to Matt. "Do you really want her here if they come for them, or do you want her in the truck, halfway to a successful escape?"

"Fine." Matt walks toward the hall and back door, stopping near Daddy. "When Mama gets home and none of us are here, she's going to freak out. That's on you."

"I can handle your mother."

———

Floating in this river that holds so many of my childhood memories, I wave to Jessie as she walks up the ramp and hops back into the truck. She and Daddy pull away, and the normalcy of this—putting the boat in the water, Daddy in the truck ready to drive home, Matt and I taking off upriver—feels out of place considering there is nothing normal about our mission. It's not normal to be searching for a child, especially one that has been abducted. It's not normal to search for him with no help from law enforcement, no help from the community. There is no law enforcement to help us. The National Guard doesn't count because I question how much they care about some random kid. The community? Most days, I wonder if there is still a community at all.

I stoop down and dig binoculars from my bag. Knowing the lenses will need adjustment, I focus on the first throng of homes —the former Knight compound.

"You don't think they'd go there, do you?" Matt asks as he pushes the throttle to trolling so we chug along, slower than a snail's pace.

"No. I just need to set the binoculars at the right distance."

"Do you ever wonder if anyone will live there again? On Mon Luis?"

"I hope so. Not the Knights, of course, but someone. Families who deserve such a beautiful piece of land." Peering through the binoculars, I see a number of trees, uprooted and split during the storm, as well as damage to outbuildings. Some look completely destroyed, but the houses remain intact. "I hope the storm destroyed Dave's shed. No one deserves that shed."

As we come around the first bend in the river, I see where the water has eroded the riverbank. In places, it looks like a giant has taken huge bites out of the bank, leaving two feet of black soil exposed beneath a skin of bright green grass. Over the years, this has become a real threat for those living on the river. After every storm, desperate measures are put in place to protect the land. Bulkheads and rocks at the bank and houses were built further and further from the water's edge. But with each storm, the water takes a little more of the land—or does the land surrender to the water because what else can it do?

We ride in silence. Matt keeps the speed slow so I can scan every single house. Building after building and house after house, I peer into windows, crane to see around corners. My binoculars go from object to object, looking for any piece of evidence that might say, *hey, I'm here. I'm right here, Jules. Come and get me.*

He's waiting for me. I know he is. I feel his anticipation in my bones. He's strong, but it's been hours now. Too many hours. *Is he losing hope? Has he lost faith in me? Does he trust me enough to find him?*

We go around smaller bends, careful to avoid storm debris, cognizant that hazards may lay just below the water's calm surface. But this water is dark, even darker than the Bay. Matt pulls up on the throttle and the boat stops.

I gasp as I look up. Right in front of us is the tall, abandoned pylon, as tall as a power pole, standing alone in the center of the river. Atop that pylon are the pitiful remains of an eagle's nest. Just a few sprigs, barely bigger than splinters, cling to the top. The eagle, huge and majestic, has lived in that nest for years, decades maybe. I honestly don't know. What I do know is that if you are lucky enough to drive up on the eagle while it's resting in its nest, you know then and there why so many choose to live here.

The storm blew the nest away.

"Hopefully, he'll rebuild." Matt backs the boat up, as we've drifted too close to the pole and the tangle of cedar stumps that surround it. "I mean, he's been here so long, surely he's grown quite accustomed to his neighborhood and rebuilding after a storm."

"Maybe. I hope he just got somewhere safe before the storm." I scan the water with the binoculars, the shoreline, the thicket of reeds, looking for that eagle, but find no signs of life. "We better keep going."

"Right or left?" Matt asks.

Fowl River has many branches. Some wide, some too narrow for our boat. Some of the branches flow so far, I've never been to the end of them. Some are anabranches, flowing wayward for a bit before rejoining the main vessel. "Well," I say. "Let's go left. Stick to the main river. If we don't find him, then we'll double back and search where we can fit in without getting stuck." That solution isn't the thorough search that I'd hoped would find my boy and ease my mind, but I can't think of a better option.

Matt goes left and as soon as the river widens again, I see something floating in the water near a dock.

"Matt! There!" I point to the object.

Matt angles the boat toward the remains of a dock. The wood looks fairly new, but it's off its moorings and bobs in the water as if snagged on something or fighting against sinking to the bottom.

Looking through the binoculars, I watch in horror as the object reveals itself. "Matt, it's a body." My stomach lurches as my mind shoots off the fastest prayers I've ever prayed. *This is not your ending, Cole.*

"It's not him," Matt says, as he drifts closer. "That's a full-grown man. He probably stayed during the storm, and the storm won."

"Let's tie off," I say. "We can't leave him in the water like that."

Matt stops the boat, and we both hop into the water, lifting and dragging the man's body back up on dry land. It's all we can do for now. Every minute that passes is one more minute I risk Cole's life.

"After we find Cole, we'll come back."

Matt nods his agreement and climbs back in the boat. He offers me his hand and pulls me up, just enough so that I can swing my body over the side.

I grab one of the towels to dry off. "How are we doing on gas?"

"Fine, especially with that extra barrel Daddy gave us. We could search all night if it takes it."

I smile. "Thanks, baby brother."

Around another bend, we pass a series of stripped pylons. There's so many bare pylons from decades of dreams being built —fishing cabins, little getaways, mansions and palatial estates. Then the storms come through and rip everything apart. Some people can rebuild, so they do. Then new storms come through and rip it apart again. If you live here, in south Mobile County, that's the deal you make with God until you can't rebuild again and you pack up what you have left and leave the pylons.

"We're running out of easy river," Matt says, pulling the throttle back to idle.

Just ahead of us is a nearly 180-degree turn, followed by a series of switchbacks notorious for underwater hazards. And I'm sure Isadora created new obstacles. If Cole were here, right here with these barren pylons, we could snatch him up and be back to open water in minutes. But the further we go, the deeper they've hidden Cole, our escape becomes more treacherous.

Cole's not being held on a pylon, clinging to the wood with the barnacles. That would be too easy. So, I stand and turn in the boat, searching, and wishing a clue into existence. Anything to tell me where he is.

"What the hell?" Something about the nearest barren pylon breaks through my building panic. "Turn around," I say, just loud enough for Matt to hear me over the motor. "Turn around. Go back. Go back."

Matt kicks the boat into reverse and then turns around.

"Stop!" I topple forward but regain my footing when Matt stops the boat at the first of the naked pylons. "Go really slow, past those pylons."

When the boat turns to face the first pole, tree branches reaching out like claws trying to drag the pylon to the bank, I see it. I didn't fully register the marking before, but I see it now painted in red—the letter B. Several yards down at the next pylon another letter—D—then E. "Stop! Stop!."

Matt pulls the boat up short and we bob in the river, up and over our own wake. Through the binoculars, I peer ahead to a fourth pylon where a bright red L marks the wood about four feet above the water. Above the swollen river.

BDEL

"We found them," I say, looking around at the thick woods that line both banks and the blind turn ahead of us. "There's a dock up there. Beyond the pylon with the L painted on it. Whose dock is that?"

"Not who, but *what*. That's Bellingrath Gardens."

"There's a boat tied off it. Here," I say and hand Matt the binoculars. "Does that boat look like it has a trolling motor attached?"

Matt looks through the binos. "Sure does."

"That's where they are, Matt. Bellingrath." I move to the center of the boat and grasp the handles on the square windshields. "Come on," I tell Matt with zero patience left in my body, "let's go."

"Why would they make it so easy to find them?"

Matt's question pisses in my Cornflakes. "Because they want me to find him. I mean, I knew that. But they want me to come by way of the river. They're expecting us."

I pick up the binoculars again. Peering through them, I focus on the dock and the boat. Empty. Both are empty. Something white is strung across the front of the dock, a banner no doubt, but at this angle, I can't read what it says. I point to a cove to our left. "Pull in there. Quick before anyone sees us."

Matt obliges. "Now what?"

"What do you know about Bellingrath? Was it abandoned when all of this started?"

"I assume so. It's not like the people that work there live there."

"No. They don't. Or didn't. I don't think anyone has actually lived there since the Bellingraths died."

"I know a little of the history of the place."

"Everyone knows that, Matt." Guilt tightens the muscles of my neck at the quip. "Sorry."

But seriously, everyone knows the history of Bellingrath Gardens and Home. It's one of Mobile's premiere tourist attractions, even for locals. The Gardens were originally the second home of the Bellingraths. I can't remember the husband's name, but the wife was Bessie, and Bessie was a woman to admire. Yes, she had a knack for gardening and creating first Mobile's Azalea Trail downtown, then the gardens and the British Revival home that sits on Fowl River. But what I find most appealing about Bessie is her altruism.

Bessie Bellingrath took charity to that rare air of never bragging about all the giving she did. During the Great Depression, she sought out struggling businesses like antique shops and tradesmen and bought their wares, often for well over the fair market price. She gave her staff members bonuses for small tasks. Imagine a woman in the 1930s handing a struggling family an extra twenty-dollar bill for something well within the staff member's job or paying a family one hundred dollars for an azalea bush cutting because Bessie swore she'd been searching for that exact type but hadn't found one before stumbling upon their backyard garden. Upon her death, sometime in the 1940s I believe, the archbishop in Mobile contacted Mr. Bellingrath to thank him for all the good Bessie had done for the sick and infirm in Mobile at the Catholic-run hospital. The call came as a total surprise to Bessie's husband, as the couple were Protestants.

So, really, The Way needn't be squatters at Bessie's former home. She'd have given anyone in need in Bellefontaine whatever they needed, right up until she discovered that the group watering her azaleas now were in the business of kidnapping. I hope like hell she's haunting the assholes because Bessie Bellingrath would never abduct a child. It wasn't in her nature to harm people.

"What are we doing here, Jules?" Matt asks.

"We can't just ride up to the dock. That's what they expect us to do. I need to get on the estate without anyone seeing us."

"And how do you plan to do that?"

"I don't know, but I know who does. Mama and Kate. They know every nook and cranny of that place.

22

B ack home, I dig through Kate's memory box in the garage. She was an avid scrapbooker during her teenage years, even as the craft was out of fashion by then. Out of the corner of my eye, Jacob's survival manual calls to me.

"That book is your guide," Jacob tells me, or rather the part of my brain that keeps his memory so close that I swear he talks to me tells me.

"I will flip through it after I find Kate's scrapbook. Bingo!" I snatch the three-inch-wide, twelve-by-twelve binder out of the box. Flipping through the pages, I land on what I've searched for —a visitor's map of Bellingrath Gardens from Kate's summer of being a volunteer tour guide. Popping the metal rings that have less rust on them than would be expected—the salt air and humidity rust everything around here—I slide the map loose of the binder.

"The guide, Jules. The guide. Do not ignore me."

Fine!

I snatch Jacob's copy of *SURVIVAL, Field Manual 3-05.70* off the shelf and open it to the dogeared page in the front. Yes, Jacob committed the ultimate book lover's crime—folding the top corner down and creasing the paper. I've left it that way because I know his fingers formed the crease. As I read the introduction to chapter one, I run a fingertip over the fold.

"This manual is based entirely on the keyword SURVIVAL. The letters in this word can help guide your actions in any survival situation. Whenever faced with a survival situation, remember the word SURVIVAL."

What exactly does survival have to do with finding Cole? Sometimes my intrusive thoughts of Jacob confound me more than help me. *So, what pray-tell, man of mine, is the point of this?*

It's everything you need, I imagine him saying.

"This manual is based entirely on the keyword survival," I read aloud, and then I know. The plan is here, in these pages. Cole's survival. I just have to fill in the details.

I read the first letter and its meaning. *S—Size up the situation.* I scan the other letters and the entire chapter comes back to me. I haven't read it in months, but after Jacob first died, I must have read these few pages dozens of times, angrily searching for clues to why Jacob didn't survive.

I grab the Bellingrath map—it's how Matt and I will size up this particular situation—and rip open the door. Mama, Kate, and Lauren, all standing in the doorway unaware that I was going to tear through the door, all stare back at me. They each hold the same expression, that of a mother hell-bent to help her child.

Mama's on me first, hugging me so tightly I can barely breathe. Mama holds me until Kate pulls Mama off to wrap her own arms around me. I lean into the hug—indulgent, selfish, wasting time. After several seconds, Kate stands me upright again and holds my face in her hands.

"We will get him back," she tells me. "Now, how can we help?"

"I've got a plan," I tell them. "Well, the beginnings of a plan. But I need your help filling in the details. They're at Bellingrath."

"Kate and I know everything there is to know about that place." Mama wipes away a few tears from her own cheeks.

"That's what I'm counting on." I push past the three of them to the main house.

"Is that from my scrapbook?"

"Yes. And don't worry, Kate, I didn't damage it, but the rings are rusting. Not bad though."

Kate, Mama, and Lauren follow me inside where we join Matt and Daddy at the kitchen island. The map of Bellefontaine and Fowl River is still spread across the countertop, so I lay the Bellingrath map on top, approximately where the estate sits along the river.

U-Undue haste makes waste.

Forcing myself to be methodical, I tap my finger on the map. "Okay. Tell me where I can enter the grounds without being seen." I look at Kate, who stares at the map. It's faded a bit but still a clear enough artist's rendering to get a sense of the winding trails, thick forest, open lawns, and flowering shrubs.

"Right there." Kate taps a spot on the east side of the estate. From the drawn trees covering the spot, it looks hidden enough to work. "There's an operations path that leads to a paved road right there. It's how the gardeners can move vegetation in and out without interfering with visitors."

"That's good," I tell her. What I don't tell her is what we all know already. I've got one shot at this, so every detail must be right.

———

As Matt and I enter Fowl River, back in the boat and with adrenaline pumping, I look up at the moon, unable to decide if I appreciate its light or wish it away so that we can hide in darkness. But one thing is certain in the days following a hurricane—

clear skies. Matt slows our speed as he maneuvers around the ruins of the Fowl River Bridge—still present over a year later—and storm debris we noticed earlier in the day.

Waiting until nightfall was not my idea, but I knew why Daddy and Matt pressed for it. The element of surprise, avoiding being seen, evading capture before laying eyes on Cole. The odds are better at night.

As we approach the second bend, Matt pulls back on the throttle. "We're getting close."

I nod and point to the pylon marked with a B. It stands in a cove, close enough to the water's edge so that we will be able to hop out of the boat and onto dry land. A jut of trees, their branches sloping forward to tickle the water with their leaves, hides the cove. Idling, the boat creeps through the branches and closer to the pylon until I can reach out and grab it. I pull the boat close and tie off.

"You don't have to come with me," I say to Matt. "I can go by myself."

"We're doing this together. I'm tired of these fuckers. I'm tired of living like this. I'm tired of worrying that some asshole is coming for you or Jesse or Lauren or any of us. None of us will be safe until they're gone. Until everyone like them are gone."

R: Remember where you are.

The next letter in the acronym and its meaning flashes in my mind. I look around the riverbank for identifying marks. "When we come out of the woods," I tell Matt. "Look for that buoy." I point directly across the river from our boat where a neon yellow buoys glows in the moonlight, balancing atop a thicket. "That should be easy to spot if we pop out at the wrong spot."

"Good thinking." Matt jumps from the bow to land, then holds out a hand for me.

"Move out of the way." I give Matt a smirk, then with my rifle and pack slung across my back, leap from the boat to land. I take a small stumble forward but find my balance and stand upright.

"Graceful," Matt says.

I dig Jacob's old night-vision goggles out of my pack and loop the strap around my neck.

"Where the hell did you get those?" Matt reaches his hand out for the goggles.

"Jacob didn't exactly have time to turn in his gear." I take a few steps into the trees, careful of my footing, and affix the goggles to my face. The world turns green, like it's drenched in radium. The ground is littered with small, green orbs—rodents. *I'm going to pretend those are all squirrels.* "Looks like a bunch of critters, but not much else. Lots of low branches, so watch your face."

I hand the goggles to Matt and wait as he surveys what's ahead of us—yards and yards of thick brush and an overgrown trail. "Now or never." Matt hands me the goggles and tightens the strap on his rifle and pack.

"From here on out, no speaking."

I stalk through the woods with one arm raised in front of my face. Most of the pine branches this low to the ground are nothing more than twigs, but some are the width of stair spindles, with thorny vines snaking around them. Matt walks close behind me, keeping the river to our right. When I stray too far from the river to avoid a thicket or large rut, he taps me twice on the right shoulder, signaling that I need to move on a northwesterly path. Every time either of us steps on a branch dry enough to send a crack into the still night air, we both stop short, hold our breath, and wait to be discovered.

By moonlight, and through the goggles, I search the ground in front of me for water moccasins. Each step is so careful, I feel like it will be dawn before we get to the estate. When I come upon a fallen tree, its trunk wide and swollen from taking on water, I secure my rifle behind my neck, triple-checking the safety and tucking the butt and barrel under my backpack straps. The back of one of my calves scrapes the bark as I climb over, but I ignore the pain and push forward. What's another injury when Cole is so close?

After what feels like hours of trudging through the woods in slow motion, I raise one hand, motioning for Matt to stop. Through the goggles, I examine the road Kate told me about. We have only ten feet of cover left before the woods open up to the road.

"If this doesn't work, we're screwed," I say, breaking my silence rule.

"It'll work, Jules. We've just gotta move fast. Get in and get out. That's it."

"But they could be hiding him anywhere in there."

"Just stick to the list Kate gave us. Do you remember it?"

"Yes. The greenhouse-looking building should be up first."

"Let's go."

V: Vanquish fear and panic.

I motion toward the road and choke down a nervous laugh at the thought of going into Bellingrath Gardens like a couple of Rambo-style mercenaries hell-bent on victory. "Sorry."

"Nope, I'm right there with you." Matt smiles back at me.

We break out of the trees. It's not paved as Kate said it was, and that makes me wonder what other details she remembered wrongly. Looking down the muddy road, nature is trying to correct the human folly of clearing this path. Thick grass and waist-high weeds break through the surface in spots. I put the goggles on for good measure. I wasn't expecting the road to have obstacles.

Neon green shapes with sharp outlines run against dark green pockets of foliage. I stumble backward a step, just missing Matt's shoe as I stare straight into the eyes of a three-foot tall owl, perched on a tree limb slightly taller than me on the edge of the road. Lowering the goggles, I watch the owl spread its wings, lift off the branch, and fly out of sight without a sound, his gigantic wings catching the moonlight for a second before he disappears in the distance. I wonder how long he's been on his hushed reconnaissance mission and who else may be watching us without our knowledge.

When we come upon the footpath, I dart off the road, relieved to be behind cover again. But the canopy of trees is so thick that the moonlight disappears. I wait for Matt and instruct him to walk with one hand on my shoulder. Through the goggles, I can make out the path. In only a few steps, the top corner of the conservatory comes into view—the first place to search for Cole.

The conservatory is a greenhouse, made entirely of windows with a center dome and two narrow wings jutting off the dome in opposite directions. It holds tropical plants of all types and, when operational, is climate-controlled to mimic a rainforest. When the path opens to the backside of the greenhouse, I crouch down and scamper to the end of the nearest wing. Matt follows close behind me.

Looking through a window, I see that most of the plants have wilted, their stalks and leaves drooping, dying on the ground. I look at Matt and shake my head. No Cole. He exhales, disappointment in his breath.

Beyond the greenhouse, Matt creeps toward the rose garden, which according to Kate was laid out in the shape of the round rotary club emblem. It's on the list because it has a fountain in the center that could be used as a place to tie up a prisoner. Cole is strong but no one is strong enough to dismantle a concrete fountain.

"The rose garden contains more than 2,000 plants and thirty-six varieties of roses," I remember Kate telling me. At the time I was annoyed by the needless details she kept rattling off, but now that I'm here and doing this, her Bellingrath Gardens trivia keeps my mind occupied and my tendency to panic in check.

The rose garden is deserted, so we sprint around it to the paved path on the other side. In my gut, I know where The Way is hiding Cole, but my gut is sometimes wrong, so I will search this whole estate to know I haven't rushed past him.

Matt and I search the Asian-American Garden next, scurrying along the path, through the covered bridge, past the structure built to look like a Buddhist temple, and finally over the arched, red footbridge. Still no Cole.

The sight of lit torches stops me dead in my tracks. Matt sees them, too, and he holds my right arm as if he senses that I am about to break through the line of trees. Instead, I creep forward, scanning the area surrounding the torches. Between the torches stands the gazebo and a banner illuminated by firelight. We stalk closer, careful to step without sound. The banner looks like it is made of a bed sheet, painted and stretched between two white, wooden columns.

Whoever hates his brother walks in the darkness,
and does not know where he is going,
because the darkness has blinded his eyes.

I crouch down on instinct, positive we just walked into a trap. I fumble for the goggles, and finally, when they are over my eyes, I see past the pool of torch light. Matt crouches next to me, his rifle at the ready. I scan left and right, ahead and behind us but see nothing by vegetation and the small heat spots of rodents.

"There's nothing here," I whisper and stare at the banner again, reading and re-reading the words. Then, in the distance, another torch glows. I gesture in its direction. "Was that light there before?"

"Maybe," Matt whispers. "I didn't notice it, but I wasn't looking for it either."

"If Kate's memories are correct, that's the Rockery."

We stick to the shadows and somehow avoid being snagged or tripped by any of the overgrown shrubbery. At the overlook, we pause and peer over shrubbery toward the Rockery, a rock garden accessible by flagstone steps built into the hillside of Mirror Lake.

As a kid, I loved how tucked away the Rockery felt. When Mama met with her garden club in the cafe here, I stole over to the Rockery. There, my imagination ran wild with tales of fairies, Thumbelina and pirates, and innocents hidden away by a wicked witch. Today, a single torch stands ablaze in the surrounding darkness, presumably stuck in a crevice in the stacked shale and left to burn.

Matt and I dash from the overlook and back into the shadows. Shrubs, once groomed into topiaries fit for a royal garden, now burst with fresh growth in all directions, creating cover for our descent to the Rockery. I find the safety of my rifle and hold it with my thumb. With one flick, this rifle will turn from menacing to lethal. One little flick. That's all it will take.

With my pulse in my ears, I take stock: rifle in my hands, buck knife on my left hip, zipper pull to my right, lighter in my right pocket, ready to light the Molotov cocktails in my backpack. At the bottom of the stairs, I pause. Around the next corner could be a Way member, waiting to kill me. I could find Cole there, scared or hurt. I could find nothing but an abandoned torch. Summoning my courage, I rush around the rocky wall.

It's just another banner.

How useless to spread a net where every bird can see it!

"What the hell?" Matt asks, reading the banner as I do.

"Whoever has Cole is fucking with us."

"Yep."

Without another word, I march up the stairs, no longer concerned with being quiet or going unnoticed. When I reach high ground, I turn in a circle, searching the gardens until I find what I'm looking for. "There," I tell Matt. "Another torch."

I sling my rifle across my back and sprint toward the distant flickering flame. Hurdling storm debris, I arrive at one end of the Mermaid Fountain and eye the torch burning just outside the pool. Splashing through the narrow lead—a strip of stacked stones filled with water that extends from the fountain's centerpiece—I rush to the bronze mermaid. Her arm extends to the sky, displaying a conch shell. A white pillowcase covers her head. The sight stops me cold.

"What is it?" Matt whispers, coming up behind me.

I shake my head and clear my mind of two competing, horrid images—one of men in white hoods galloping on horseback around a burning cross, the other of Cole struggling to see and breathe beneath a hood. Sloshing forward, I yank the hood from the mermaid's head. Turning the pillowcase over, red letters—this time in marker—glare up at me.

You desire and do not have, so you murder.

You covet and cannot obtain, so you fight and quarrel.

You do not have, because you do not ask.

"Another fucking verse," I say to Matt and throw the pillowcase at him. Into the surrounding darkness, I yell, "I'm asking now! Where is he? Give him back now, dammit!" I climb the stone surround of the fountain and stand tall, exposed to whomever is watching and mocking my terror. "Take me. I'll do whatever you—"

"Jules, shut the fuck up. Do you hear that?"

I listen around my sobs and gasps. A few sputters in the distance then, yes. At last, I know what Matt hears because I hear it too—the low rumbling of a motor.

23

I f I thought Garrett would let me live, I'd chuck this rifle into the woods so I could run faster. But he'd never let me hear the end of it, and I may need it if one of these Way fuckers jump out of the bushes.

Running, I curse my naivety. I knew the pylon markings leading us to Bellingrath were too easy. The Way isn't going to serve up Cole on a driftwood platter. Of course they're going to toy with me, torture me, as long as they possibly can. So, with every step, the verses run through my head. The words rearrange themselves, bleeding each verse into the others. They must be clues. The Way is playing with me. Playing with Cole. Playing with his life.

I can't hear the motor anymore, which means whoever they were and wherever they were going, they're long gone. All we got out of our search at Bellingrath were Bible verses and the knowledge that Cole isn't there. All that running back and forth and reading dumb banners was a waste of time. Knowing that I don't know how much time Cole has robs me of my breath and forces me to pull up short of the tree line.

"What's wrong?" Matt jogs up beside me, barely winded.

"Where is he?"

"I don't know. But we have to get to the boat and keep looking."

I swipe sweat from my brow with my equally wet arm, which does nothing to dry my face. "I don't even know where to look."

"The boat we heard was heading to the mouth of the river. We'll start there."

I follow Matt out of the woods to discover we came out close to where we left the boat. At least my sense of direction isn't shot like my nerves are. Wading into the water, I see our next gift—a piece of white fabric tossed into the boat. I'm not surprised that the red-faced assholes saw our boat. They probably waited for us to come, then started placing their banners. Of course, we seemed to move faster than they expected with how soon after the third torch was lit their boat sped away.

"What does it say?" I ask, pulling myself into the boat after Matt.

"At least red ink on white is easy to see in the dark." Matt holds the fabric out of the shadows to read by moonlight. "The burning sand becomes a pool, and the ground springs of water. In the haunt of jackals, the grass becomes reeds and rushes." He stares at me confused. "What is that supposed to mean?"

"My guess would be either nothing again, or where we're supposed to go next." I mull the words over in my mind, then out loud. "Sand, water springs, reeds and rushes."

"That could be anywhere along the coast."

"Not really. Most of the beaches here are gone. Replaced by rock."

"Mon Luis Island has beaches, a small bit at least. And up near the canal has a strip of sand left."

"Those have plenty of reeds around the land. It's mostly undeveloped except that old factory."

"What about the springs part?" Matt asks.

"The only springs I know of are along Dead Man's Beach. They wouldn't hold him so close to our house, would they?"

"I wouldn't put anything past—"

"Matt," I say, cutting him off. "Cole's camp from a year ago was right there. Near the beach and the springs. That's how he got fresh water half the time."

"There's that big clearing."

"Big enough for several tents. A dozen at least."

"Sit." Matt points to the passenger seat nearest the steering wheel. He cranks the boat and backs out of our cove. Once he has the bow pointing southeast, he pushes the throttle as far as it will go. "Hold on," he yells. "And pray I don't hit anything."

———

Arriving home empty handed is not what I intended. As soon as we tie off the boat, not even bothering with the boathouse or cables, I pull myself up onto the main deck. The crab pier, catwalk, and stairs have all been washed away. A board or two hangs on, having refused surrender to Isadora's waves, but they're so bent they've been rendered useless.

On the deck, I retrieve the binoculars from my pack. Peering through, I scan the stretch of beach a few hundred yards north of our property. "All I see are torches. But there are several and they're lit and seem to be arranged in some kind of pattern."

"How do you want to play this?"

"I want to go in guns blazing, then burn the place to the ground."

"Okay, cowboy, do you have a real plan?"

"Kind of. I've got a concept of a plan."

"So, no plan."

"It just needs some flushing out. And people. Several more people."

"We've got people." Matt looks to the house. As if on cue, ten Martins file from the house and onto the porch.

"Jules! Matt!" Mama stands at the edge of the giant hole that was the front yard before Isadora arrived and overstayed her welcome. Hours of storm surge and waves crashing over the bulkhead and onto the lawn washed out most of the grass and dirt between the rocks and the house, leaving a five-foot-deep pit between the porch and the pier. Isadora's second act was much worse than I thought.

Matt and I make our way down the pier with more caution than usual. I can feel the instability of the structure beneath my feet as our walk feels shaky and at places, leans to the right. The ramp of the walkway that used to slope into the yard, now dead-ends into the pit. I watch Matt as he lowers himself from the pier into the hole, then do the same. The ground beneath my feet is muddy, but walkable. On the porch side of the hole, Daddy lowers his green, 6-foot ladder to us. When I step on the first rung, then second, I grip the upper rungs for stability as the ladder feet sink into the ground, leaving just enough height to climb out and onto the porch.

Now on solid ground, Mama forces Daddy out of her way to wrap me in her arms. She stands back and peers into the moonlit pit. "Cole?"

I shake my head, unable to form words, so Matt updates the family for me. "A bit of a wild goose chase, but we know where he is now."

"I've got a plan," I say, in control again over my erratic emotions. "But I need your help."

"Anything," Mama says and places her hands on my face, one on each cheek so that I have no choice but to look her in the eyes. "Whatever you need. We will bring Cole home."

"I have to, Mama."

"*We* have to. He's ours."

———

I: Improvise.

After the immense frustration of Bellingrath Gardens, I feel back on track. Moving forward. Following the survival manual guidance. More than anything, my hope lies in the fact that every Martin has a role in my improvised Plan C.

Daddy and Jessie are fire support from the beach. Mama, Kate, and Garrett are the guards, securing the house from the driveway gate and pier. Lauren, with Lucy, Mallie, and Kate's boys for good measure, is the informant. Matt and me? We're the extraction force.

With one last check of our supplies and a review of a hand-drawn map scratched out from memory of a year ago when Cole first showed us his makeshift home among the trees, we are ready to go. Whether we will succeed or not, that is the question in everyone's mind.

Jacob always talked about single points of failure, how to identify them when making a plan, and the importance of not having one. I'm sure Plan C, after Plan A and Plan B attempts at finding Cole produced nothing, has multiple single points of failure. All of them compete for space in my brain as Matt and I set off into the dark woods just north of Bay Aire Road.

Failure point one: Lauren reaches the Holy T checkpoint to inform the military police there that she heard screams near Dead Man's Beach and people need immediate help, but the soldiers are too eager to help. If the soldiers arrive at The Way camp too early—before Matt and I extract Cole—the plan may fail. I don't know how Shahin will react, other than sweeping up Matt, me, and possibly even Cole in any detainments he may order.

Failure point two: The soldiers don't act on Lauren's information. Instead of containing The Way at their camp, the soldiers do nothing and the red-faced assholes pursue us, overrunning Mama, Kate, and Garrett standing guard at our property.

Failure point three: Daddy and Jessie don't reach the beach in time. Their support comes too late or not at all. This is a big one and by far the riskiest part of the plan. Without long distance walkie-talkies, cell phones, or radios, we are heading out both deaf and blind to each other. Jacob would shut down this operation on this point alone.

But what choice do I have, Jacob? Without equipment or batteries, I have no solution. So, shut it, please.

Failure point four: We don't find Cole. This is the biggest one of all, and the one I shut down.

He will be there. He will be alive. This plan will work.

A half-mile—approximately, because I am not a human GPS—into the woods, I hold up a tight fist. Matt sidles up beside me, and we both crouch behind the trunk of a fallen tree. The massive trunk provides plenty of cover and should muffle our whispers.

I slide my pack off my shoulders and open it. Four wine bottles, each corked and swaddled look up at me—four one-eyed monsters. Matt does the same with his pack and gives me a serious look. I nod.

I pull two plastic baggies of grease-soaked rags from my pack and hand one to Matt. On our haunches, we prepare our makeshift bombs in silence, pulling the cork from each bottle and shoving the rags down in the necks, ensuring the rags fit tightly in the necks.

"Okay. Only light these things if you have to."

"No shit." Matt grabs his two bottles with one hand, wrapping his fingers around the necks of the bottles.

"Check your lighter."

He pats a pocket with his free hand. "Got it."

I watch as Matt tightens his rifle strap so the gun sits snug against his back. "Ready?" I ask.

"Ready."

"Remember, only use that gun if you absolutely have to."

"For the last time, Jules. They have your kid. This warrants deadly force."

"Please. Just think before you shoot."

Our steps are swift but silent as we move through the woods, every step drawing us closer to Cole's clearing, closer to the glow of torches, closer to the assholes that took my kid. Storm damage makes the trek more difficult than I prefer, but the remaining kudzu and shrubbery—those Isadora didn't tear down or rip out by the roots—conceal our final push. When the actual flames of the torches come into view, I raise my closed fist again, halting our progress.

Peeking through the shrubs and ravaged pine trees, all but stripped clean of their branches, I see tents arranged in a circle. "Follow close." As I scurry to the edge of the clearing, allowing only the balls of my feet to touch the ground, I feel Matt on my heels.

"Do you see any guards?" I whisper. Matt shakes his head. "Why wouldn't they have guards?" Matt responds with a shrug, then gestures for us to move on.

Crossing over the imaginary threshold of The Way's camp, we tuck behind the nearest tent. I try to quiet my breathing as we hide in the shadow and pray my thunderous heartbeat won't signal whoever may or may not be inside the tent. I move to peek around the tent, but Matt holds me in place. When I glance at him, he places one finger over his lips. His otherworldly, "I can hear fish" sense has alerted him to something.

That something ends up being someone, or rather two people emerging from a neighboring tent. I see the rounded top of a head, covered with a baseball cap, saunter away from the tent and away from us.

"Come on," one man says to the other. "They're 'bout to start."

We wait a few seconds, then creep between the two tents to discover another tent just ahead. But to the left, a sliver of space provides a sickening view. Downed tree trunks make for crude benches with two or three men and women sitting on each, their backs to us, face a makeshift stage designated by a row of torches, like a backdrop of an altar.

"Oh my God," I whisper and clasp my hand over my mouth.

Two men drag a boy, shirtless, barefoot and filthy, up to the stage. The boy's head is covered, a hood or pillowcase maybe. My mind's eye flashes on my own captivity when members of the Knights led me, practically suffocating beneath a hood, onto the platform on Mon Luis Island. Are these people going to try Cole for made-up crimes as the Knights did me?

Just as my stomach lurches into my throat, sick at the scene playing out before me, the men turn the boy toward the crowd and yank the headcover away. Cole. My kid. My foundling. My whole heart. His eyes light with panic like a wild animal operating on nothing but pure adrenaline and instinct. He jerks his body against the strength of the two adults holding him in place. He bends his knees and tries to drop to the ground, but the men won't allow it. They yank him back to standing, but Cole doesn't give up the fight.

As Cole writhes against his captors, my mind races. The plan is good. Not perfect, but solid enough. But my plan may not be fast enough to save him. Then, I see two more men walking toward the stage. One carries a long, thick reed in his hand. They pause when they reach Cole, then turn their bodies to the crowd. menthe other man—tall, rail-thin, lifts his face into the torchlight.. Days ago, that same face stared at me as I rode away from the Town Hall meeting. That's him. The stranger from the parking lot. I know it is.

"What you see here is a sinner, a doubter."

That voice. I know it in my bones. In that voice is my worst nightmare come true. Dave Richardson is alive and well and has my boy.

"He has been found guilty of denying the one true God. By aligning himself with the Martins—enemies of God—he has turned his back on God. By turning his back on God, he turns his back on each of you. You the righteous. You, The Way!"

The crowd, in unison, calls out, "Amen, Prophet."

"Are we to allow this behavior to go unpunished?"

"No, Prophet!" A man on the front row stands but is pulled back into his seat by his neighbor.

The two men hold tightly to Cole's arms as he struggles to free himself, twisting and squirming in their grip. My feet move. Forward. I must go to Cole. Save him. Protect him. Then, I'm on my back with a thud.

"Not yet," Matt says through gritted teeth. "Hold."

Dave's voice fills the air around me. "Cole Aarons was given the opportunity to repent, to deny his sinful association with jezebel Jules Martin Jones, but he has refused."

Like Cole, I try to break free of Matt's grip. "Hold," he commands.

"I, your prophet, begged this boy to be saved, to accept Christ into his black heart. To know The Way. He refused. Repeatedly, he chose damnation."

Dave Richardson's voice has taken on the same evangelist effect as his Daddy's, guiding the crowd to his desired response. Only, his father never threatened damnation. His father doesn't call himself Prophet. I force myself to stare through the tents at Dave and at Cole, still struggling against his captors. *That's it, honey. Do not give in.*

"Warriors of The Way, we must see justice done if we are to survive. We are the harbingers of God's word, the enforcers of

God's justice." Dave turns to Cole. "Cole Aarons, you have been found guilty of a crime we cannot ignore. And as the Lord God teaches us, if we spare the rod, we spoil the child. For your crimes against God, you will receive ten lashes."

Ten lashes. A true caning. *God, help my sweet boy.*

Wait. Fuck that. I'll save him myself.

V: Value life.

"Now," I tell Matt and shove him hard away from me. I light the first of my bottles. Looking up, I watch as Cole jerks violently to no avail, unable to break free of his captors as the men lift him and turn his smooth back to the crowd. Dave takes the reed from one of the men, preparing to whip Cole. "Now," I hiss at Matt and hold out the lit bottle to him.

Matt takes the bottle, stands tall, and throws it high in the air. It lands directly on a tent, and with a whoosh, the tent catches fire, ablaze in seconds. The crowd turns to the fire, confusion and fear on their faces.

"Run, Cole," I yell, charging from behind the tent. "Run!" I toss another lit bottle to my right, lighting a second tent on fire. Out of the corner of my eye, a third lit bottle hurdles through the sky from the direction of the Bay.

Relief renews my fervor because I know who threw that fire-bomb. Jessie is there, and her aim is true. On Dead Man's beach, she peers through the night vision goggles, firing off homemade bombs. The first lands near tents with a loud, glass-shattering spray.

The crowd bursts into chaos as I sprint toward Cole and Dave. In the confusion, one of Cole's captors abandons his post and rushes toward the burning tents. Several Way members follow the man, rushing toward the burning tents.

Another firebomb lands and explodes. Cole kicks his remaining captor in the balls. The man doubles over and, in doing so, releases Cole.

"Run!" I yell to Cole.

"Not without you." Cole leaps onto the back of one of the men, clawing at his face from behind.

In a split second, Dave pulls a pistol from his waistband and points in Cole's direction. Jacob's voice screams in my mind, "Run from a knife. Charge a gun."

I hurl my body forward, tackling Dave and forcing him to the ground. His pistol bounces away and we both scramble through the mud, trying to reach it. Then Dave is on me, pressing my face into the wet ground.

"Get off her!" Matt's voice is close and loud.

"Shoot him, Matt!" I fight against Dave's body and brace for gunfire, but the blast doesn't come. Mud fills my mouth, and I struggle to breathe, then gasp for air as the pressure dissipates and Dave's weight on my body disappears.

Spitting and coughing, I push up to my feet and unsheathe my buck knife. My eyes register Matt's arms wrapped around my attacker. Then, I leap, catching Dave in the shoulder with my knife. I rip the knife out and blood pours from the wound. Dave's agonizing scream is a blessed symphony in my ears. A kill-shot would have been better, but I'll take his pain as a small victory.

Matt drops Dave to the ground as another Way member charges toward us. I swipe at the woman, but the blade misses her. She stumbles backward. I rush her and kick her hard in the ribs, hopeful that will keep her down long enough. Behind her, behind the benches, flames stretch skyward, skipping from tent to tent.

Several feet away, Cole wrestles with one of his captives. I grab Matt by the arm and drag him away from Dave, still recoiled on the ground. A man has Cole pinned to the ground, his meaty hands around Cole's neck.

"Shoot him," I order Matt.

"Jammed," Matt responds, panting.

"Fuck."

We pile on the man. Matt strikes him with the butt of his rifle as I plunge my knife into his bicep, ripping in and out of his flesh. Matt lifts the man and tosses him from Cole.

"Trees. Home. Now." I jerk Cole up to his feet and push him toward the woods. Turning to run after Cole, my ankle catches and I fall to the ground. Glancing at my foot, I see Dave clinging to my leg. With every bit of force I have, I kick, landing the sole of my shoe hard against Dave's face.

A: Act like the natives.

"Go! Go!" I jump to my feet and run from the clearing, following Cole and Matt into darkness.

As if raised in these woods, Cole runs, confident in every step. He winds around thick shrubs and under low-hanging oak branches as if he knows each obstacle in advance. He leaps over fallen tree trunks and splashes through puddles. In the distance, the roar of diesel engines breaks through the trees.

"Lauren did it!" I call to Matt, fast on my heels.

The ground it took Matt and I a half-hour to traverse, Cole covers in minutes, running with abandon. Running for his life.

24

"Cole," I say as Kate pulls the gate closed behind me. I hear the clank of the lock, then pull Cole to me. "Are you okay? Did they hurt you?"

"I'm okay, Jules. I promise."

"Inside. Now," I command everyone. As I run down the driveway, with Cole beside me and Matt and Kate behind me, I let go of my emotions. I allow the tears to fall unencumbered. Free. *My boy is free.*

Lauren, Mallie, Lucy, and Kate's boys wait for us under the carport.

"You did good," I tell Lauren. "Really, really good."

"I don't know what all they will do, but they should at least stop them from coming after us tonight."

"Let's hope so," I say as I hold the back door open for everyone to get inside.

When Matt passes me, I see a burn on his arm. It's red and blistering in places with black, charred patches near his wrist. His face is pale.

"Your arm." I grab his good arm and turn him to face me. "Lauren, Matt's hurt."

"I'll be fine." He stumbles, catching himself against the hallway wall. "One of the rags got me a little."

"No, Matt. That looks serious."

"I'll be fine."

Lauren comes to him, examining the arm without touching it. "You'll be infected if I don't take care of it for you. There's a first aid kit in the kitchen." Lauren leads Matt to the pantry.

When I walk into the living room, Mama rushes to me. She pulls me to her, kissing my cheeks and then my forehead.

"Mama," I say, stepping out of the hug so I can breathe. "I'm okay. The plan worked."

She pushes me aside and grabs Cole standing right behind me. "Cole, honey. We were all scared to death over you," Mama says, now smothering the boy with one of her hugs.

When he breaks free, he turns and looks at me, half dazed like an animal released from a trap.

"He's okay," I tell her.

"You are such a brave boy," Mama says through tears.

"I knew Jules would come for me."

"Every time," I tell him and snatch him into another hug. "You best get used to these."

"My turn," Jessie says and throws her arms around Cole. The grin on her face brings fresh tears to my eyes.

As soon as you throw the four bottles, get out of there. There's nothing more you can do. I'd told Jessie and Daddy that when we were walking through the plan. Trusting that they would follow my command was one of the toughest things I've ever had to do. Not because they aren't trustworthy, but because losing them, losing any member of this family, would end me. Letting them risk their lives for me, for Cole, was more than I've ever asked of anyone.

"There's something else," I tell the group. "Dave Richardson is alive. He's who had Cole."

"He's running whatever those freaks are doing." Cole's eyes flash with intensity and I feel his energy level rise. "Calls himself Prophet. Matt conked him on the head pretty good though. He's probably still out cold."

I can't believe what we did.

We saved Cole.

We started a fire.

Matt possibly killed Dave Richardson.

"It was all necessary, right?" I ask Daddy.

"Yes. We had no choice. It was them or us." Daddy's pride shows on his face, but so does grave concern.

I swipe the tears off my face and force my emotions back. Now is not the time to fall apart. My family has no idea of the full scope of what we just did. The reality of it lives in the burnt smell in my nose, the taste of ash in my mouth.

L: Live by your wits.

"They will come here," I tell the family. "We need to be ready. Be on alert."

Garrett, from the kitchen island, says, "I'll take first shift by the gate. Dad, will you take first shift in here?"

"Yep. Already planning to."

"I can watch with you," Matt says, fighting back a wince as Lauren smears a salve on his charred skin.

"No, Matt. You won't."

Matt curses under his breath, then swats Lauren away. "That burns more than the actual burns." Turning his attention to me, he says, "Jules, I'm perfectly fine to take a guard shift."

"You need rest. So does Cole. And food."

"On it," Jessie says and disappears into the pantry.

Mama sits in her chair, a plaid glider with matching footstool. She pats the stool, indicating for me to sit. When I do, she reaches for my hand. "Cole, come here, honey."

Cole obeys, and when he does, she squeezes one of his hands, too. I watch as her lips tremble around her words. "If we had lost you, Cole—"

"Mama, we got away. We're okay. We're safe here," I lie. I don't know where I will be safe until Dave is dead and in the ground.

Mama's expression is one of fear and failure. "They got to Cole. What's going to stop Dave from coming onto our property to hurt you?"

"Round-the-clock guard shifts," I tell her. "We run this place like an Army post on lockdown. We build the garden inside our gate here. We fish off the pier only. I am the last person to want to be penned in, but we don't have a choice. No one leaves unless it's absolutely necessary, and when we do, we go in groups. In fact, we will tell Shahin that we will get our rations only when Daddy and I go to the outpost for council meetings. Other than that, no one off the premises. Not even for church."

"Jules, church?" Mama asks.

"I'm serious, Mama. God will understand."

"But what if they come?" Kate asks.

"Then we defend ourselves. We still have the right to defend ourselves. That means everyone needs to learn how. Jessie is good with a rifle already. Matt, will you get Cole up to speed?"

"I know how to shoot, Jules. My dad took me skeet shooting all the time."

"Have you ever shot anything not made of clay?" I ask Cole.

"Have you?" Cole's eyebrows shoot up to his hairline.

"He got ya there, sis." Matt stands, his good arm wrapped around Lauren's waist. "But what do we do when we have to turn in our extra guns?"

"Then we get creative." I force my voice to sound far more assured than I feel. The truth is I don't know how long we can keep The Way out. I don't know if Shahin or anyone else will be on our side fighting them. I don't know much right now except that I will never let them get to another person I love.

"One more thing," I say to the group. "I think we should all sleep in the main house for the time being. At least until Dave is out of the picture."

Everyone nods in agreement except for Matt who protests giving up his and Lauren's privacy. "How are we all supposed to fit in the main house?"

"We'll put your mattresses and Cole's and my cots in the living room. We're just going to have to be a little closer until we can figure out what to do about Dave."

"What's to figure out?" Daddy says. "We tell Shahin where to find Dave."

"Sure, but what if Shahin does nothing? My gut says he either won't care, or he'll care for the wrong reasons."

"Meaning what?" Kate asks.

"Meaning I think Shahin knows way more about all of this than he is letting on."

25

The sun blinds me as it crashes through the living room windows. I'd almost forgotten how rude the early morning sun is if you sleep in this room. One night down, and I already miss the garage with its single window and blinds. Blinds would be a great addition to this room. More drapes, fewer orchids. I'm tempted to accidentally-on-purpose kick the plant at the foot of my cot from its stand, just to rid this room of one.

Yes, I'm cranky. And with good reason. I know I have myself to blame for my current sleeping arrangement, but I've never known Matt to snore like a 1989 Chevy with no muffler. Sleeping on a cot is difficult enough without having to hold a pillow over my head so that I don't turn that same pillow on my brother, holding it to his face until he chokes out his last breath. But I can't be too angry with him. He took in a lot of smoke for me, for my boy.

The sound of bare feet hitting the ground breaks my fuming and festering, so I turn onto my side. "Cole," I whisper before he can make a break for the door.

Cole offers me a tired smile, then nods toward the back door. I stand and grab my flip flops. Carrying them in my hands, I follow Cole out the door and to the garage.

"I was kind of afraid I'd never be in here again," Cole says, heading to where his few belongings are stored. "Do you think I could bring some of my stuff inside if that's where we're staying now?"

"Of course," I say, then stop short at the sight of Cole's wrists. Purple rings encircle both like bracelets made of bruises. "Cole, your wrists," I say, but can't think of anything else other than those inane words.

Cole places a cardboard box on the worktable then looks at his wrists. "Yeah. They tied me up pretty tight."

"Do they hurt?" Another stupid comment as I get a closer look at his arms. His wrists aren't just purple. They're rubbed raw in places. "Oh, god. We need to get some aloe or something on those." I glance down at his feet and see that his ankles are even worse. "Cole—" Tears force my throat closed.

"I'll be okay," he says, digging through his box of hand-me-down clothes and trinkets.

"Do you want to talk about what they did to you?"

"I caused most of the bruises myself. I was trying to break out of the ropes."

"You didn't cause those. You didn't cause any of this. You were only trying to escape, to protect yourself." I wipe away a few straggling tears. "I understand if you're not ready to talk, but I will be here to listen if you ever are ready."

Cole nods but says nothing. He pulls a book from the bottom of the box. "Here it is," he says mostly to himself. He shows me a copy of *The Lion, the Witch, and the Wardrobe*. "I'm going to want this if we have to sleep in the living room with Matt again."

"Something to do other than contemplate if you're strong enough to smother him?"

Cole smiles and a quiet laugh escapes his mouth. "Definitely."

"That's one of my all-time favorite books. I'd love to discuss it with you when you're done."

"Okay," Cole tells me with a smirk in his voice.

"I'm going to choose to ignore that," I tell him. "I'm so impressed with you, Cole.Leaving your shoe was clever."

"I figured they didn't care if I was barefoot." Cole looks down, disappointment clouding his expression. "I lost the other one in the woods."

"No worries. I'm sure we can scrounge you up another pair. Are you hungry? I can fix you something. I'm not sure what we have, but there's got to be something left in the pantry."

"No," Cole says, and I see by his expression that his response came out harsher than he intended. "No, thank you. I'm not hungry."

"Cole, you don't have to worry about being polite with me. It's going to take time for you to work out what happened last night and the one before."

Has it really been only one day and night? One sun and moon cycle since Cole was kidnapped? It feels like he's been away from the garage for weeks. Yesterday feels like it lasted for a year, maybe longer. I know in my gut that this will become a day of demarcation—the day before the kidnapping when I thought Cole was safe, the day that Cole was taken and my mind and heart broke into two, and every day after.

"Jules," Cole asks, looking inside the box again. "Do you think Dave has been here the whole time?"

"You mean in Bellefontaine?"

"Yeah."

"More than likely." I look at Cole, gauging how deep I can dig into his time with The Way.

"He's leading them. How can he be allowed to just roam free?" Cole pulls his homemade slingshot from the box and lays it on top of the book. "They're all so weird. Calling him 'Prophet.'

'Oh, Prophet… My Prophet,' like it's his name. When we first got to that place, the men that grabbed me brought me to him like they were giving me to him like a gift. Piled up all the stolen rations around me like I was just another thing. All grinning and everything. It was so creepy."

"But you recognized him? You remembered Dave?"

"Of course I did. I knew exactly who he was, even though he's really skinny now."

"But Dave wasn't the one who took you from here?"

"No." Cole fiddles with the slingshot, but his fingers tremble. "Three guys. They were waiting for me when I came out here for the gig."

"They were?"

"Well, for someone. They probably would've snatched up anyone from here, so long as the person was close to you. Or was you."

"I'm so sorry, Cole." I move beside him and try to take his hand in mine, but he pulls away and closes his arms across his chest.

"I don't need babyin'."

"I know. But it's okay to be upset. It's okay if you're angry at me."

"I'm not angry at you," he tells me, but the hurt in his eyes makes me question his words. "I just don't think it's fair is all. Bait. That's what Dave called me. 'A sweet, little piece of bait.'"

"That's awful."

"And I knew you'd come. That you'd take the bait and risk your life, so I tried to get away before you got the chance, but I was too weak to break those ropes. They were too tight. So, you came and risked your life for me and that's not fair."

"Cole, that's what you do when—"

"Stop it!" Cole turns to me and the tears pour down his

cheeks. His nose and ears and eyes go pink with the hurt bursting inside him.

"Cole, honey." I reach out for him, but he pushes me away.

"Don't you get it? If I lose you, I have no one. No one is left for me."

I grab him and pull him into my arms, squeezing him hard as he wriggles around to free himself. "Shhh. It's okay. You're okay. I'm okay." Cole tries to shove me off again, but I squeeze him tighter. "You're mad at me and you're scared—"

"Am not."

"You're scared and so am I, and that's okay. Neither of us is going anywhere. I promise."

I hold him through his tears. When his body stops shaking from sobs, I stroke his hair, then hold him tight again. "You will be okay," I tell him. "I promise."

"You're squeezing me to death, Jules."

After several minutes, I feel like we both can be around other people again, so I convince him to start storm cleanup with me. The few glimpses I've had of the property haven't been happy ones. Branches cover the yard—big, skinny, huge, long. It's like every tree in Bellefontaine threw all their branches into our yard. Shingles dot the mess with torn, black strips, and the front slope has a gaping hole in it where the water eroded the land behind the rock bulkhead. Soon, we're sure to discover dead birds and fish among the wreckage. They'll start to rot in the sun and give off an odor so strong, the whole place will stink of death.

I open the garage door and spot Lauren and Matt surveying the yard from the carport. Lauren has on a wide-brimmed hat and work gloves, ready to do her part.

Matt holds up a hand at me, the universal sign for stop. "Is Cole with you?" he asks, his voice low.

"Yes. He's going—"

"Tell him to stay in there." Matt nods toward the end of the driveway.

Sitting on the street are two military vehicles.

"Cole," I call through the open doorway. "Do not, under any circumstances, come outside. Go upstairs and wait for me to come get you. Stay away from the windows." I watch as he turns up the stairs to Matt and Lauren's former apartment, then I close the door and head down the driveway.

Shahin stands at the gate, waiting, and we've got a lot to talk about.

"You can come through," I tell Shahin. "Your vehicle stays here, though."

Shahin gives me an annoyed look.

"The ground's too wet for your vehicle." I motion to the Humvee and its oversized wheels. "Those tires will leave huge ruts in the yard and we're trying to get cleaned up to plant the new garden. Since, you know, our first one was destroyed."

"Understood." Shahin walks to the Humvee, says something I can't hear to the driver, then returns to me.

I unlock the gate and let him through. If he's hoping for a cheerful greeting, he won't get one from me. I'm way past pleasantries.

Walking down the driveway, I steady my breathing and affix my poker face. As much as I want to believe that Shahin is here to ensure justice is served in Cole's kidnapping, I have a nagging feeling that, in this case, justice has three perspectives—mine, Dave's, and whatever Shahin's may be.

"What can we do for you today, Captain Shahin?"

Maybe Shahin has no idea what transpired last night. After all, due to the storm, we are back to square one as far as communications around here. The radio still puts out nothing but static, the power is out, and, I imagine, several roads are blocked by fallen trees. He may have his hands full with damage reports and distressed residents. Who knows if he was with the soldiers that showed up at The Way camp while Cole, Matt, and I ran for our lives.

Just play it cool, Jules. "Anything I can help you with?" I glance at Shahin as we join Matt under the carport. A cloudless sky makes shade a necessity today.

"How did you all fare through the storm?" Shahin directs the question to Matt.

"Not great, but we're okay," Matt answers.

Shahin retrieves a small notebook and pen from one of the cargo pockets. "I'm riding around today assessing damage to determine greatest needs."

"Gasoline rations," I say. My mind jumps to the all the gasoline we went through last night. "That's our most immediate need. We've got a large branch through the dining room and the rest of the tree is up against the house. It'd be nice to know we're not going to run out of gas for the chainsaws before removing them."

Shahin makes a note of it on his notepad.

"And," Matt says, "we just discovered the well and outhouse tank flooded."

"Is that what that smell is?" I ask.

"Yep," Matt says. "What else did you think it was?"

"I figured the dead animals were already stinking up the place."

"No, no. That treat will come tomorrow, if we don't get them burned or buried today."

I wonder how long Shahin will let Matt and me go on with this cordial banter before he tells us what he really wants. Shahin never shows up anywhere without an agenda and his own list of needs and wants. I've learned that much about our current overlord. His little notebook of resident concerns has to be a convenient ruse.

"We could use potable water," I tell Shahin. "So we don't

have to constantly boil water. That really uses the propane up." I look to Matt for him to pick up the conversation. "Do we need more propane?"

He obliges with, "Well, Jules, if Shahin can get us gas for the chainsaws, we'll have plenty of wood to burn. It'll be like the early days after we ran out of propane and cooked everything over an open fire."

"You say we, baby brother, like you did any of the cooking." I nudge Matt in the ribs, smiling at Shahin while Matt feigns injury.

"I didn't see you standing over the fire, roasting fish and wild greens."

"Well, we all have our part to play." I look directly at Shahin and say, "And I'm willing to give credit where credit is due. Kate is a fantastic campfire cook."

"Stop," Shahin says. "I know what you're doing."

"What? Us?" I ask him. "Well, we're just trying to figure out which Shahin is here today. The George Shahin who plays nice and acts concerned about the people here, or Captain Shahin, who likes to puff up his chest and pretend things like destroying our garden aren't a major problem?"

Shahin stares at me for a long moment, and I can see I'm under his skin. I must admit that I like this position—me getting the better of him instead of the other way around.

"Are you aware of the fire near here last night?"

I press one hand to my chest in surprise. "Oh no. I hope no one was hurt."

"The fire burned out quickly thanks to all the standing water."

"So, no damage?"

"There was personal property damage, but luckily no lives were lost."

"Well, that's a relief. God is good, huh?"

"God had nothing to do with what happened last night." Shahin takes one step, closing the distance between us.

I force my feet to hold my ground. "Ask me how Cole is doing this morning."

"I assume the kid is fine."

"Barely. Maybe you should ask Dave Richardson about that."

"Excuse me?" Shahin takes another step, close enough that he could reach out and grab me. Matt, too. But I can't back down. I can't show fear, even though it's burning beneath my skin.

"Dave Richardson is alive and well. He's calling himself Prophet and is apparently leader of The Way."

Shahin's face is stone. Not one flinch. But the absence of emotion on his face is confirmation enough for me.

"You knew that already, didn't you? You've known he was here for a while now, haven't you?"

"I'm just as surprised as you, I'm sure."

"Not just now, you're not." Matt says, and shifts closer to my side. "Right now, when Jules told you, you didn't look surprised one bit,"

"George," I say, using the familiar purposefully. "What am I supposed to do about this? The man who tried to kill me is back, and he kidnapped a child." Shahin says nothing, so I keep pressing. Eventually, he will slip and reveal something. "Am I supposed to ignore that it happened? Are you going to ignore it? Did you arrest him last night?"

"You sure have a lot of questions for someone I could arrest here on this spot."

"For what? Please, name my crimes."

"Arson, for one."

"That's bullshit. How did I supposedly start that fire?"

"I know you were both there last night." Shahin's frustration paints his face almost as red as the freaks with their war paint.

"How do you know that? Did Dave tell you? Is he your Prophet, too?"

Shahin sticks a finger in my face. "You and I both know how that fire started."

I swat his hand away. "You and I both know that you've been hiding Dave Richardson this whole time."

"And what proof do you have of that? I haven't seen Dave in years."

"Liar. I know you're involved. And I think this goes all the way up your chain of command. Is Freidman in on it, too? Is that why she pardoned the Knights? Let them morph into The Way? I know this is all connected. I just don't know to what extent or why. But trust me, I will find out." I cross my arms, uncomfortable with how close Shahin is to me. He's so close I feel heat coming off his body and the hot air of his breath. "What else would explain the fact that you couldn't care less about a child being kidnapped? Or is it that this particular child doesn't warrant your time or effort? Maybe I should file a complaint.. Dereliction of duty is a pretty serious charge."

Shahin leans in and that hissing voice of his blows into my ear. "You're not exactly in the position to make threats, Jules. Especially against me."

"So, is that the aim? Build up Dave and his religious freaks until the rest of us fall in line or leave? Or maybe you want me dead, too."

"My aim is to help the people of Bellefontaine through this crisis. If you haven't noticed, Ms. Jones, a hurricane just went through here and a lot of people need a lot of help."

"But Cole was never going to be one of them, was he? He's not worthy of your help."

"You got him back."

I lunge forward, but Matt catches me around the waste and holds me to him. "Don't, Jules. You're playing into him. He wants you to give him a reason to arrest you."

Shahin steps back, holding up both hands as an innocent man

would. But frauds aren't innocent. "Hey, I'm just here to check on you and your family."

"Bullshit. You're here to scare me. You had them take Cole to scare me. You did all of this to scare me into leaving. Is that it? Was all of this your plan?"

"There's a lot of people here who blame you. You may not have started all of this, but you made it worse. All the problems in Bellefontaine. You're the one that escalated the violence here. A lot of people are upset about that. Either I take you in or you leave, and we forget you ever came home."

"So that's it? I leave and everything is great again?"

"Not exactly, Jules. I mean, sure. At first that was the aim." Shahin steps from under the carport, places his helmet on his head, and tightens the chin strap. "But now, I want all of you Martins gone. Every last one of you. Bellefontaine doesn't want you here anymore. It doesn't belong to you."

Shahin strolls down the driveway. After a few steps, he stops and turns back to us. "No need to unlock the gate. Anyone with legs can hop that thing. You should really reconsider your safety measures around here. I'd hate for anything bad to happen."

Matt and I stand under the carport, watching Shahin walk away until he climbs into a Humvee and he and the vehicles disappear around the bend in the road. Matt and I walk to the gate and lock it tight. Just like the outpost, all anyone would have to do is climb a few feet, and they'd have free reign of our whole property.

"No one else gets in here today," I tell Matt. We wave down Garrett to guard the gate, knowing we will have to build it up, add more barbed wire, somehow secure it while also cleaning up debris, repairing the well, fortifying the pier, and rebuilding the dining room. The growing list in my head is exhausting, so I shut it down before full-blown overwhelm sets in and paralyzes me.

Back in the garage, I call for Cole. He bounds down the stairs. Strong, healthy, ready. I motion for him to come with me.

We join Matt on the carport, and I ask him, "You ready to talk to Daddy? Now that we know where Shahin stands?"

"Lead the way," Matt says.

At the end of the pier, Daddy hammers a loose piece of aluminum to the rafters. Matt, Cole, and I wait until he hops down from his perch on a beam.

"This looks ominous," Daddy says. "Another storm on its way?"

"You could say that," I say. "Shahin wants us all gone. He doesn't care how, but he doesn't want a single Martin living in Bellefontaine anymore."

"Oh." Daddy says. He lays his hammer on top of his closed toolbox, then turns back to me. "Well, what do you think we should do about that?"

"Stay," I say. "This is home. We're not going anywhere."

EPILOGUE

Dear Jacob,

I have so much to tell you, but don't have enough pages left in this notebook to explain everything. It's been a week since Hurricane Isadora, and we've made good headway with cleanup—as much as we can on our own. Yes, we are very much on our own with this. I don't think the new captain is interested in helping us. He's actually said as much, and I'd rather avoid him and these National Guard soldiers altogether, so we will carry on. What choice do we have?

I've heard your voice in my head a lot lately. Probably because I've never been so scared as I was last week. Cole was taken, but I got him back. Yes, my crazy plan worked, and we didn't burn down all of Bellefontaine in the process. The plan involved some Molotov cocktails. Don't start with me. And no, I will not tell you the plan because you would have hated it from start to finish. All you need to know is that we are both alive and mostly well. Isn't that what you told me when I asked questions? That the Army is on a need-to-know basis, so sometimes I must be, too. Sorry, babe. That's just the way it is.

What else?

Oh, yeah. Bellefontaine now has its own official religious cult. Maybe not official, official, but they're here, and they are complete freaks. Yes, they took Cole and are led by Dave Richardson. If only I had your marksman ability, I could take him out with a single shot from two hundred yards away. I know you don't think I have it in me to take a life, but if he touches my kid again, I will end him. If you were in charge here, or even someone with half your moral fortitude, I could depend on you to arrest Dave Richardson, as kidnapping should warrant some justice, but you're not here. I'm afraid George Shahin isn't going to do a damn thing about this. At least that's the impression I got when George paid us a visit last week.

Is it odd that I'm getting used to living in fear? It is, isn't it? That shouldn't be normal, should it? How often did we talk about how surreal it is that violence can become normal?

I miss you. I still miss you every day, and even that is starting to feel normal. Some days, I can even make it through the day without feeling like I want to punch something so hard and so long that my knuckles bleed. But I don't think I will ever stop missing you, *missing the life we had, the life we should have lived together. That feeling will never go away.*

But I will look for you. In the trees and on the water, in the empty space next to me, the air around me. So, send me a message now and then, just to keep me strong. Because I'm going to need all the strength you can give me. I don't know what's coming, but I know this is long from over.

I know you're watching over me. Thank you, my love.

--Jules

I close the notebook, knowing how much more I want to tell him. Namely that I'm starting to understand why he had to leave me so soon, too soon. If Jacob were still alive, I wouldn't have come home. If I hadn't come home, I wouldn't have met Cole. And with Cole is where I belong. But I can't tell Jacob that, not yet. I can't tell him that a tiny piece of me is starting to accept his absence.

I know it's pure syrup to say, but I think Cole is my life's purpose. He must need me more than I needed Jacob. Why else would the world be this cruel? Cole must be the reason I was made to be tough. Because only the toughest of people will be able to do what must be done.

Over the last week, as we cleaned up from the storm, I made a decision. I'm tired of living like this. I'm done with waiting for the authorities to figure this out. Every time I bend to pick up a tree branch or stare down the road on guard duty, I get a little more tired of waiting for rescue or waiting for The Way to come. I don't know what yet, but it's up to me to change what needs changing.

Soon, I'll figure out what I must do. I feel that in my bones. But for now, I will bide my time and keep rowing this boat.

I peek out the window to see the sun has moved lower in the sky, signaling my respite in the garage is done. I tuck the notebook under Jacob's old tanker pajamas at the bottom of his trunk, and head outside. Looking toward the driveway gate, gnats swarm in the late day sun. The first hour of my guard duty shift will be brutal as I swat away the annoying buggers with my lips pressed closed. Few things are more disgusting than gnats inside your mouth.

"Reporting for duty," I tell Garrett, taking the rifle from him. "Your boys were begging to go fishing earlier, so you better get to it before Kate comes searching for you."

Garrett gives me a smile, and I watch as he trudges down the driveway, probably ready for a jug of water. When I turn back toward the road, a man stands at the gate. My heart lurches in my throat as I ready my rifle and point it in his direction.

The man is in plain clothes with a baseball hat pulled low. When he removes it, I let out a breath.

"Captain Johnson? Brandon?"

Johnson gives me a smile; one I didn't see often when last he was in Bellefontaine. "Glad you recognized me."

"What are you doing here? How are you here?" I look around and see no car, no way of transport at all. "Did you walk here all the way from New Jersey?"

"We need to talk. Is there somewhere private we can go?"

"I can't leave my post," I say, dizzy from his sudden appearance.

"Like I said, we need to talk. I think we need your help."

"We?"

"Yes. *We.*"

Johnson turns toward the trees across the road. He waves an arm and a woman appears. She's Black with a buzzed haircut and white tank top over a full bosom. Somehow, I know this woman. I have a feeling I think I will know her voice.

"Libby?" I ask her.

"Yes, my darling. In the flesh."

***

The End

ACKNOWLEDGMENTS

It was Mama's idea to live on the Bay, and Daddy loved Mama. For forty years, we loved and played and prayed and grew on the western shore. So, the first people I must thank are Mama and Daddy. I would not be who I am without them. Kim, Kellie, and Leo, I bet you feel the same. We are rich beyond measure because of two people. What a debt we owe!

Thank you to my fabulous agent, Amy Collins, who puts up with all my freak outs and insecurities but sticks by me anyway. There will be more moments of panic in my future. Thank you for not only repping me and advocating for me, but for teaching me about this crazy industry.

To my team at Aethon Thrills, thank you for investing in my books and me. You've taken a risk on this series. That reality is not lost on me. Once again, you've helped me polish my words, created a gorgeous cover, and given my story a publishing life. Thank you.

To my critique group, beta readers, and writing buddies. I'm fortunate to have you as peers and damn lucky to have you as friends.

To my chosen family—you know who you are—you all have a home on my future compound. May it be green with fresh air, good wine, and lots of love.

To my readers, here I am again, full of gratitude for you. Of all the books in the world, you chose to spend your time with mine. I hope you found it a worthwhile expenditure of your time and energy. And yes, book three is on the way. Jules has a few more adventures in her and another story to tell.

Lastly, to my guys, Jay and Bay. My heart is full of love for you and from you. You are my security blankets. Yes, I will continue to take the middle cinnamon roll, and you will continue to love me despite my insane tendencies. Bay, I can't wait to watch everything you do with your life. That big brain of yours knows no boundaries. Jay, thank you for speed reading all those pages during the crazy rewrite month. Your devotion to me should be studied.

The pier on the cover of this book is the pier Daddy built and rebuilt after every storm that tried to wash it away. It is where my siblings and I as children jumped from and into the brackish water and where our kids took that same leap. It's where we fished, ate countless watermelons, spit the seeds at fish and birds, swung with Mama and Daddy, and made out with childhood crushes. In times of despair, I hope each of us in the whole, wide world, has a memory that fills us with love and wonder. For me, that memory is Mama and Daddy's pier. Whatever yours is, hold it close.

Ta-ta for now, my darlings. More soon.

THANK YOU FOR
READING BLACK CLOUDS

We hope you enjoyed it as much as we enjoyed bringing it to you. We just wanted to take a moment to encourage you to review the book. Follow this link: Black Clouds to be directed to the book's Amazon product page to leave your review.

Every review helps further the author's reach and, ultimately, helps them continue writing fantastic books for us all to enjoy.

BRACKISH WATERS
Splintered Reeds
Black Clouds

———

You can join our non-spam mailing list by visiting Thriller Books: https://aethonbooks.com/thriller-newsletter/ and never miss out on future releases. You'll also receive five full books completely Free as our thanks to you.

Don't forget to follow us on socials to never miss a new release!
Facebook | Instagram | Twitter | Website

Want to discuss our books with other readers and even the authors?
JOIN THE AETHON DISCORD!

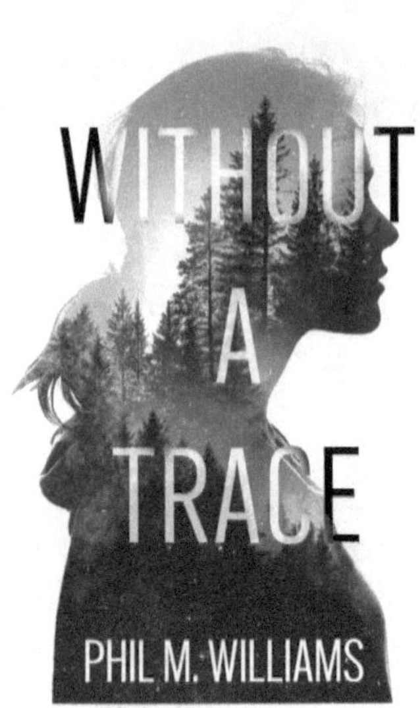

A missing girl. A team of unlikely misfits. One terrifying descent into darkness. When a teen girl vanishes without a trace, everyone assumes she ran from her strict father. But Justin Boyle knows something sinister is afoot. He saw her at the mall. He saw the twisted intentions of the strangers with her. And he knows she's in danger. The police dismiss his warning. So Justin turns to the only allies he has: Edwin Arroyo, a disgraced UFC fighter living in a homeless camp with his loyal dog, Grace Turner, a true crime fanatic stuck working the food court, and Rakesh Abbasi, a quiet tech whiz running his family's crumbling electronics store. Together, they form an unlikely team of amateur sleuths, diving headfirst into a twisted mystery that exposes depravity, danger, and the limits of their own courage. Time is running out. If they fail, a young life will be lost—and the evil will spread. **From bestselling author Phil M. Williams comes a heart-pounding crime thriller perfect for fans of gritty thrillers, razor-sharp twists, and flawed heroes who refuse to quit.**

Get Without a Trace Now!

**For all our Thrillers, visit our website at
www.aethonbooks.com/thriller**

ABOUT THE AUTHOR

Jodie Cain Smith is the founder of the Mobile Literary Festival and a Page Turner Award Winner. Her novels include *The Woods at Barlow Bend* and *Bayou Cresting: The Wanting Women of Huet Pointe*. Her short works have appeared in *The Petigru Review, Pieces Anthology,* and *Chicken Soup for the Military Spouse's Soul,* among others. When not creating fictional worlds on her laptop or planning events at her favorite indie bookstore, Jodie hangs out with her long-suffering husband and the most precious little boy ever created. Seriously, the kid is amazing, and the husband puts up with a lot.

9 781964 505190